I0761296

IF A FACE COULD KILL

Also by Becky Masterman

The Brigid Quinn Thrillers

RAGE AGAINST THE DYING
FEAR THE DARKNESS
A TWIST OF THE KNIFE
WE WERE KILLERS ONCE

A Brigid Quinn Spin-Off

HER PRODIGAL HUSBAND *

Novels

MATERNAL INSTINCT *

* *available from Severn House*

IF A FACE COULD KILL

Becky Masterman

SEVERN
HOUSE

First world edition published in Great Britain and the USA in 2026
by Severn House, an imprint of Canongate Books Ltd,
14 High Street, Edinburgh EH1 1TE.

severnhouse.com

Cover and jacket design by Piers Tilbury

British Library Cataloguing-in-Publication Data
A CIP catalogue record for this title is available from the British Library.

ISBN-13: 978-1-4483-1789-9 (cased)
ISBN-13: 978-1-4483-1898-8 (paper)
ISBN-13: 978-1-4483-1790-5 (e-book)

All Severn House titles are printed on acid-free paper.

Typeset by Palimpsest Book Production Ltd., Falkirk, Stirlingshire, Scotland.
Printed and bound in Great Britain by TJ Books, Padstow, Cornwall.

The manufacturer's authorised representative in the EU for product safety is Authorised Rep Compliance Ltd, 71 Lower Baggot Street, Dublin D02 P593 Ireland (arccompliance.com)

Praise for the Brigid Quinn Thrillers

"Masterman keeps the tension high throughout this page-turner"
Publishers Weekly on *We Were Killers Once*

"A twisting, high-stakes story with characters so real and so recognizably human that it breaks your heart a little. Brilliant"
Shari Lapena, author of *The Couple Next Door*, on *A Twist of the Knife*

"Will compel both new readers and old fans to cheer Brigid on"
Library Journal on *A Twist of the Knife*

"Gripping . . . [will] draw in fans of Michael Connelly and Dennis Lehane"
Booklist on *Fear the Darkness*

"Fans of Lisa Gardner and Tess Gerritsen will love this book"
Booklist on *Rage Against the Dying*

"Masterman lives up to her name in this masterly combination of compelling character and plot to keep the pages turning"
Library Journal Starred Review of *Rage Against the Dying*

"One of the most memorable FBI agents since Clarice Starling"
Publishers Weekly Starred Review of *Rage Against the Dying*

About the author

Becky Masterman has worked as an actor, playwright, and an editor for a forensic science and law enforcement press. Her debut thriller was a finalist for the Edgar and the Anthony Awards for Best First Novel and for the CWA Gold Dagger. She won the Tony Hillerman Fiction Award for *A Twist of the Knife*, and her books have been translated into twenty languages. As well as a series of novels featuring retired FBI agent Brigid Quinn, including spin-off *Her Prodigal Husband*, she is the author of standalone thriller *Maternal Instinct*. She lives in Tucson, Arizona with her husband.

beckymasterman.com

For Boodle

Acknowledgments

Much gratitude to my new editor Sara Porter for her wise recommendations and lavish encouragement, and as always to the rest of the very professional team at Severn House.

Thanks to Anne Siren, Julie King, Jeannie Johnson, Bruce Wray, and Vicki Bergesen for their thoughtful reading and kind praise. You were right about everything.

Thanks to Larry Trumble who provided me with some manly military talk.

Writing is hard and takes a long time. I'm grateful to all those people who made one small perfect comment, at just the right time, to help me through. You don't know who you are.

Dr. Gail Anderson's book *Biological Influences on Criminal Behavior, 2nd edition*, plus her counsel, gave great insight to the impact of fetal alcohol syndrome on judgment.

Besides the writing critiques and the information, both scientific and social, that inform this story, I acknowledge what people do for others, who make a difference and live so kindly:

Lynn Speth, with her long-time devotion to the foster children of southern Arizona, provided not only background, but inspiration and drive. For more on her group, see www.AVIVA.com

Deacon Kim Crecca of the Episcopal Diocese of Arizona introduced me to the art project at Perryville Women's Prison. She is now in charge of Camp Genesis, which runs summer camps in Arizona for the children of incarcerated people. The royalties for this book will go to that and Bridges Reentry, which aids women being released from prison as they struggle to make a new life. If you want to know more, see www.prisonministry@azdiocese.org.

I'm grateful that Della, my newish little border terrier, has figured out a way to stay asleep in my arms as I write this. And as always, Fred, who asks if I've written.

ONE

No one was supposed to be in the house.

Instead, Royce is trapped in this bedroom with nothing but a pistol he has never fired and a pathetically skinny white woman dressed in denim shorts and an extra-large T-shirt that says Guilty As Charged. She's pressing herself against the wall as if she hopes it might dissolve.

Sirens in the distance. Were they coming here? Royce should run. But a running Black man doesn't end well. Neither does a non-running Black man.

"What's your name?" he asks, having nothing against this woman. Hoping that being nice will give him some cred. That she'll tell the cops when they arrest him that he never meant to hurt her.

"Nicki."

"I'm Royce," he says.

She doesn't say anything else. Considering the circumstances, what else was there? As he gives Nicki a second look, you notice dots of paint in different colors—blue, yellow, black—on her T-shirt. You connect the dots to an easel by the window that has a half-finished portrait on it. He gestures, not wanting to appear as stupid as everyone says he is, saying the only thing he can think of: "Oil painting?"

"Acrylic," Nicki says.

He nods as if he knows what that is. He understandably has a lot on his mind, so only now he notices, leaning against the wall next to her, a whole stack of paintings. The one that's showing is of a beautiful child, with a face like a GIF if you search for "beautiful child." Royce has got no option but to wait, so although he doesn't really care he asks: "Who's the kid?"

"Ramona." And beating him to his next question, "They're all Ramona."

"Nice name. Who's Ramona?"

"My daughter."

"Mother with such a beautiful child." This makes the woman's face light up. He's never seen a face "light up" before, but now he'll always know what that looks like. On closer inspection an odd face, a little flattened, features a little off in a way hard to describe. But who is he to judge with a nose mashed in a bar fight, meth-riddled teeth, and acne-scarred cheeks? "How'd a mother with such a beautiful child come to be in this house?"

"I killed my husband," Nicki says. Her voice is as flat as her face, speaking as if she's giving him the time.

"We all make mistakes," Royce says.

"It wasn't a mistake," she says. "I'd do it again."

Sirens closer. She had lied; she must have called 9-1-1 from the bathroom. They were so fast in responding they might as well have been waiting on the next block.

It feels as if his heart has moved up to the base of his throat, climbing to get out. Funny how people never think about how scared an intruder can be. On TV they're just vicious maniacs. No, you always heard about things from the perspective of the poor person who lived in the house. Take this woman, for example, who seemed to be slightly less terrified than him. More like tired, down and out, like him. Though maybe with her strange face, it was harder to tell how she felt.

Or you hear about the perspective of the brave SWAT team with their invincible body armor who break down the door. What about the intruder? He's taking a greater risk than anybody else. Would anyone ever feel sorry for him?

Per the simple plan, Royce had approached the property as if he had business there. His hand supported the unfamiliar weapon in the front sling of his hoodie. That way it wouldn't sag and give itself away like a hard-on under Lycra. The hood pushed down so he wouldn't look suspect on an afternoon that was already too hot for late spring. Big old shorts that had been beige when they were clean. They sagged, too. He needs a belt. When this was done he would stop by Goodwill and get a belt. These were clothes meant to be unnoticed. The only people who got noticed in the desert were the ones who dressed nice.

The yard was empty, not just of people, but of vegetation and gravel, too. Some concrete blocks piled three-high at the corner of the yard looked like they were meant for something that hadn't happened yet. Otherwise, the house, one of those prefabricated deals midway between a frame construction and a mobile home, was pretty neat. The paint job didn't look washed out and dark wood trim around the windows added a nice touch. The car that was sometimes parked in front was also gone. He had been watching the place for a while and knew that the car missing was a good thing. No one home.

It was so easy. People often didn't lock their front door during the day. More burglars should operate at three p.m. in the afternoon. With an empty cardboard box under his arm, he planned, if anyone asked, to say that this had been accidentally delivered to his house and he was just being a good neighbor. He looked to the right and left, and out to the road in front of the house. Nobody around, not even that nosy woman who he had seen peeking over her wall when he had scoped out the place. He turned the doorknob and was in.

No one in sight at first. He tossed the empty box on the floor and got out his gun instead. The house so quiet, the sound of the old refrigerator turning on made him jump. It should all have been easy. He put the gun back in his hoodie rather than leave it on the counter where he might forget it.

But there was nothing in any of the kitchen cabinets where he might have expected drugs to be. Not even in the cupboard where they kept nothing but allergy pills and vitamins. Except they had a bunch of Narcan stashed there, the overdose drug. *Just in case?*

Royce moved down the hall to the left of the kitchen. One bathroom had a medicine cabinet with shaving cream and some prescription drugs that didn't look like anything good. Four toothbrushes stood upright in a yellow ceramic holder by the sink. That should have tipped him off that there was more than one person he had to watch for, but he sort of had tunnel vision looking for only one thing. He was back in the living room when he heard the toilet flush at the other end of the house. The bathroom was where the woman had been, and she came out now, pulling up her elastic shorts.

"What the—" said the woman. Even at that point she looked more tired than terrified, like she'd seen this kind of thing before and knew everything that was coming in advance.

Royce reached in the front pocket of his hoodie to get the gun, too late. The trigger snagged on the fleece and he fumbled, giving the woman time to run into the bedroom next to the bathroom she'd come from. She tried to slam the door on him, but he got to it just before it closed and blocked it with his shoulder. The force of his body not only opened the door but made the woman trip backward and fall on her ass. She crawled backwards on her hands and feet like someone possessed in a horror movie until she hit the wall. There she stopped.

Standing over her, now in better control of the situation, he said, "OK. Just tell me where it is and I'll be out of here." For emphasis he was finally able to pull the gun out of the hoodie and brandish it a little.

"Where what is?" she said, looking genuinely confused, and not terribly impressed by the gun, like she was a bad actress in that horror movie.

"Do I have to spell it? D-R-U-G-S?"

The woman shook her head. "We're not allowed to have drugs here." And as if it would make a damn bit of sense, added, "It's against the rules. We're not even allowed to have alcohol." She thought a little and admitted, "Maybe there's some of those little bottles of tequila in the kitchen. You could take that."

Royce didn't have all the information after all that might have warned him about this place. If he had, he might have asked upfront who was "we" and who made the "rules." But the sirens told him the time for questions was past. His heart provided a percussive beat to their wail.

"Goddammit," he said. "Did you call nine-one-one?"

"I was in the bathroom!" she yelled, losing her patience, as if that explained all, as if people never took their cell phone in the bathroom to play a game while they were on the toilet.

She looked a little scared at the sound of the sirens, but a little watchful, too, as if to see what he would do next. Whether she would be hurt before the cops showed up. He figured he could duck into the bathroom and be back before she could get up off the floor and run. He expected she was his ticket out of here alive.

Royce found the phone resting on the edge of the sink next to the toilet. She had known there was an intruder, even though she pretended not to. The line was open and she was the one who called for help. He disconnected the call, but knew it was too late because of the sirens.

Running back into the bedroom, Royce slammed the door shut and locked it. Nicki had not moved, maybe fearing he would shoot her when she ran past the bathroom to get out of the house. Anger began to take him, countering his fear with the unspent fury of years.

He turned on the woman. She raised her hands because she saw it coming when he shot at the stack of canvases. Now she howled, dove for the paintings as if she cared more about them than because he had accidentally shot her instead. A trickle of blood called her attention to the wound on the back of her upper arm. She lifted her arm to lick it off. As she did so, he revised his picture of her from skinny to more of all muscle and bone. Her tongue wasn't long enough to reach, so she wrapped her fingers around her arm. It was done so casually, that lick, that he wondered if she'd been in this kind of situation before. Was she pretending terror?

"Ow," she said.

"I'm sorry," he said, running his left index finger down the barrel. "I've never used one before. It was an accident. You have to tell them it was an accident. I didn't mean to hurt you."

"You shot me!"

"I was aiming at the paintings. It was an accident."

"Why? What did I do to you?"

"You lied to me. You called the cops."

"I swear I didn't! I didn't know you were here until I came out of the bathroom!"

Royce crouched down on the opposite side of the room where he could still see her without the bed getting in the way. He turned his fury on himself. He was so goddam stupid. Had he ever been not stupid? Like before the meth? It was hard to remember himself before. Oh, that's right, that's what he expected to find in this house. Drugs. Only there wasn't any. Nicki insisted on this even after he showed her the gun. No drugs on the premises. They were very strict about that, she said. No tolerance. Something wasn't right, here.

This bedroom was at the back of the house so Royce couldn't tell how many police cars were out there. He might have been able to tell from the sirens but they were silent now. There was probably an ambulance too, to cart off whoever ended up alive when all this was finished. He pressed up against the wall opposite from the woman who didn't seem to realize that, by taking advantage of his confusion, she could probably get out the door before he shot her again. That's how it was with terror. It kept you from thinking things through. A flash of black went by the window between them. She saw it, too. Shiny, and round, a helmet catching the sun. They were surrounding the house.

They must have been satisfied that they had the place surrounded, because the next sound he heard was from the bullhorn just like in the movies. A man's voice, of course. Were there any female SWAT police? Oh, the funny things you think about when you might be about to get killed.

"COME OUT WITH YOUR HANDS UP!"

This was escalating way beyond and faster than anything Royce could have imagined. Wasn't there supposed to be a hostage negotiator? So much for the step where the hostage negotiator talks you down, talks you into letting the hostage go and everyone comes out alive. They had skipped that step and gone straight for the megaphone and probably the shooting. What he wouldn't give for a hostage negotiator about now. He would give up so fast. Maybe this town only had one negotiator and he was busy talking someone out of jumping from a building.

The woman whimpered loudly. At least she was aware of the

situation, how she could get hurt way more before this was over, way more than just a nick from a stray bullet. He looked at the weapon. He probably didn't want to be caught holding it.

"Shut up," he yelled, and then said more quietly in case someone else outside could hear and overreact, "Just shut up and let me think." Only even then, when she obediently shut up, he wasn't thinking so good. Put the gun under the bed, maybe? They would find it, but he would look less threatening that way.

Royce wondered what would happen next. Didn't they have tear-gas canisters to throw through the window so he could leave the house with his hands up to show he wasn't going to hurt anyone?

"LET THE WOMAN GO!"

How did they know she was in here, barricaded with him? Had the guy who left in the car come back and told them? Did they know because of her 9-1-1 call? If they knew he wasn't alone, maybe they wouldn't use tear gas. He'd never been tear-gassed, never been in a situation anything like this one before, and had no real clear idea of police protocols beyond what he'd seen on TV. How long would they give him before . . .

. . . boots pounding in the hallway as if they might go straight through the thin wooden floor. The bedroom door, too, like the rest of the house, was pretty flimsy. He wouldn't have been able to separate the first noise from the second. Whether it was the bedroom door splintering into the room with the help of a battering ram, or the sound of the gunfire as he raised his hands . . . in protest? In defense? In surrender? He reminded himself that he meant to put the gun down.

There was impact like when you're punched in the gut, but no immediate pain. Royce grabbed the sheet on the bed but his fingers had lost their feeling and it slipped away. He slumped over onto his side which, all things considered, felt the best at this point. He watched a pair of thick black boots coming toward his face. Christ, those boots were big. The boots stopped a few inches away. One of them kicked away the gun that had dropped near his hand when he went down.

A voice somewhere, not belonging to the boots, said, "Thank God he has a gun, Jim."

Then the boots were replaced by black knees. He felt nothing except a bit of moisture at the sensitive corner of his mouth. If his brain was still fully functioning, he would wonder if it was spit or blood. The boots, whose name was Jim, leaned his big gun against the side of the bed. A glove was removed and fingers pressed to the side of Royce's neck. He could have told the cop his heartbeat was much slower than it had been just a few minutes before, but it wasn't worth the effort.

Royce was still alive at that point. Only just. All he wanted to do was close his eyes, but he couldn't seem to send them the signal to do so. His vision blurred, gentling the harsh black of the SWAT uniform.

No accounting for cerebral activity as each lobe shuts down; surprisingly his speech is the last to go. "I didn't put in for this shit," were his last words, in a blood-soaked whisper, just loud enough for the SWAT guy to think he heard right when he saw Royce's lower lip was moving up and down and he leaned closer to listen.

TWO

I'm Brigid Quinn. The event recounted here is made up partly of what Nicole Gleason told the police in multiple interviews, the 9-1-1 operator's recording, the SWAT body-cam film, and my own imaginings later. The full report added he was a Black male, age twenty-seven, named Royce DeWitt. There had been no identification on him, but fingerprints taken at the autopsy revealed priors in petty larceny and drug possession. This was public record.

Too bad they killed him, but how could they know? The rest of the story might have played out much easier and faster if he could have been questioned. Saved a couple more lives, too. Even dead, we should have cared more about that guy, asked ourselves a few more questions rather than jumping to the conclusion that he was just a junkie looking for drugs in a group home likely to have them. That was our first mistake. Dorito—my take on her real name—was the second.

Even before they killed the burglar in the group home just outside our development, there was something about Dorito that irked me. Something so purposeful about her. Maybe it was the crisp striped blouses over white capri pants. Or the way her reddish bob swung forward, punctuating each step as she walked. Or the way her sandals clacked on the sidewalk as if for all eternity she was headed toward a homeowners' association meeting to lodge a complaint about the color someone had painted his house.

Meanwhile the rest of us shlubs in tattered shorts and soiled sneakers drifted listlessly through the Arizona heat, looking like we'd lost the shopping cart full of our belongings. But don't go thinking I'm petty. It wasn't her looks that got to me. We had our falling-out over dogs. Dorito didn't like dogs and didn't like anyone who did. By no fault of our own, at the time we had three. She had yelled at me through her screen door when my pug peed on her gravel. I don't like being yelled at under any circumstances, so I yelled back, "It's gravel. It's not like my dogs are going to kill your gravel."

She responded, "It attracts other dogs and they pee, too."

As we stood at an impasse I tried, "So what should I do, lick it off?"

She slammed her door, and from then on when walking the pugs or the schnoodle I'd steer them in a wide swath around her property, just a couple of streets from my own, entertaining myself with imagining how she'd react if I took a dump next to her sign that read: Beware of the Owner, with the outline of a rifle.

This time of year, early July and the desert monsoon rains late in coming. People were already cranky, turning on each other. Incidents of road rage spiked. I tried to avoid Dorito on my early evening walk without the dogs, who sniffed endlessly. But on this day she rounded the corner of the next block as I was headed out. At the sight of her I felt my body cinch up in that physical *oh-shit-now-what?* feeling. I couldn't very well cross the street, wave, and move on. No matter how you feel about the neighbors, there is protocol. Instead, we approached on the sidewalk like a couple of gunslingers, each waiting for the other to draw her weapon.

My temporary doglessness didn't soften her stance. It may have even stiffened her resolve. Now I noticed that, instead of a pistol, she carried a clipboard. When we had come face to face, the pointy parts of her bob poked at me. "Here's the latest, Brigid," she began, starting in the middle as if we'd been in contact before and I cared to know the rest.

Her words pinned me against the concrete block privacy wall that ran parallel to the sidewalk. The wall was still radiating the heat it had soaked up during the 100-plus degree temperature of the day. That and the way Dorito had a habit of invading your personal space made me crankier than I usually was during the dog days of summer.

She went on. "The cops have been called out like twenty times over the past year because of fights and stuff."

"Like twenty times. I was not aware of this. Where?"

"At the group home." If she wanted to add "you big jerk" to the end of that, she refrained. She ignored my implied skepticism and pulled my focus closer to her grievance. "Now they killed a burglar."

I knew that, of course. How could you have a SWAT team show up two blocks away and not hear it on the evening news or through the Neighbors social media site? I thought of reminding her the burglar wasn't part of the group home, and that it was actually the cops who killed him rather than one of the residents. But Dorito never seemed to process what someone else said, only concentrating on what she would say next. Also, given our dog pee debate, I knew logic was useless. Besides, *Jeopardy* would be on soon and I didn't want to miss my husband Carlo answering all the questions. I don't know why, but watching his mind in action always made me feel friskier than watching *Bridgerton*.

When "now they killed a burglar" didn't appear to get a rise out of me, she loomed even larger and pumped the drama, "They're roaming the streets!" She took a step closer so I could be impressed by how her evangelical hair, each strand in lock-step with its rigid partner, was able to hold its shape through the afternoon heat.

I couldn't resist challenging her *Walking Dead* imagery. It was also fun to just poke her back a little. "Seems like some would say you and I are roaming the streets. Are you sure a few of them weren't just taking a walk?"

I should keep my mouth shut. That's one of my biggest faults. When other people talk about how they wished they could have thought of something to say, some snappy retort, I wish I could Just. Not. Speak. Some might call me a social anarchist. Others think I'm just a douche.

Dorito wagged the clipboard too close to my face. "There's no one around to control them!" she declared. Seemed like everything with Dorito was a declaration, and that angry. I suspected her of hoarding exclamation points.

"No on-site manager?" I asked.

She shook her bob so vigorously I welcomed the slight

movement of the air it caused around us. "No one! Nada! Zip!"

"You're sure of that?" I said, trying to remember who said "say it three times and it will be true." Goebbels? But being sure didn't seem to count for much with her as she changed the subject, going on. And on.

"I called the Pima County Board of Supervisors and they said they're not responsible, that the home is run by the state. So then I called the state and they said they would 'investigate.' You know what that means, that they won't do a thing. So I called back the person in the county who was very understanding."

"Hm," I murmured.

That was enough encouragement for her. "And on top of that, I heard somebody in Scottsdale bought the property and two others nearby for the purpose of creating these group homes. Maybe they got the money from the state to do it? What do you think of that?"

Mildly interested despite my best intentions, I asked, "What kind of group home is it, behavioral health?"

"That would be bad enough. All kinds of drug addicts and schizophrenics and such. No, these people are convicted felons."

"Ah. Formerly incarcerated folks. On parole."

Whether or not she saw a distinction between conviction and release, she wouldn't say. "But they did tell me, that woman on the supervisors' board, that I could start a petition to have the house closed down. Or rezoned for residential only. That's what this is. Get them out of our neighborhood." And here she delivered her actual truth, bringing down the blade in a coup de grâce, "And just think of the property values."

I held out my hand for the clipboard, seeing it as the easiest exit from her aural assault and knowing the petition had no legal standing. Someone was just humoring her, so I might as well follow suit. "OK, OK. I'll sign it." As I did so I asked, "Do you know how many of them are living there?"

"No."

"Do you know what crimes they committed? Violent? Non-violent?"

She glared, and stepped even closer if that were possible. Her proximity made me fully appreciate for the first time her very large face, the size of a small skillet, and out of proportion to the rest of her body. The eyes, nose, mouth were average size, just set in a vast amount of pale flesh, making her look like pictures I'd seen of the Red Queen in *Alice in Wonderland.*

"Could be murderers. Could be sex offenders, for all I know," she said, with a drop of saliva falling on my hand that held the pen. I would have wiped it on my pants but it dried immediately in the low humidity. "Human traffickers. Pedophiles right there, three houses from the school bus stop."

Her lack of any factual information led me to step aside, grab the back of her hair and slam her large face into the wall *bap bap bap bap bap bap bap*, seven times to refocus her. Hey, just kidding, I haven't done anything like that in a long time. Even as I say that, I understand I can't judge Dorito or anyone else for coming in hot. See, I've been there.

I finished signing Brigid Quinn with a fake address and handed back the clipboard. "Does this thing have any teeth to it?" I asked.

Dorito didn't answer because Jake Walsh had come out to water his bottlebrush tree and Texas sage. She said, "Blessings," out of the corner of her mouth and then wiped it with the back of her hand as if the word was oily. Then she bolted across the street toward him with her body as upright as a quail going for seed. I saw the trapped look in Jake's eyes and kept on walking, with all the gratitude of a person who escapes at the expense of another.

On my way back I saw that Dorito was gone and Jake was just wrapping up his hose. He was singing a cheery little tune and smiling, perhaps thinking of the coming Apocalypse. I should explain here that Jake is a Jehovah's Witness. He'd tried to convert Carlo and me on several occasions before giving up. I never asked if that meant he'd consigned me to hell. Whatever the case, I'm sort of resigned.

I asked him, "So did you sign it?"

"No. I told her we should try to help with the situation rather than just make those people homeless."

I said, "You're a better man than I am, Gunga Din."

He smiled, appearing to know the poem I was alluding to, or at least the classic movie. Just because you're a Jehovah's Witness doesn't mean you've never read anything but the book of Revelation. "It's just biblical principles," he said, and went back to putting away the hose.

Any other time I would have mentally rolled my eyes, but not this time. "Well, you're still a good man. By the way, what kind of name is Dorito?"

"You know it's Dorita," he said, though he couldn't help smiling again. "With an 'a' at the end, not an 'o.' Not like the chip."

"Or if chips had gender." But now I could see the word "gender" troubled him and I said goodnight and headed home before I got myself in another culture war skirmish.

When I looked out the back door, I found my husband Carlo putting out a tin plate of water by the big statue of St. Francis in the backyard. He'd recently reported seeing a bobcat break the dish of the clay birdbath as it tried to get at the water. Rather than hold that against the bobcat, while the desert baked in preparation for the summer rains, Carlo worried about the animals. No matter how angry I still felt from time to time, the sight of Carlo always brought me peace.

I wanted to tell him about my encounter with Dorito. Seeing that he was occupied, I went into my front office and turned on my computer to see if there was talk about the group home on the Neighbors site.

Scrolling.

We're looking for a pet sitter for just a few days, three dogs all very friendly. Large. We like them to be walked morning and evening.

Scrolling.

Has anyone heard any more about that rapid coyote that bit someone's dog the other night?

I mean rabid.

They have to give you a bunch of shots right in your stomach if you think you MIGHT have been bitten by a rabid animal. Otherwise you get what's it called.

Hydrophobia. You're thirsty but you can't drink. That's why animals go crazy when they're sick.

Scrolling . . . ah, there you go, someone late to the party.

What is it with the trouble at the group home, I heard a SWAT team was sent there and killed one of them?

It wasn't one of the people who live there, it was a stranger who came looking for drugs.

Did the stranger find any?

No. It was pretty pathetic.

Well, there's another drug addict off the streets, at least. Why put them in group homes, anyway? Why not just keep them in prison? Don't they still have that three strikes and you're out life conviction?

Wow, that's pretty harsh.

It's a hundred and fifteen degrees but we got a snowflake in the neighborhood.

Fascist.

Who you calling a fucking fascist, Libtard.

Hitler. I hear they're having a sale on tiki torches at Home Depot.

There it was, what Carlo called Godwin's Law, that any political conversation would devolve to Nazi name-calling in just a few exchanges. Then, typically, a critical thinker who must have come online after finishing their daily podcast:

The vast number of people in prison are just people who haven't come to terms with the fact that they're poor and there's nothing they can do about it except be angry. So prison is not so much punishment—their life is punishment enough—as a warehouse for discontent.

And just as typically from the other end of the spectrum:

I bet you listen to NPR and hang a Communist flag. Know what to do with the group home? BURN IT DOWN. Problem solved.

(Fifteen thumbs-up and two crying faces.)

They'll just move them into another one.

Yeah, they're like subterranean termites, exterminate in one house and they move to the one next door. You got to keep burning.

I hardly reacted to the threats, having seen their like before. A couple of the comments could have been posted by Dorito, but she didn't identify herself by name so I couldn't be sure.

The pugs were outside with Carlo, Peg sniffing poop for reasons known only to her, and Al splayed panting on the back porch, trying to soak up as much coolness from the concrete as possible. Al had been diagnosed with congestive heart failure several months before. He was on meds but was also aging, and we both worried a little without admitting it to each other. One of the things we didn't admit.

Our latest acquisition, a three-legged schnoodle named Achilles, was called that because of his missing hind leg. Carlo had told me the story of how the Greek hero's mother dipped him in a magical river, holding him by the ankle. Achilles was invincible except for that ankle and Hector's arrow slew him. Something like that. I might have it a little wrong.

Anyway, Achilles clung to Carlo physically the way I did emotionally. They'd both been traumatized, and instinct had told me they might help each other through it. They did. Of course, there's no discounting the benefit of some drugs and therapy as well.

Carlo looked pretty chipper, the corners of his mouth turned up in a way that spoke to his doing something good, filling the bird feeder, putting that pan of water out for the quail family (difficult to count as they ran around, but we estimated eighteen of them, cookie-cutter images of their parents down to the little black spike on their heads). They were too little to fly up to the birdbath even when it wasn't broken. That's why Carlo put out the pan, for the littles. I liked the way Carlo got even brighter when he looked at me. "You were gone a long time," he said.

"Was I?"

"It's pretty hot still."

"You've got that right."

"I hear the Catholic Church is going to reinstate the existence of Purgatory now that they know where it is."

He'd said that before, but it wasn't so lame, always worth a grin and a headshake. "I'm going to take a shower before *Jeopardy.*"

"I'm right behind you. Soon as I water the fig tree now that the water won't steam the leaves."

I said, "Adam looks like he's got a lot of figs coming in."

His turn to say, "Yes, they're still green, but I think we'll have a good crop."

Oh, but there it was, that thing we still kept returning to sometimes, the small talk that shielded us from intimacy, like a lie that isn't told. The therapist had worked with us on this. *Don't protect him from you, Brigid. Say it. Say it all.* Carlo was supposed to say what he was thinking too, but I could never tell for sure whether he did.

The sun was on the west side of the house, and where there was shade there was a 10-degree drop in temperature. I walked the short distance to Carlo, took his hand, and we both (as well as Achilles, who followed us) walked back to the porch and sat down in the brown wicker chairs. From these chairs a serial killer had made his confession to Carlo because Carlo had been a Roman Catholic priest and a sucker. I had suggested getting new outdoor furniture to replace the ones with bad memories, but again, the therapist had advised against it. She said you could change everything in the world but that wouldn't blot out memory. Memory was just too good at supplying facts, real or otherwise.

"I ran into Dorito," I said.

Carlo half-smiled. He'd long ago given up on correcting me when I renamed people in the neighborhood. "I'm sorry," he said. "How angry was she?"

It wasn't so much whether Dorito was angry, but at what point on the spectrum. Like those pain charts where you're supposed to say whether you're at a two or a ten. The last time she carried around a petition it was because she reckoned homosexual teachers were grooming children by letting them read *Cathy Has Two Daddies.* She appeared before the school board to complain about that and didn't seem to think it made a difference that she hadn't read the book. They should have anger charts that go from mildly disappointed to murderous rage.

"About an eight," I said. "Spitting mad."

"Poor woman." Carlo looked down at Achilles, who was plastered to the side of his foot. He moved the foot up and down a bit, rubbing the dog's side to reassure him of his continuing affection. "Maybe she should have a dog."

"I think it might take more than one," I said. "I'm not sure how many it would take."

Then I took a deep breath and told him the whole story: how Dorito was stomping pissed about the group home on Randolph Street and was collecting petition signatures to have the property rezoned. I didn't hold back on any of the details, though that meant reminding him of the burglar who'd been shot.

"But that's not their fault," he said. Carlo's logic has a hair trigger.

"I know! OK, a couple of them had a loud fight in the front yard a few weeks ago, and more than two of them like to occasionally take walks together, but still." I confessed that I had signed the petition just to get her overly large face out of mine, and how Jake down the street had refused. Carlo nodded approvingly at that.

"What should we do?" he asked, jumping from problem straight to problem-solving as he always did. It's a guy thing.

"I was just thinking," I said cautiously, still sometimes hesitating to tell him what I was thinking. "I could, you know, go over to the house, introduce myself, hint that they needed to get their act together and be model citizens if they don't want to be out on their collective ass."

Carlo blinked a couple of times. Stared straight ahead, and I hoped he wasn't considering that maybe I should move back into the casita in the yard where I'd spent some time when he was afraid to sleep in the same bed with me.

I backed up a little. "First I could call that deacon who works in the prison system, find out whether these are just your run-of-the-mill petty thieves and such, or whether they're truly bad guys." Even as I said that, I thought about how the truly bad guys weren't the ones who got caught, usually.

Carlo took another moment to process that. "You could," he concluded.

I took another breath, less deep this time. "I could bring cookies," I said.

"And books," he said, warming to the idea. For Carlo, books are the universal cure-all. He got up, again that thought-to-action thing, and went into the house. Achilles and I followed him to the room that had been his library from before the time I married him. He was already tickling some book spines midway down the second aisle. "Bill Bryson, I think. And some Dave Barry. Nothing like humor to put things in perspective." He pulled out half a dozen paperbacks and handed them to me. "That should do for now," he said. "Do you think the woman is still there?"

"What woman?"

"The one who the burglar had in the room with him."

He must have read the details in the newspaper, about the woman, her terror, how she had bravely called the cops. The news hadn't identified her, for the best, her being formerly incarcerated and all, plus the fact the home was getting slammed on the Neighbors social media site. Better for them all to stay under the radar. "I don't know any reason why she wouldn't still be there. Maybe depends on whether she's gotten a job, found a place of her own. Those group homes probably aren't the ideal. People want to get out unless they're a hopeless case. I don't know. I'll find out."

"That would be good." Carlo frowned. "I'm afraid I don't have any women's books. I hope they're all male."

"I like Dave Barry," I said. I've never said Carlo is perfect.

THREE

I'm not saying I have this mental health thing down pat. Though I told him of my intent, I purposely waited until Carlo had left for his yearly retreat to an ashram near San Diego. He'd missed the one the year before, not because of Covid, that was pretty much gone, but because he was too scared to leave me by myself. I couldn't quite get clear whether it was because he was protecting me from getting killed, or protecting someone from me killing them. In our marriage-counseling sessions he wouldn't say, and the counselor appeared to fear asking.

"You're sure you'll be OK?" Carlo begged before leaving.

"Hey, you're the one driving through Death Valley in June. You got water?"

He picked up his cooler cup from the kitchen counter and waggled it to show there was ice in it. "I'm serious," he said.

"Cell phone?"

"It's in the car."

I put my arms around his waist and gave him the tightest hug possible, short of going straight through him. My cheek pressed against the third button down on his shirt. He hadn't flinched in months, me touching him, and he hugged me back, twining my white ponytail between his fingers for extra reassurance.

"I love you," he said.

"Thank you," I said, not daring to tell him what that meant to me without a sloppy sob. "Call me when you get there. I'll be here watching *Jeopardy*, like any other normal retired wife who has never killed anyone."

When I waved him off and went back into the house, I sat on the floor and gathered Al, the pug with heart disease, to my body, transferring the hug. He didn't object. I rubbed my nose against the top of his black head (I love the smell of dog fur). It wasn't just dog I smelled this time, it was aftershave. "Daddy kissed you goodbye, didn't he?" Al gazed at me with those bulgy, black-olive eyes and kept the secret. I smiled, knowing what Carlo smelled like and how he must have kissed Al before he left. Just like I never called us Mommy and Daddy in Carlo's hearing, he had never kissed a dog in front of me. I love the smell of Gillette aftershave and felt like I was getting a two-fer, Al and Carlo in one breath.

This was the first time since we married that Carlo would be gone for two whole weeks rather than one. That of course didn't count the several months that I lived out in the casita. Even when we were going through that rough patch, when he found out more about me than I'd ever willingly shared with anyone. He didn't come out and admit he was afraid to fall asleep in the same bed with someone who was a monster, but I understood. That had happened once before when I was dating a concert cellist/single dad named Paul, and accidentally left some crime-scene photos on the kitchen counter that his kids saw.

I've recounted Carlo watching me enjoy the sight of a man having his eyes burned out with hydrochloric acid, his body practically jumping from the floor with the agony. It didn't matter that he was a very bad man and had just smothered his girlfriend in the nearby bedroom. Carlo had known for a while that I occasionally had killed people, and I guess he thought I did it reluctantly. But from that moment when I sprayed the guy's face with acid, Carlo saw this look on my face. I don't know what the look was: Joy, maybe. It shocked him.

While we got back together after those few months, when Carlo had reconciled himself to the fact that I might actually relish killing other monsters, we both still had the notion that I was some hard-boiled broad who never felt as deeply as other people. I'd lived that way a long time; it was one way to survive before he found me.

Before he left for his retreat, I had assured Carlo I would take every precaution before I risked anyone's life and limb. I called that deacon we knew and asked her about who was in the group home. She didn't know, but referred me to a parole officer. He told me he couldn't give me details over the phone, but in general there was nothing to worry about. So I went over to Basha's and picked up a bag of Oreos. I put the Oreos back because what if they were suspicious of me? I could have been one of the neighbors out to get them. I could have tampered with the cream filling. These are the things I think.

Separate bags of chips seemed like a safer option. The books were already in the car, as was my pistol in the glove compartment. Chances were good these people weren't bad, just a bunch of sad sacks who hadn't figured out how to get through life yet. But like I told Carlo, every precaution. I also took my walking stick to add to my small old woman look. It wasn't obvious that the stick has a blade attached to the bottom. It had come in handy in the past for the occasional rattlesnake, or once, a femoral artery.

This was a Sunday morning, so unless they had jobs as Walmart greeters, all the residents might be at home. I pulled up out front, got out and grabbed my stick and the box filled with individual snack chips. I couldn't bring all the books in the same trip but tucked a few under my arm.

I didn't have to knock on the door because someone, a resident I hoped, and not someone stealing concrete blocks from the side of the house, was at work already on a morning hot enough to roast a small turkey. He looked pretty big, but I was still taken aback when he stood up, taller even than Carlo. He didn't seem inclined to be the first one to speak, so I did.

"Hi. I'm one of your neighbors. Brigid . . ." I considered adding my last name but didn't. Why? Maybe Dorito's fear was rubbing off on me. This guy sure was big. Big fuckin' guy.

He still didn't speak, so I said, "I brought youse some chips. Replace the sodium you lose from sweating."

The man dropped his trowel in a nearby tray of wet cement, took off his work gloves, wiped his dry face on a dirty towel hanging from his belt, and walked over to where I stood in the open. I had positioned myself there with purpose, wanting to appear unthreatening and yet ready to deal with an attacker if I had to. Given this man's size, either of those scenarios seemed laughable now. I put out my hand for a shake and he took it in a paw that made mine disappear into its depths. "Thanks," he said, and added, with a southernish accent in a higher pitch that didn't match his physique, "That's right neighborly of you."

"I see you're building a wall," I said.

"Good fences make good neighbors," he said with a dry smile and sad eyes.

Anyone capable of irony is generally not immediately dangerous, so I countered with a line from the same poem, about not loving a wall.

Without pretense, he asked, "Who said that?"

"Same guy." Having spent what was probably our sole knowledge of Robert Frost, if not all poetry, we turned our heads to watch two other guys emerging from the house. They were both way shorter and scrawnier than Big Fuckin' Guy (who from that moment I began to think of as BFG). It was good they had less surface area, otherwise they'd never have been able to afford the tats that covered their chests and arms.

Ever hear about ermines? They're smelly, curious, and not to be trusted. They're kind of cute, but they have a very bad attitude. A few years ago, someone in Vermont who thought they were doing nature a favor opened an ermine farm to let the creatures out so they wouldn't get turned into coats. The ermine showed their gratitude by killing all the wildlife and house pets in a 10-mile radius before most of them were either exterminated or trapped and returned to the farm. About the size of a ferret, they can kill animals much larger than themselves, especially if they come in packs.

These guys, salt-and-pepper shakers—one lighter, one darker. So far they didn't present much of a threat, but that's how it sometimes is with ermines. They appeared busy trying to come up with one-liners about little old women and not having much luck.

I began to rethink Dorito's opinion and my own options. I figured I could take the two little ones all right, but if the big one came to their defense, he would take more work. I wasn't in the mood for it, it was too hot, and besides, I had to honor my promise to Carlo not to hurt anyone.

Time to make a bit of a show. It would pre-empt any aggression on their part, as well as push the envelope a bit to see just how much aggression lurked in that house. Luck would have it, an opportunity appeared in my peripheral vision from the right corner of the house. Not another person, something much smaller. A brown and black striped lizard, about seven inches long, was making a foolhardy dash across the yard. Foolish because there were no bushes for him to run to where he might have had cover. I stood very still so as not to frighten him away and, sure enough, he ran in my direction, just close enough.

I whipped my walking stick out and snapped off his tail, glad I had aimed well and not hit the poor thing in his center mass. Yep, reflexes as good as ever. He could always grow another tail, and this was enough to make my point without a tussle that would get sand in my pants.

"Sorry," I said, wiping the blade on my shoe just for show and then leaning on it to reveal I had no further intention of using it unless I had to. "I have a lizard phobia."

The ermines were duly impressed, which they expressed by punching each other's arms and hooting. The big guy just tilted his head with mild appreciation.

"Be nice to her. She brought chips," he said. He came close, made a bear-like swipe at the top of the box to open it, and took out one of the bags, which he ripped open with his teeth to pour the contents down his throat.

As I watched with admiration his snacking finesse, two other people appeared at the front door. One stayed in the shadows, so my attention was first taken with the man, this one average height, which was to say about a half a foot taller than me. His height, his build, his close neat haircut, his face you wouldn't recognize again if you saw it in a line-up next week—everything about him screamed the villain of the piece, the one you never suspect because he's so . . . normal. So one was too big, two were too small, and one was just right. I felt like Goldilocks. Mr. Normal gave me a once-over, took in my stick, my gender and my stature in one glance, scanned the other three guys for signs of aggression and said, "Somebody getting froggy out here?"

"Everybody's very cordial." I knew the term "froggy" from working with military men. I in turn gave him my one-second assessment, his age, his remaining bulk that would never go away. "Navy?" I asked, to ratchet down any tension by changing the subject.

He scoffed, "Marines. What are you doing here?"

I confessed I was just bringing chips. "And books."

"Thanks," he said. "I don't know who you are, lady, but maybe you should go now before I call the police. We've had enough trouble with neighbors."

I could tell from the way he said that, telling me to go before he called the police, that calling the police was the last thing he wanted to do this morning. My thoughts flashed to the burglar who had been killed on the premises. There was no telling how the police would react to this kind of caller.

"Look," I said, "I know this didn't start as well as I'd planned, but I don't mean anything. I really did just bring some chips as a gesture of goodwill. And some books." I nodded first toward the ones tucked under my arm, and then toward my car. "I brought some books."

One of the ermines closed the gap between us and put out his hand for the chips. I gave him the whole box, trusting he wouldn't bite my hand.

"See, part of the reason I came over is that there's someone in my neighborhood who doesn't like the idea of a group home here." Rather than state the obvious, I lied just a little, calling Dorito "he" so I wouldn't get her on their radar. "He's making moves to get your place rezoned as residential. That means no group home and no place for you and future folks to stay when they get released. You don't want that, do you?"

The first ermine had his mouth full of potato chips and couldn't speak, but the second, darker one did for him. "Fuckin A," he said, and turned to the guy who'd told me to get off the property. "Can they do that?"

"Maybe they can," Mr. Normal answered.

"So you see, I'm here to say that you gotta lay low for a while. Get your act together. Not do anything that might get attention, no fights or noise where a neighbor has an excuse to call the police." I stopped short of telling them not to step off the property in any numbers someone could call a "roaming band." That's just offensive.

"It's not like you're helping much," BFG said, gesturing at my walking stick. "Anyone else around here can discharge a firearm and no one blinks. But with us, if anyone saw us with a homemade weapon like your stick, they'd call the cops in a heartbeat."

"Admitted," I said. "I can be a little . . . impulsive. I'm Brigid." I went from man to man, holding out my hand for a shake. I saved the chip-eating ermine for last so I could wipe the grease on my shorts. Even then I still didn't give my last name, reserving a little privacy for safety's sake, so they couldn't be sure which house I came from. None of them said their own name, maybe for the same reason. "So. Is there someone in the position of manager here?"

"Who are you that we need to answer that?" Mr. Normal asked.

I nodded my agreement. "I'm nobody right now. But maybe someday I'll be your best friend. You never know. And even then you never know." I smiled as I said it, and he smiled back. Nothing funnier than an old lady claiming to be your protector. "Would you just confirm something that I already assume?"

"What's that?"

"None of you were in for violent crimes, am I right?"

Did Mr. Normal respond immediately, or was the pause wide enough to drive a truck through?

"We got theft, drug sales, fraud, arson . . ."

There was that pause again but, satisfied that he was telling me enough of the truth, I nodded and asked my original question again. "And what about the manager? Do you have anyone looking in on you, to see if you need anything, help with job applications and interviews, anything?"

"We had a guy, but he quit unexpectedly. It was after . . . the shooting. We're waiting for our new guy. They won't be on-site, but they call or check in every day without telling us which one it will be."

I nodded, accepting that he could have kept that piece of information from me, but didn't. "All righty then. Let me just get the rest of the books out of the car."

When I turned to leave the yard, I saw Dorito of the large face watching at her back wall. With her fingers curled over the concrete and her nose appearing to rest on top, she made me think of that graffiti character from World War II, "Kilroy was here." Wow that was a big forehead. I wished she'd go away and leave well enough alone. *Stand down before they put two and two together*, I thought.

The felons' math skills were apparently good. BFG whispered, "Fuckin A" as she called, "What are you doing!" It was a statement rather than a question so I didn't answer. Hoping to squelch her, I walked across the street so I could talk to her without the others hearing. I walked slowly, giving her time to cool her ballistic system. No such luck. She went on. In a loud whisper, she said, "Are you over there warning them that we're trying to get that property rezoned?"

"I didn't mention that," I lied. "I just thought it would be interesting to see for myself who's living there. Whether they felt like an actual threat to our neighborhood."

"How would you know?"

"I was once in the business."

She was too self-absorbed to ask what business that was. "And?"

"They're a bunch of third-rate criminals," I said. "They don't pose a threat to anyone."

"We disagree."

There's that "we." It always shows up sooner or later with people too cowardly to speak for themselves. "Who's we?" I asked. "You got a mouse in your pocket?"

Undeterred, she said, "I've got twenty signatures on my petition. Everyone except that Jehovah's Witness signed it. Even you."

"I was rethinking."

She frowned as if put off by the thought of someone capable

of changing their mind. I took advantage of her temporary silence. "So the way my thinking went, I should do a little more fact-finding before I jump on your bandwagon. See the situation for myself."

"And how much fact-finding will it take for you to understand those people are vermin?"

Ooh, the slur did it for me. I knew where it came from. When I'm in a good mood I can joke that in the last election I was scum, so vermin is several evolutionary steps up. I could even call the group home residents ermines because in a sense they were my people. Indeed, some of the things I'd done were way worse, like killing a man and staging it to look like an accident.

"What evidence makes you come to that conclusion?" I asked, barely, just barely controlling myself.

She might not have noticed my voice had cooled by several degrees. "Just look at them. They're low-life, and they've got a woman in there. Heaven knows what they're up to with her. I've seen her and she looks weird, something wrong with her face, a little on the Down's spectrum. Or something. I heard she was mentally depraved."

I didn't turn to look. I did not respond. Would not give her the gratification of having a point of view that could be confirmed or denied.

"I get it, live and let live," she said, when the quiet got to her. "You're probably one of those people who says 'you do you.' Am I right?"

"Not at all. We both know you should do me."

Now it was her turn to be quiet as she tried to sort that out.

I understand that to name-call is to admit defeat, but I was too worn out from making peace with the guys for further conversation.

"Pain in the ass," I said definitively but with some wonder, as if having just been surprised by that discovery.

"That's un-Christian," she said, narrowing her eyes and lifting her nose a couple of inches off the top of the concrete wall to display the judgment of her neanderthal jaw. She was one to talk about another person's odd face.

I stared, thinking it probably wasn't worth drawing the breath needed to speak. And then I nodded agreement with her assessment of my religious ideology. "You got that right. And you're still a pain in the ass."

Now her expression was totally closed for business. All her features sucked together in the middle of her face. When she said, "Have a beautiful day," I could swear I heard, "Go fuck yourself."

We both turned our backs on the other, me returning to the car where I'd left the back door open to get out the rest of the books. The four guys had stayed in the yard, watching with interest my interaction with Dorito, even if they couldn't hear much of it. Just as well. Neither Dorito nor I were the kind of people who were good influences.

"What was that about?" asked Mr. Normal, who was appearing to be the de facto leader of the group.

"Nothing," I said helpfully.

The lighter ermine said, "Aw, come on, we see her all the time looking over that wall like she done just now."

"She gives me the creeps," said the other.

I said, "I know how you feel, but you've gotta ignore that woman, right? Leave her alone. Don't speak with her. Don't even look at her funny."

"Trust me, I'm down with that," the darker ermine said.

Racism might be one of our lesser problems right now. I reiterated, "She can make trouble for you."

There was that last person who had appeared in the doorway, behind Mr. Normal. That figure I'd noted was wispier than the others and I didn't know if it was a female or just a trick of the shadows. Then I remembered how, according to the news, it was a woman who the SWAT-shot burglar had held hostage in one of the rooms of the house. As I walked back into the yard, she finally stepped all the way out.

She was greatly changed, but I was nearly certain. "Oh my God," I said, surprised, and pleased, and ashamed all at once. "Nicki?"

"Brigid?"

She had the same close-cropped brownish hair I remembered,

the same tall and lean body that made her look a little boyish. I dropped the books and walked toward her without thinking how I'd be received, whether she'd be happy to see me, slam the door in my face, or something worse. Except for her one step out onto a four-foot square piece of concrete I supposed you could call a front porch, she didn't take another move in my direction.

As I got closer, I could see the conflict of her reactions to me, welcoming or angry, flow across her, her prominent top lip stiffening as her oddly shaped eyes softened. I kept coming, though, and when I reached the wannabe porch, she stood still enough to let me hug her, raising her arms to almost return the embrace.

I felt humbled. I don't know about her hug, but mine expressed that old regret for all the times I'd failed, the way I was responsible for what had happened to her. You see, it was my fault she was here. As my own rage has settled down to a low-level grumpiness with occasional elements of snark, I thought I had finally learned the lesson: Violence begets violence.

"Please forgive me," I said.

She didn't answer.

FOUR

Nicki was in really good shape when she went into prison. I know, because I was responsible for training her. Four years later she was, if anything, even more physically fit. As with the male prisoners, working out is one permitted way to pass the time. And apparently the extra fat and carbs from prison food didn't do any damage. She was still as lean as ever, which made the muscles even more prominent than before. I thought for a moment that if the burglar hadn't had a weapon, it would have gone worse for the burglar. Or gone better, since he probably would have been unconscious before the SWAT team got to the house and killed him.

Apparently, Nicki was the darling of the group home, the only woman living there for now, and much respected additionally as the only one who had actually killed someone. She told me she had a bedroom to herself while the four men bunked together in the two rooms at the other end of the house. Illogically, the men felt she needed their protection, especially after her experience of being barricaded in the bedroom with the burglar when none of the rest of them were home.

She told the guys who I was, how I'd trained her in self-defense. She didn't mention how I ended up screwing her at her trial, and I was grateful for that. Maybe she'd mostly forgiven me. Hard to tell; she didn't appear thrilled to see me. Maybe prison hardened her in more ways than one.

Mr. Normal introduced himself as Tyler Wrobleski, more gentlemanly than the others, and apparently the one who owned a laptop. "That training might come in handy," he said. "The Neighbors site, do you know it?"

"Yeah," I said.

Tyler said, "It's been lighting up again lately about us, probably because of that woman across the street. They're calling for an HOA meeting. Maybe a better name for them would be MOB."

"Brigid isn't here to talk about that," Nicki said, and invited me to come inside, pointed me to an armchair in the living room.

That's when I regretted not wearing longer pants. The fabric on the armchair she offered me was a little too shiny to be actual cloth, and vaguely sticky, but I'd be damned if I would refuse it, hoping the backs of my thighs wouldn't adhere to it when I tried to get up again. The whole house, as much of it as I could see, was like that chair. Filled with stuff that would make a thrift shop cringe, but on the whole not as dirty as it might have been.

The smell though. Vaguely of curry, which was all right, but also a cat who didn't have its litter box cleaned out nearly enough.

"Have you got a cat?" I asked.

"No," Nicki said.

I ignored the guys who had come inside and split off into various rooms while pretending to ignore us. I may have been the first and only visitor they'd had. Nicki flopped on the grimy couch across from me. She had taken a couple of bags of chips out of the box I brought, and threw one at me. More assertive than I remembered, a little tougher. "So who is that bitch, anyway?"

"You mean Dorito?"

"That's her name?"

"I should get it right or I'll accidentally use it if she ever speaks to me again. It's Dori-*ta*."

I told her about getting waylaid the day before to sign her petition, and even how I'd imagined *bapping* her head against the concrete wall. Nicki looked uncomfortable at the image. Too close to reality for her, I thought. It was good she didn't laugh.

"So did you sign it?"

I wished now I hadn't brought up the petition because . . . "Certainly not!" I said.

Nicki squinted at me and appeared satisfied that I was lying. Suggestions of her being mentally slow were greatly exaggerated during her trial. Plus, it's likely that naivete dies in prison. She squinted a lot, her flattish nose raised a bit as if she were looking through the lower half of bifocals, the part you use to read things. Reading me. Controlled.

I remembered her as passive when we first met. Now she was not.

I also read that—despite her superficial friendliness—she could very well harbor some resentment for the part I had played, no matter how unwittingly, in her incarceration. But she wasn't going there today. I got the tough facts out of the way first, ripping off the conversational bandage. I had nothing to lose.

"You got out early," I commented. "How long?"

"Good behavior and all that. Been out about two months."

I shook my head with added regret. "I had no idea."

"Why should you? I guess I could just as easily have called you but . . ."

I left that "but" alone. When someone gives you a way out, take it. "I see you didn't stop working. Some brilliant stuff here." I gestured at several unframed paintings that hung on the walls, one of a blonde woman coated with a sheer blue cape. Another of a man and woman in profile, both of them gazing at an apple in the woman's outstretched hand. All of the figures with one or more unusual facial traits, the oddly shaped eyes and flat upper lip. Self-portraits all. Except for one of a child at work on her own drawing. She was an angel with ponytails.

"I'm sorry that didn't work," I said. "I don't know what else to say. Would it help if I crawled on my bloody knees in your direction?"

She knew that what I meant was the part I played in her defense at trial, that backfired, but she wanted to talk about better things. "I learned so much at Perryville, I finally became one of the teachers," she said. "There was lots of talent there, given the restrictions."

"Restrictions?"

"Like we weren't allowed to use glue for the collages. I think they were afraid we'd sniff it."

I smiled obligingly. Nicki always had a good sense of humor, proof of the mind behind that face.

She went on. "So the gals used toothpaste, instead. They were so inventive, one woman who wanted extra texture used sand from the yard. I've volunteered to go back and keep up the instruction. As soon as I have a car."

Nicki didn't say it like she was poor-mouthing or hinting for help. Besides a dry wit, she was remarkably free of self-pity. Long resigned to the way life treated her, maybe. Nicki had been born to another child of sixteen who drank herself to death at age nineteen, leaving Nicki with the dead body in the house for several days. Father unknown. Put in foster homes, she stumbled through school because they didn't know what else to do with her. In some ways she appeared "slow," but there was this artistic talent that none of the special ed teachers could explain away. She would sketch them during class instead of learning how to read.

If anyone cared they would have breathed a sigh of relief if they knew she grew up, got a job at a grocery store, and even married a guy who owned his own mobile home. If anyone cared about her they would have said she made it. Until she didn't.

There was that painting on the wall that I didn't have to ask about. The beautiful little girl. I knew it was Ramona. I'd seen the photograph that she took to prison with her. Those funny ponytails sticking out from either side of her head. Big sky-blue eyes. In the picture Ramona was three, her age at the time when Nicki went to prison.

I had no right to ask Nicki questions about Ramona. Where she had been, where she was now. Foster care, I presumed. Growing up in someone else's house just like Nicki had.

Did I dare to ask about her? Fuck it. Thinking about that song, "Fools Rush In" I asked, "Where's Ramona right now? She must be around six, right?"

I half-expected to see pain, Nicki gripping her mid-section or starting to cry, but instead I perceived a kind of shift in the light as unmistakable joy swept over her face. "That's one good thing that Eleanore did."

"Eleanore?"

"My mentor."

"Ah, I've heard of that. How is it working out?"

"She's great. When she became my mentor, I told her I was worried about Ramona because I couldn't get all the information on what it was like with the family who had her. Would you believe, Eleanore visited them? Was able to reassure me that Ramona was happy enough. She's finished first grade and got good marks. She's smart, you know?" This was especially important to Nicki. "I wrote her letters the whole time I was away. Even before she could read. Eleanore told me the foster mother read the letters to her. Wait." Nicki left the room and came back with a pile of those pictures that children create. The paper all ruffled from the dampness of the watercolors. "Look, I think she has my talent, don't you?"

I could only agree. I would have bitten off my tongue before I'd say that the pictures of "Ramona and Mommy in front of a big house with a dog," struck me as anything but the typical figures of a little one.

Instead I turned back to the one hanging on the wall, the one of the couple with an apple.

"Is that one Adam and Eve?" I asked.

Then I looked harder. "Wait. Is that . . . Vincent?" I remembered seeing his picture in the news repeatedly after she killed him. There were lots of photos of him in the news, that birthday thing where he was holding Ramona, maybe for the only time, but what the fuck. He was as ugly as I remembered him, one of those baggy-eyed disaffected incels who finally attracted Nicki because she didn't have the experience to be warned. Then he punished her for it.

Nicki nodded.

"You really . . . captured him," I said.

The look on her face when talking about Ramona slipped away. "He won, and he didn't even have to be alive to do it."

At that point I could have jumped in and said, "Oh no! Look how lucky you are, to be alive! To have Ramona!" That's about as useful as cheering someone up by telling them to cheer up. Like when Mom would tell me I "shouldn't feel that way." So I stayed quiet and let the feeling flow.

She didn't give me much to work with. Just took a deep breath and sighed with the exhalation, "It's always been Eve's fault, hasn't it?"

"Nicki, I'm sorry," I tried again. "I wasn't at your sentencing to speak for you because I was . . . I was . . ." I could have told her how I had problems of my own; how Carlo was in danger from a serial killer blah blah blah, but it all seemed like nothing but an excuse.

"Shut up, Brigid," she said wisely. "I'm not going to make you feel better."

I had met Nicki while she was clerking at Walmart six years ago, two years before she went to prison, and couldn't ignore the cigarette burn on her right hand. She didn't know it's easy to tell a cigarette burn. Rather than embarrass her with questions in public, and from a stranger, I gave her a card with the address of Desert Doves for abused women and left. The next day I went back and she'd put a Band-Aid over the sore. I didn't know enough about fetal alcohol syndrome at the time to notice anything unusual about her facial features. As far as I was concerned, you still had to look really hard to notice any difference between her and anyone else. But she would be forever judged, forever marked, and I'm not talking about that scar on her hand.

"Well listen," I said. "We've got this clunker that we seldom use. I could loan it to you until you're able to get back on your feet. Are you working?"

"Got a job at Basha's. They won't let me handle money, but I'm allowed to restock the shelves at night. And I can walk there after the sun goes down so it doesn't matter how hot the days are."

I knew the shortest route to the grocery store was via Golder Ranch. "You need to be careful after dark," I said. "The area is still pretty safe—"

"Except for the occasional burglar with a death wish."

I tilted my head back and forth in that maybe-yes maybe-no way, "That was pretty terrifying. I didn't want to bring it up, but you were the woman." It didn't need to be a question.

Nicki told me the story from her perspective. It all seemed rote, as if she was reading from the police report. That made a lot of sense, seeing as how she would have been interviewed at some length. Just because the burglar died didn't mean there wasn't an investigation.

"I was in the bathroom." She looked a little embarrassed,

"Playing angry birds on my phone. Didn't realize the front door was unlocked. Usually anybody who leaves locks it. So the burglar just came in. He must have had the time to look around the house for drugs."

"How did you know that's what he was after?" I asked.

"Later, when he had me trapped in my bedroom, he said so. Besides, what else?" Nicki said, waving her hand around the more-than-modest furnishings of the room. "Would he think there was money here?"

BFG was passing through the room slowly, and grunted, "I think he took my Rolex."

Nicki answered me straight without the sarcasm. "When I came out of the bathroom, we practically ran into each other in the hallway. I ducked back into the bathroom, slammed the door, and sent a text message to nine-one-one so he couldn't hear me doing it. But then I came out."

"Why?" I asked.

"What?"

"Why did you come out?"

There's a look that tries not to be a look. Hard to say exactly how I knew, but the room got just a little quieter.

She held her stare as if she'd practiced it. "You know me, not thinking clear, right?"

Defensive? All I could do was glance down and not respond. Affirmations (oh no! you have good judgment!) bounced off of Nicki. She could read through them, which tells you that her mind was actually just fine.

"It sounds like he had a plan," I said. "Not some random reaction."

Nicki ignored me and went on with her version of the events. Still talking as if it was scripted. "That's when he asked me about where the drugs were," she said. "I told him we were clean. Didn't even have liquor in the house. At least not most of the time. Erroll and Jackson sometimes sneak beer in, or those little airplane bottles."

I started to ask if those were the ermines, but she wouldn't get it. "Are those the little guys, by any chance?"

Nicki allowed herself a smile. "Yeah. The big one, Henry,

he doesn't drink at all. Anyways, the burglar got pretty mad when he heard the sirens going and saw a policeman in a black helmet go by the window. I guess he knew then that I'd called. He had a gun with him and he shot me with it."

"That was stupid."

"Well, no, he wasn't aiming at me. I think he was shooting at the paintings against the wall. There were six of them and the bullet went straight through on his second try."

"You could have been killed."

"I've had worse," Nicki said, looking a little embarrassed by what she would consider an overreaction.

"You didn't try to defend yourself," I said, remembering our training.

Nicki startled—at the memories, I thought—and then dropped her eyes. "I was really scared. Besides, didn't go so good the first time, did it?" she answered as I mentally kicked myself for the suggestion. "The SWAT team came in and killed him, and that's it. I felt a little sorry for him."

"I can feel that."

She shook her head. "Poor schmuck. He was terminally stupid. I had to pretend to be scared so he wouldn't do anything extra idiotic like hurt himself. As far as doing anything to defend myself—been there, done that, got the orange jumpsuit."

"Are you sure that burglar didn't have anything to do with you?"

"Like my husband's family is trying to get revenge? They asked me all those questions when they were getting my story. They asked for details about the SWAT team, too, making sure I wasn't going to spread another story about a cop killing a Black man."

"Do you know any reason why you might have been targeted? Vincent's family?"

"I didn't hear anything about them since Vincent's sister spoke at my sentencing hearing. It was pretty brutal, her saying they should execute me for what I did even if I was a moron. I wouldn't be surprised if they heard about my getting out early and were pissed, but that guy?" Here she put an end to any further talk. "That guy was just after some drugs; in the wrong place at the wrong time."

I nodded. Still, it would be a good idea to keep Vincent Gleason's family in mind and I could do a little snooping to make sure they were behaving themselves, but changed the subject to her walking at night. "What I wanted to say is Golder Ranch has a lot more traffic than it did a few years ago, and with the road work that's going on next to that new housing development, a car trying to stay in the correct lane could clip you one without seeing you."

"I'm OK. I wear a head lamp and walk against traffic."

"Is the pay enough to get a place of your own?"

Nicki shook her head regretfully. "Not so far. Minimum wage has gone up since I went in, but so have rents."

"I just want to be here for you."

One side of her mouth lifted in a sign of half-wanting to believe me. "Well, I'm doing OK. I have these guys, and we're all pretty supportive of each other even if they're a bunch of doofuses." She hesitated for just a beat. "Plus there's my mentor."

"What's she like?"

"She's pretty rich, got a rock on her finger." Nicki put one hand with fingers extended to the size of a baseball over the back of the other. Then paused as if regretting saying anything that, no matter how slight, even hinted at negativity. Not knowing where to go from there, she added, ". . . but she's supposed to be really good with ex-felons. Really supportive."

"Who is she again?"

"Eleanore Turner. That's Eleanore with an e."

Being a bit of a reverse snob when it comes to wealth, I smiled and lifted a pinky finger. "Or is that the wrong finger?"

Nicki ignored my innuendo, said, "You haven't heard of her?"

I remembered a friendship with a wealthy woman that had gone seriously awry. Someone like Nicki might think that all the people who weren't out-and-out poor would know each other. "Me? I'm hardly part of that social circle. You said *supposed* to be really good. Does that mean you don't have any personal experience with her beyond her making sure Ramona is OK?"

"Hold on a second." Nicki unfolded herself from the couch and disappeared into a back room that was close enough I could hear a drawer opening and closing, ruffling sounds. She came back out and handed me a letter. I read.

> Dear Nicki. May I call you that? I know your name is Nicole but I always think that nicknames express a kind of closeness that formal names do not. I would like to be your true friend. You may call me Ellie if you want.
>
> I've been told that you're a painter! More than that, you teach others at Perryville to explore their own gifts. I understand that there are many restrictions on the kind of media allowed. That certain things like glue are off limits. How funny, do they think you will glue one of the guards to the wall and make your escape? I hope you don't mind my joking. I remember reading my mother's copy of the *Reader's Digest* and always liked the section called "Laughter is the Best Medicine." In my family, no matter what happens we turn it into a joke.
>
> Any-hoo, a little about myself. I live with my husband Ian in Tucson, and won't be far from the group home you've been assigned to. Ian is a veterinarian/developer/Pima County Supervisor (!), who is even busier now that everyone got themselves a pet during the pandemic. I'm fifty-two (yikes!) and spend my time working on various nonprofits in the area, notably Sister Jose's Women's Center—a place for homeless women to get their lives back on track.
>
> And, of course, this mentoring of formerly incarcerated women coming out of Perryville. I humbly mention that this isn't my first rodeo, so to speak. I've mentored three other women over as many years. Each one is different, with her own past history, current challenges, hopes and fears. And here is where I get serious ☺ I extend my whole heart to you, to do whatever I can to help you begin your life again. A big part of that will be helping you make a home for your child who you haven't seen in a while. I'll be finding out more about her, and how I can get the two of you together again. With the long-term goal of getting her out of foster care and back into your

arms for good. Having not been blessed with children myself, the difference in our ages makes me especially hopeful that I can be a mother to you. I hope you don't think that's too forward. I tend to "let it all hang out."

But I don't want to take charge of your life or boss you around. I hope you will write back to me and tell me about yourself, what family you have waiting for you, your goals—your dreams—for the next chapter of your life. To let the past go and embrace your future. I'm at your service. I can't wait to begin! My goodness, this is a long letter. I promise you I'm a good listener (reader?) too!

Respectfully, Eleanore Turner

I gave the letter back to Nicki. "How lovely," I said. "Is she like her letter?"

Nicki's words were energetic. "She's wonderful. My parole officer told me she's mentored a few other women and was really good for them, got them started back in the world or something. She wrote me some other letters while I was still in prison. And she's been around a lot."

She was repeating herself and it reminded me vaguely of brainwashed guys in *The Manchurian Candidate*. I brushed away that thought. "No downsides?"

Nicki considered, appearing to choose her opinions with some care, maybe sensing my skepticism. "Oh, maybe a little hovery."

"How is that?"

"No. I don't mean that. She's found out just how much fixing I can use. To be a better mother, you know? After not having a chance to do it while I was in prison."

All I did was listen for more.

"She takes me to meetings with my parole officer. Gives me things like this pillow." Nicki pulled it out from behind her back. It said, Live. Laugh. Love.

"How about refrigerator magnets?" I said, doing my best not to sound sarcastic, which might have smacked of jealousy. "Today is the first day of the rest of your life?"

Nicki couldn't help but smile. "Yeah. That."

"Can't you just throw them away?"

With a brief flash of her eyes, she didn't answer me directly. "I was so happy to have my time inside shortened, and I still have to report to the parole officer for a couple of years. The parole officer likes her. I'm crazy not to do anything that will rock the boat. And you know I'm the first one to say I don't trust my own judgment."

The humiliation of the trial, when a psychiatrist speaking in her defense tried to establish that she wasn't altogether responsible for her actions because of having fetal alcohol syndrome. That was another track not to walk down if we didn't have to. So much to avoid. I cracked my neck to get rid of some stress and only said, "There's some who'd say the executive function in my own brain isn't always up to snuff. Who's your parole officer?"

Nicki shook her head even if she smiled as she did it. "Oh no you don't. I can see you thinking. Don't you get involved trying to fix things too, or I'll go completely nuts," she said. "I shouldn't have said anything. It's really not a big deal. Don't sweat the small stuff, right?"

I wouldn't be surprised if she had a refrigerator magnet for that one, too. Not that I was going to get involved. Nicki certainly didn't need another person messing around with her future. And I hadn't been much use the first time, to put it mildly. But we did have that extra bedroom. My niece Gemma-Kate had moved out when she moved in with a boyfriend closer to the university. I'd have to run this by Carlo and get approval from Nicki's so far unnamed parole officer before I offered the room. I would remind him of her case, how I had taught her how to kill someone, without realizing she'd actually do it. Carlo and I would discuss whether, in his words, I was doing it to "assuage my guilty conscience." I would say, "sure," and then I'd put clean sheets on the guest bed and give Nicki a call to pack up her stuff and come.

FIVE

There's nothing social about social media. I always promised myself I wouldn't look, but with Carlo gone, the dogs walked by six a.m. to avoid the heat, and half a pot of coffee left, I poured myself a cup and went to the Neighbors site the next morning to see what new outrage and/or "can you foster this cat," and/or "is this snake venomous?" and/or "big yard sale Saturday!" was there. I particularly wanted to see if there was any more residual buzz about the group home. Getting reacquainted with Nicki had made it personal.

Postings were typical, the group think flowing from one topic to another like a school of fish going after chum:

We went to Billy's Barbecue for dinner last night. Service was terrible! We had to ask for silverware and when it came, after about twenty minutes, our food was cold! Plus the knives and forks were plastic! Made it really hard to eat the ribs. Barbecue sauce was way too vinegary. Will never go back.

There were a dozen hearts (meaning they liked what they read or in this case felt the poster's pain). And a few comments, illustrated by this:

We agree. It's way too expensive for what you get and the portions are tiny. Try Bubb's Grubb instead, the portions are HUGE! The barbecue is great but did you know you can get scrod there? We always go for the Wisconsin fish fry on Fridays.

And this wit:

Get scrod! LOL!

And this:

That's terrible that you complain on this public site about such trivia at a restaurant! Have you ever known anyone who owned a restaurant? It's a really hard business. Next time if you don't like plastic forks tell the manager, not everyone in the goddamn world!

And this sage pondering the ways of the world:

You let your food get cold waiting for utensils? Who the hell eats ribs with a knife and fork?

No matter what anyone said there would be someone outraged at it. Turns out that outrage wasn't only addictive for me but pretty much for everyone. It was like coming up on a traffic accident, slowing down and rubber-necking to see if you'll be rewarded with an honest-to-goodness fatality. I was sick of it, not only in that anonymous "They and We" way, but in myself. With the work I'd done I was long desensitized to violence, but I wondered when it had happened to the rest of the world. All the way from the Red Wedding in *Game of Thrones* to babies in body bags. Which mass killing tipped us all over the edge? Oh look, we observed. Twenty-three people mowed down at the mall.

Still, I scrolled down, telling myself this was all about supporting those people in the group home in general, and Nicki Gleason specifically. Ah, there it was:

Anybody know why there was a SWAT car in front of the house on Bowman? Crazy lights and sirens.

A helpful neighbor posted an internet link to the local news without comment. That gave enough alleged facts to resurrect the old news and allow everyone to immediately pile on.

Too bad there was only one person in the house. He could have shot them all at once.

There's a group home in our neighborhood? Aren't they supposed to let us know? Or do they keep it a big secret until somebody gets killed?

My neighbor told me that one of them went into a friend's house in the middle of the night.

OMG. What happened?

He was just standing in their kitchen and asked for a drink of water when they asked him what he was doing there. High on something. They called the police who said, 'Oh that's just Earl, and they took him away.'

Like he does it all the time? My God! Everybody keep your doors locked.

Interesting that no one questioned whether the Earl incident was apocryphal.

Apociphal? What the hell does that even mean?

Too bad that burglar didn't kill them all. That would solve the problem.

What good would that do? They'd just send more.

That was the end of it for now. The outrage spends itself in looping without someone to fan new flames. The next posting was about someone looking for a home for two cats because their person had to go into assisted living. After that was a note about the new housing development and that sparked another, if less intense, rant:

I moved to Catalina so I could get out of the city. Now what do we have? A new housing development with NINETY houses going up just off Twin Lakes Road. Before you know it the traffic will be tied up all over the place and we'll have to stand in even longer lines at the grocery store.

That garnered thirty-six hearts and one laughy face. I didn't realize people were so protective of the village status here in Catalina. It was like a little country pocket between the big city of Tucson (a smidge over one million people) and Saddlebrooke a little further up the road, which had been settled in the eighties and had no limits on desert encroachment for miles around into a larger and larger community.

Carlo called. I told him about my visit to the group home because he asked, and about my dust-up with Dorito. As usual at a time like this, I felt like I was talking to my confessor, complicated by the fact that we were engaged in sexual relations.

"That was pretty harsh," he said when I told him I called her a pain in the ass, but he said it with a laugh. "Are you going to apologize to her?"

"Do you think I should?"

"Certainly not!" he said. "I'm sure your observation was spot-on, and totally appropriate."

There it was, not justified, not intelligent, not diplomatic even, but "appropriate." The mildness of that word made me want to punch myself in the face. "OK, I'll go over there," I said.

That was how conversations with Carlo always went. He agreed with me until I saw things from his perspective.

Apparently knowing he'd made his point, he didn't belabor it. "How's Al doing?" he said. "I've been feeling like I left you hanging with all kinds of stuff."

"Oh stop it. You haven't been gone that long. He's hanging in there." We disconnected without me mentioning Nicki Gleason. That story was just too fraught and long to go into it over the phone, especially as Carlo was supposed to be retreating. I didn't want to distract him.

So there I was, knocking on Dorito's door, whispering to myself *Dori-ta, Dori-ta*, until she answered. It struck me that her large face wasn't so much like the Red Queen's as like a painting of Martin Luther on the cover of one of Carlo's books. That's it, she looked like a transitioning Martin Luther. I banished the thought. They say people know what you're thinking even if they don't know they know.

"Hi," I said, even then not trusting myself to get her name right and thereby ruin all attempts at reconciliation.

Her hi was even more cautious than mine. She did not invite me inside, but clung to the edge of the door, as if slamming it would be an option. I wished I'd brought a casserole. There must be an easy recipe somewhere that even I could have accomplished without scorching a pan or sending anyone to urgent care. I made a mental note to find this recipe before the next time I called someone a pain in the ass. An asshole casserole.

Without actually repeating that word, I managed to get out what I hoped would come across as a heartfelt apology. Heartfelt. No sense in doing this in half-measures.

I even got the name right. "Dorita, I've come by to offer you my heartfelt apology. I really went off the rails yesterday. It seems like we're all just so . . . so angry these days."

She stayed quiet while I waited a beat or two to let her say yes, she understood, she was angry too. The beat dragged out. I changed my tactic. With my hand tucked under her middle I picked up Peg and held her in front of me. You do that and people always comment on what a funny face pugs have, or instinctively reach out to pet them. Something. She couldn't hate dogs that much, right?

Not happening. I vigorously rubbed Peg's head to encourage Dorita to do likewise. I added a line that seemed to work with other neighbors. "Seems like there are three kinds of people in the world these days: Democrats, Republicans, and people who love their dogs."

Still nothing. Maybe she was newly offended that I'd suggested she might be angry. Maybe I was the only one here who was bad bad bad. That made my mind wander back to smashing her large face, this time between the edge of the door and the door jamb if I grabbed it and pulled it towards me. Man oh man, I needed to do a little more time in therapy. Meditation or mindfulness. Something to get over this residual anger that invaded me, not all the time, but too often.

She broke through my lengthy reverie by saying, "Well, thank you for coming by. I really appreciate it."

There. Done. But no use letting the moment pass without something really useful. "May I ask about your progress in getting the house rezoned? Dorita?"

She sighed elaborately, with a combination of exasperation and weariness at dealing with my ignorance. "It's apparently not an easy process. When Pima County said it was a state-sponsored home and they couldn't do anything, I got a contact at the state level and they said they'll investigate the incidents I've documented for them." She scoffed in a conspiratorial kind of way now that I'd groveled sufficiently. "I had to go to the sheriff's substation on Oracle and file paperwork to get a full report. That's how the government is these days. We all have to do the work ourselves just to stay safe. Good heavens, why would these people even want to be here? Why would anyone want to live where they weren't wanted?"

I felt my body rock a little as I figuratively bit my tongue to keep from suggesting that could apply to a hundred million Americans who were unwanted by one group or another. Someone is always not wanting somebody else. "Ain't it the truth," I said, letting her think that an apology was the same as agreement. "So who's the person?"

"Person?"

"Your contact in the state government."

Dorito looked suspicious for only a moment. Just because she was a pain in the ass didn't make her totally clueless. But she couldn't think of an excuse to not give me the name of the guy. I repeated it inside my head a few times because I didn't have a piece of paper to write it down on, and besides, that would have confirmed her suspicions about me getting involved if I'd done so. As for getting that report from the sheriff's department, I knew who would have authorized it, and I cringed at the mere thought of Max Coyote. More on him later.

Dorita said, "By the way, last night there was a loud argument outside the house. I could hear it all the way inside my house even though the windows were closed and the air conditioning on."

"What were they arguing about?" I asked.

"It had something to do with the garbage bins. Who was supposed to bring the garbage bins back into the garage after pick-up. It was after ten p.m., and they were going at it in the front yard. I watched them over the wall and the biggest one shoved one of the little ones. I called the police."

"Those idiots," I said, and felt it, even if calling the police was a tad over-reactive, and maybe it would have helped if she knew their names instead of consigning them all to "one" like a herd of javelinas.

She could tell that I at least sincerely wished they wouldn't have fought, and she smiled. "You wouldn't have called the police, though," she said. "And they knew I was the one who did it. When the police came and found everything quiet, and left, that woman came to my backyard and shouted over the wall with her fists balled up that I should come out and we'd settle this once and for all. Can you imagine?"

"Nicki?" I asked, and no, I could not imagine her doing that.

Dorita shrugged. "What did she want, a wrestling match in the dirt? How low class can you get?" Her large chin lifted in a show of disdain. "I think she's a lesbian."

I wanted to go pretty low class at that point, beginning with, "You got a problem with that, bitch?" Maybe Nicki didn't have the greatest restraint, but this apology business was getting harder and harder. Not wanting to have to start from scratch with my groveling, I just gave my head that little rocking motion. But she wasn't finished with me. She narrowed her eyes to the size of dimes and said, "I know what you think, Brigid, that I'm some sort of Karen, or at least a NIMBY. But don't go getting all righteous on me. Are you really all that much better than I am? You take the felons into your house. See if you change your opinion then."

You might think this came as a tirade, but it was all said gently, without a hint of the brazen mouthiness you might think would issue from Dorita. It felt as if she was as tired of the whole thing as I was, tired of the fighting. Tired of the moral high ground. I was, too. I guess she had a point, small as it was.

When I didn't answer her question, Dorita's features got smaller, as her eyes and lips pulled toward her slightly wrinkled nose in her expression of judgment, the way they had when last we talked. "My point is, you can stop judging me now," she said.

I couldn't go so far as to agree with what she said, perish the thought. But I could lighten up the moment. "Stop judging me judging you," I finally said with a straight face.

She stopped, and thought. And laughed. We both laughed. She finally loosened her grip on the edge of the door. She invited me to come over sometime for a glass of wine and I agreed and walked back home with Peg, both of us knowing that would never happen.

The next time I heard anything about her was the following morning on the Neighbors site that ran something like:

Who reported it?

The neighbor next door to her. Said he happened to look over the wall between their houses this morning. She was near the fire pit.

Didn't he hear anything? Cries for help?

I don't know. This is all I know.

I turned on the TV local news but didn't see anything yet, which probably meant it wasn't anything too serious.

SIX

I had Peg on the leash in my left hand, my iced coffee in a cooler cup in my right, and a blue plastic poop baggy tucked in the waistband of my shorts. Al had for some time given up his walks because of his heart condition. We stopped for Peg to graciously let Bentley the Airedale sniff her butt while Jake the Jehovah's Witness and I behaved more human-like.

"The cops are over at Dorita's house," Jake said. "A neighbor found her this morning."

I'd gathered that from what I saw on social media. I certainly hadn't wished Dorito to come to any harm, but never one to pretend feelings I did not have, I sipped my coffee before saying, "How unfortunate. What was wrong with her?"

Maybe through the Jehovah's Witness grapevine, maybe because my toned-down reaction made him realize I didn't know as much as he did, Jake added casually, "She had her face set on fire."

This time I did react, sucking air through my teeth as I imagined what "face set on fire" looked like, and a teeny part of my brain remembered that *bap bap bap* thought I'd had about that face. I didn't ask Jake any more questions, but walked the few houses down to see for myself. Turning the corner gave me a full perspective: ambulance, three sheriffs' cars with lights ablaze, someone already stringing crime-scene tape. A few other neighbors were standing about, talking quietly, pretending not to gawk.

I saw Detective Max Coyote from the Pima County Sheriff's Department, who had once been a friend, wasn't now, but still respected me enough to help when I needed him. Maybe I could return the favor.

The side gate to the backyard was open, so I slipped under the crime-scene tape and walked through as if I belonged there. It was easy to do, having belonged in scenes just like this one on many occasions, both as an FBI agent and as a private investigator. But a security detail stopped me before I got halfway, asking who I was and telling me I shouldn't have a dog at the crime scene. I picked up Peg so she couldn't pee on any evidence.

"Coyote asked me to take a look," I said. "I'm FBI."

He looked doubtful and turned away, probably seeking some corroboration, so I had to move fast. Here's what I saw:

Dorita's body lying on the gravel close to an outdoor seating area that included four Adirondack chairs surrounding a brick fire pit. A forensic tech was interested in that fire pit. A medical examiner, who I should have recognized but didn't, attended to Dorita. She was wrenched in a bizarre position. One arm thrown back over her head and one arced over in what looked like a thwarted attempt to put out her face. Legs bent at the knees, curling her body in what I would guess was agony.

I walked closer to get a better look at the part of her face that her arm didn't cover. Blackened, as Jake had indicated. Something about the features I couldn't quite put my finger on—not quite concave, but rather rearranged; her nose appeared to have moved over to one side of her face. It couldn't have burned away; that would have been really intense. In this case the fire had barely incinerated her hair, only burning that perfect coif to about two inches up from her high forehead. The rest was intact. Maybe she was enflamed long enough to kill her, but whoever set the fire put it out before it could call attention. I could see a blackness where her teeth should have been. No lips left.

"I work with Max Coyote," I said to the medical examiner. "Brigid Quinn." He didn't return the courtesy by giving me his name but at least heard me when I asked, "When do you figure?"

"Real fresh," he said. "It was warm last night and that factors into it. If there was rigor mortis, it's eased, and no livor mortis that I can see, but I'll be able to tell more back at the lab."

"So less than twenty-four hours." If you watch crime shows you start to think that a pathologist can call time of death to the minute, but that's just hooey.

He gestured to another tech who stood nearby awaiting instructions. "Get her bagged and tagged."

I knew the main forensic pathologist, so I was certain I would be able to be present at the autopsy. For now I wandered over to the fire pit. "Whatcha got, anything?" I asked.

The tech, maybe an arson expert, gave me an unrecognizing look that indicated he wasn't sure I belonged there but nonetheless said, "Looks like this was the source of the fire. And it smells like gasoline."

Anybody knows you don't start your fire pit with gasoline, it's too smelly. And on a hot summer night, this would have been utilitarian rather than esthetic. Whoever set the fire did it to get things started. So it wasn't a surprise attack. But you don't wait around watching a stranger light a fire in your yard. And if you run out of your house to stop them, how do they pin you down long enough to set your face—and only your face—on fire? Was this a two-person job? Or someone who was strong enough to immobilize her with one arm before holding a torch of some kind on her face until . . . no, she would have screamed. It all added up to Dorita knowing her attacker or attackers. But the houses here were far enough apart, and no one in the summer opened their windows, not even after dark. My mind raced from one scenario to the next in a way it hadn't done since I almost broke Carlo the year before. I admit it was delicious.

"Quinn. Get the hell out of my crime scene before I have you arrested."

"Max," I said, turning around to see him standing with a pad in one hand and his other on a hip, as if wondering where all to start. "I heard it's a homicide."

"No shit? I was thinking she tried to light a cigarette with a blow torch."

"Who discovered her?"

Max stared.

I tried again. "I just wanted to let you know I'm here if you need me. I talked to the woman just yesterday."

"What time?" Looks like he was the one who'd be asking all the questions.

"Mm, mid-morning?"

He made a note on his flip pad as I added, "We're . . . friends."

"That right?" he said. "Not what I heard."

I idly fingered some crime-scene tape while he looked like he wanted to smack my hand. "So what *have* you heard?" I asked.

"You called"—he flipped back a few pages of his notepad, which were probably already covered with information gleaned from surrounding residents—"Ms. Dorita Gordino a quote asshole unquote. Twice."

"Twice?"

"Yep."

"There were witnesses?"

"Yep."

"I deny it. What I said was that she was a pain in the ass. Quite different." I guessed I'd spoken louder that day than I'd meant to, and the group home residents standing outside across the street had heard me. The question now was, *Which of them had ratted me out? Were they in a hurry to avoid suspicion themselves?* "Well, you know, these days everyone has their differences. So polarized."

Max thoughtfully poked some of the gravel in the yard with the toe of his shoe. As I watched him do that, my glance went to the ground beside him. There was a track in the gravel. A slight depression, as if someone was dragging something. A body? Not Dorita. The track was too well defined, less than a foot wide, and it stopped a foot from her body. I wouldn't mention this to Max. If he wanted to solve the case on his own, fuck him.

He was on his own track. "You said you talked to her yesterday. What did you talk about?"

I adjusted a squirming pug on my arm while deciding what to say. "I apologized to her for what I said. I was really good at it, too. Who told you I called her an asshole?"

Coyote flipped his pad open. "Was she living alone?"

"I don't know."

"Do you know of next of kin? Did she speak of a parent, or relative?"

"I don't know."

"Friends, right." He flipped the pad closed. "If you'll excuse me. I've got some questions to be answered and a long list. Church, homeowners' association, Elks Club, people who signed her petition to have the group home rezoned for residential. Have I missed anything?"

I could have said yes, but I wasn't about to mention the residents of the group home. Him not mentioning them meant they were at the top of his list. Did he already know that there had been words between Nicki and Dorita? Had anyone besides the group residents heard what could be judged as a verbal assault? Would one of her roommates tell Max about it, the way they did about me calling her an asshole, to take suspicion off themselves? With another glance at that drag mark in the gravel, I shook my head at his question about missing anything and pretended to be distracted by the sight of a gurney clunking over the graveled ground with a soon-to-be-filled black body bag that shone in the too-bright sun.

SEVEN

As I've said before, your past doesn't die; it doesn't even wrinkle. Max Coyote was such a sweet man, the kind of man you could call sweet, combining two flavors like salted caramels. His wife, Crystal, Carlo and I used to be dinner friends. He'd often come around to the house on his lunch hour when he would teach Carlo to play poker and Carlo would teach him philosophy. But then came that time when I killed a man and staged the crime scene to look like his van had overturned in the nearby wash. Mind you, the man was a serial killer and I was defending myself, but it was in the early days of my marriage and I was terrified that Carlo would find out what I was capable of. I know, I know, it was a knuckle-headed thing to do. The suspicion of my crime that took hold in Max was sort of cancelled out when I saved his life a few weeks later. We both knew I could have let him die, so my secret would die with him. We both knew I wouldn't go that far. I never confessed. We never spoke of it. But we weren't friends anymore.

That's why he treated me the way he did, and that's how I knew trying to get information out of him would be a dead end. My first inclination was to go to the group home and make sure Nicki wasn't traumatized, but I might be watched. It was better not to see her until things had settled down some. My second inclination was to find out what the mood in the house was, whether they were understandably concerned that one of them would be suspect in Dorita's murder. I gave in to that inclination.

BFG, who I'd first seen working out in the yard, opened the door at my knock before I had time to draw my hand away. He must have been watching out the front window. It also occurred to me that maybe not that many people knocked at this door. People were either part of the group, or people stayed away because they were afraid. Either way, being a felon was hard.

"Go away. You'll call attention," he said, not opening the door enough to let me in.

"Hey, I was just walking my dog." I held Peg up facing him and she didn't deny it.

Unlike Dorita, he was unable to resist reaching out and scratching Peg under the chin.

"You could be a little more hospitable," I said. "I was the one brought the chips, remember?"

"Henry, let her in," called Nicki from somewhere inside. "She's not with the cops."

"Retired FBI," I admitted.

He lifted one side of his upper lip, skeptically, I assumed, as he opened the door wider and stepped aside.

I entered, my eyes slowly adjusting to the dim room after the blaze outside. They had closed all the blinds. "Hey, Nicki, I'm glad I caught you awake."

Only just, it seemed. Nicki sat on the couch where she had been when I first visited her. She looked pale, with a paleness that owed nothing to sunscreen but to fatigue. The dark smudges under her eyes were thrown into greater contrast with the rest of her face.

"I didn't work last night," she said, sounding like she wished she had. The alibi would have come in handy. I thought I knew why. You get caught once, forever after you'll assume you're suspect.

BFG, or more properly, Henry, hadn't left the room. He stood leaning against the entryway to the kitchen, arms crossed, with a bodyguard kind of look about him. I thought this was endearing, that this guy, maybe all these guys, had Nicki's back.

I took everything in at once, including an out-of-place woman sitting in the shabby armchair where I'd been a few days before. Certainly, there was a lot of silent communicating going on, not just with BFG but with me too. Nicki looked at me with a less than welcoming face, as her eyes shifted to the chair across from her in both an introduction and, oddly, a caution. The woman or me: which of us was not to be trusted?

Just to be on the safe side, I'd be careful with what I said, or what the woman said, don't *rock the boat* or give away anything that might be taken back to the parole officer. You're in prison, you stop trusting anyone, and it takes a while to stop looking behind you to find out who's listening so you don't have to talk out of the corner of your mouth anymore. If Nicki at some other time might have gotten up to greet me, right now she looked too exhausted (was it a rough night, and if so, why?) to even think of it.

It only took four steps across the small room to where the other woman didn't bother getting up, either, with less of an excuse. Without saying hello, she did deign to slightly raise a hand off the arm of the chair, as if to either shake or, with the fingers curved downward, let it be kissed. With both arms extended, her gauzy, multi-hued top would have made a good butterfly costume.

I pretended I didn't see the hand because I was adjusting Peg in my arms. The hand got the message, patted Peg on the head with a vigor no dog ever liked, then went back down.

"I bet you're the mentor Nicki told me about," I said. Nicki's heavy eyelids went up a little as a further warning to behave myself.

The woman dismissed my remark with a wave of stubby lacquered nails. "Mentor seems so superior, don't you think? Like I'm a wise woman with all the answers. I learn as much from the formerly incarcerated as they learn from me." As if revealing a flaw, she lowered her voice. "Maybe more."

"Eleanore with an e," I said.

"That I am," the woman said. "Four e's if you count my last name, Turner. And you are . . ."

"Brigid Quinn, no e's at all," I said, and smiled to make it a quip. "They were all taken."

As we spoke, I was able to give her the three-second once-over. I assumed she was there to show support for Nicki, the kind of intimidating woman who'd come in wearing her King Kong pants whenever she wanted her way. And it would most often work. The King Kong image combined with the top made me drift toward more of a don't-mess-with-the-butterfly vibe.

If we went with that theme, she was the ugliest butterfly you'd ever seen. Startlingly ugly. She didn't have a mustache but it wouldn't have surprised me. A long, gaunt face, with uncooked dumplings under her eyes to make up for the lack of flesh elsewhere. Her lipstick appeared to be a gallant attempt at redeeming her face, but even that failed as the shade contrasted severely with the colors in her top. An overbite. That was my three-second observation, but I don't think I'm missing anything. This was a woman who flaunted her lack of looks, reveling in it, her ugliness her brand.

And yet she was somehow magnificent. Maybe it was her style. I could imagine her big personality bursting into a room and making it laugh with her. Like now. She had hooted her appreciation of my comment about the 'e's like a drunk mechanic at a lame off-color joke. It was the way of some wealthy and educated people to convey 'hey! I'm just like you!' when in the company of those on a social rung of the ladder below them. Clearly that's where she saw me as well as Nicki. Yet . . . there was something about her, maybe what would be a non-threat to both men and women. The whole package taken together might make her hard not to like, but I determined to do my best.

The next typical social question at that point would have been how Nicki and I knew each other. But it would appear that either Eleanore wasn't very curious or already knew. Besides, what to say about how Nicki and I knew each other? It could hardly be as pleasantly easy as Eleanore's *I'm her mentor.*

I trained her to kill her husband would only lead to more questions.

"Has Sheriff Coyote already been over here?" I asked. "If not, you should be prepared for it."

Eleanore gave a shaky grin that hinted she was making her best effort at smaller talk than the murder across the street.

Still standing, just to see how long they'd leave me there, I put Peg down on the floor where she set about hoovering up microscopic crumbs and marveling at the smells. I tried a different tack. "So he was here already?"

Nicki opened her mouth to speak but Eleanore put the words in it. "Oh, let's not go over that again. How many ways can you say you don't know anything? What with that burglar who got shot in her bedroom, Nicole has been through more than enough. Show her your arm, Nicole, where you were shot."

When I—not to mention Nicki—paused too long before picking up on the burglar remark, Eleanore picked up the slack.

She said, "Nicole has told me that you want to help her. By getting her a place to live other than"—a distasteful wave—"here. And that your husband is an Episcopal priest. We go to an Episcopal church, St. Philips, the historical one on Ina. We've been trying to get Nicole here to come with us."

She didn't wait for me to answer her questions, to explain that no, Carlo was a Roman Catholic who had left the priesthood when he fell in love, not with me but with a first wife who had died of cancer some years before. It was all too complicated, and I didn't care enough to explain.

"It would do her good, don't you think? Going to church? I bet you do, with your husband being a priest and all."

Again, instead of trying to explain, I cut to the important part of her questioning. "My husband is away for a while, but I'm sure when he gets back and we talk, that Nicki will be welcome to move in with us. As I'm sure she would be at your home." *Take that, bitch.* I glanced at Nicki with a conspiratorial smile. "Carlo is a real sucker for sinners."

Eleanore frowned briefly and straightened her diaphanous top. I guess it was to show that my remark affronted her. I think the top was an effort to look casual in these surroundings that were beneath her. It wasn't terribly expensive, but it didn't cry poor either. Neither did her drop earrings made from real turquoise. All in all, I'd give her a D+ on blending in.

As I stared at her, the conversation having momentarily stalled, I realized she was doing the same thing with me. I felt my face peeled back to see what was inside my head—both of us so intent on discovery that we didn't wonder why the other was doing the same thing. If that meant Eleanore was as protective of Nicki as I was, I would cut her some slack.

If only to fill the silence, Eleanore shifted again to the topic of Nicki escaping the influence of the low-lifes that inhabited the home. As if convincing us both that it had been her idea all along and we were resisting to no avail, she said, "I can't tell you what a fabulous idea it is to get Nicole out of this place." She inadvertently glanced at the shiny arm of the chair on which she had declined to place her arms, keeping them cleanly in her lap. "I urge you both to follow through on this. She deserves much better. I feel like I've known her forever." Acknowledging suddenly that Nicki was in the room and might be addressed, "We're like old friends, aren't we, dear? Like best buds."

I didn't like being urged to do something I'd already planned to do. Nicki drew her head back an inch and acquiesced that yes, they were just like best friends. That done, Eleanore turned her attention back to me. "We shared so much in letters before Nicole was . . ." Here I could feel her searching for the woke word, avoiding ex-felon in favor of . . . what would she choose? Re-entering? She went with ". . . returned to society where she belongs. I won't tell you all the things we wrote about. It's up to her to share the personal things with you that we did . . ." (Here a fond little smile for all those secrets.) "And isn't it wonderful that you live nearby? Nicole says you're just a block or two away in that development with the sweet little track homes."

It didn't take me any more time to understand how Nicki's feelings about this woman might be as ambivalent as my own. Eleanore with an "e" seemed to get larger as she spoke, her fluttery top billowing out until it filled the room. The woman was a champagne fountain; she bubbled, she burbled, she gushed. Like I said, some might like her and some might find her overbearing. While she was no match for me, Nicki was no match for her. I remembered the passivity I'd first seen in her, a victim of domestic violence. It was there again.

The secrets Eleanore mentioned sharing with Nicki? Compared to what Nicki and I had experienced in life, what we'd seen and what we'd done, I guessed that Eleanore had no good secrets to share. She went on, now clutching her purse that had been resting bravely on the carpet so worn it was mostly made of grime. "When the dust settles, we should all get together." I wondered if by "dust settling" she meant the ash from Dorita's face. Then, as with so many social people, she extended the invitation and then immediately withdrew before it could be accepted. "Ian, that's my husband, is busy with his veterinary practice and of course the Pima County Board of Supervisors. Both of us are alike in that, always wanting to, you know, do a little good, *give back* to the community. Speaking of which, have you told Brigid about what we've planned?" She waved her hand around the room as if I'd understand the gesture.

Nicki said, "Eleanore knows someone who owns one of those art galleries around Campbell and Skyline." Here she crooked one corner of her mouth, like the whole concept was a little nuts. "She's scheduled a . . . whadya call it?"

"A showing!" Eleanore said. "We're launching Nicole's work in Tucson—as a start. Are you familiar with Nicole's work, Brigid?" She turned to Nicki, now totally sunken into the couch, as if her bones had been removed. "So much more interesting than the nasty things going on. Show her your studio, Nicole."

"It's not so much my studio, more like my bedroom," Nicki murmured.

"Oh now, you won't make it in the art world denigrating your work that way." Eleanore waggled her fingers. "Go on, show her your paints."

"You know, I can look at her paints another time," I said, as Nicki pushed herself from the couch.

No good. I could tell what this was; one of those times when friendship, or whatever you called this relationship, turns competitive. Eleanore knew more about Nicki, is what she was saying. *I know her better than you do*. Maybe it was one of those radical chic things, Eleanore feeling good about herself for befriending women who were hard up.

And poor Nicki, caught between two strong women in a battle of wills. I can be stubborn, too. Instead of going in the direction that Eleanore was indicating and Nicki was heading, down a hall to her "studio," I stepped over to the wall where some of her paintings were displayed. There was a new one of Ramona, her face close to that of a calico cat, both of them enraptured. "Ramona," I said, and Nicki turned around. "I didn't see this the last time. Did you just finish it?"

Eleanore answered for her, "Yes!" Her face went into one of those expressions that mimics an ice-cream brain freeze. The image fitted her comment. "That child is so adorable it hurts. I've taken Nicole for supervised visits with Ramona. And her foster parents are wonderful. We have a good relationship with them, too. Ramona is learning to swim at our house."

"I'd like to see her again sometime," I said.

Silence from them both.

"I still don't know if the showing would be a good idea," Nicki said. "With who I am and all."

Eleanore burst from her chair, strode forward (I couldn't imagine her simply stepping anywhere), and held out her arms, summoning Nicki. "Hugs!" Nicki, who was standing next to me gazing at the painting of Ramona, did as she was told. I remembered that doing as she was told had been what got her in trouble before: doing as she was told in foster homes, and in her marriage. Until she stopped. She wouldn't repeat that mistake again, resisting. Now she knew better than to resist.

"Nonsense," Eleanore said. "You're a good person, isn't she, Brigid?" Eleanore crushed the slighter woman to her bosom and looked at me over her shoulder. I nodded obediently. Even I was giving into her.

"I'm not going to listen to people who haven't even met you yet!" Eleanore kissed Nicki on one cheek, then on the other, though Nicki had thought the kissing was finished and had tried to pull away, which made it a little awkward. The cheek having escaped Eleanore's extended lips, she finally let go of Nicki, shook my hand, and fluttered her blouse out the door.

Noting the significant warmth of the chair Eleanore had vacated, I sat down, thinking again that—despite her so-called class—she hadn't objected to leaving me standing during her performance. Nicki I could understand that way. She had simply been too cowed to offer a seat next to her on the couch. I didn't recall her saying much since my arrival, but maybe I'd missed it. With Eleanore sucking up all the space around her, it would be easy to do. From this vantage point, the chair where I'd sat at my last meeting with Nicki, I could see her paintings again. They were very good.

Right now, reacting to Eleanore, "Wow," I said. "Is she always that manic?"

Nicki's eyes went blank, either because she didn't want me to see how she felt about the woman or didn't understand the word. So I switched tack. "Is she serious about the gallery thing?"

Nicki nodded. "Please come. All these people are her friends. I'll need someone I know."

OK, so maybe I wasn't her most loyal friend, but at least I was a face that she knew from before she was convicted. And, she'd have to admit, someone who tried her best.

"She's a really nice woman. Just one of those people who thinks they know how to live life perfectly and want to tell you all about it."

I went home and gave the dogs their lunch. Peg and Achilles were good eaters as always, but Al looked like he was weighing whether it was worth it to hoist himself off the tile. I leaned against the kitchen counter and watched for a while, at which point he decided to forgo it, so I picked up his dish that Peg was eyeing. She seemed to be gaining the weight that Al was losing. I placed the dish in front of Al's face so he wouldn't have to stand up to eat. He put his chin on the floor next to the dish and sighed, so I picked it up again.

Moments like these I missed Carlo extra. I've never gotten in the habit of living on my phone to stave off loneliness, but I wasn't averse to seeking distraction at the computer.

Having found nothing more on the Neighbors site, I went to Facebook. My niece Gemma-Kate had put me onto that when she came to live in Tucson and go to school here. It used to be challenging to investigate people. Now you just had to open their Facebook page to see their naked souls laid bare for the world. Even if they think they're fooling us, posting the fabulous vacays, hiding the disappointment that was their children, it's easy to use a little basic psychology to find the person underneath the person. The virtue signaling. The plea for help. The airing of the grievance du jour. The only reason I had an account was to be able to check out other members—their loves, their hates, the groups they participated in.

Dorita Gordino turned out to be an uncommon name worldwide; there were only three, and it was easy to pick her out. Her profile photo pretty much matched her face when it was intact yesterday. Forty-two years old, born in Phoenix, went to Arizona State, more than six hundred friends, realtor, single. No mention of a divorce. I'd find that out separately to see if she had a troubled ex in her past who might want her dead. Boyfriend? That would be harder, but possible. Would fit a crime of passion, and setting someone's face on fire certainly fitted that bill.

As I would have expected, Dorita's (I shall call her that from now on out of respect for the dead) page, like many others, was a carefully constructed person. Noncommittal on anything political, in religion just the occasional God-post followed with "can I get an Amen," leaving her open for certain kinds of political phone calls from candidates who had her number in more ways than one. Often changing her profile photo in various stages of glam while revealing nothing new about her. At least she wasn't always as angry as I knew her to be. Some travel, photos taken of her. By whom? Her perfect life didn't include a man.

And posts to her page, three happy birthdays from about four months ago. Someone named Elliott Gordino, usually shown with another man (her brother, his partner?). I shifted to Elliott's page and found he lived in Flagstaff. And aging parents in an assisted living facility in Tucson. Too bad they'd be the ones to be informed, to identify her remains. I wondered if she had something else, a birthmark or something, that her parents could use to confirm it was her without the trauma of having to look at what remained of her face.

Enough Dorita, what about Eleanore? What was her last name? Turner. Ah, Quinn, mind still working on all cylinders, thank God. I searched, found five of them, three with an e. Easy to narrow it down from there to the one who lived in

Tucson. Four hundred and sixteen friends. Lots of photographs of smiling people draped over one another in restaurants, bars, sporting events, and formal gatherings indicated by the glittering gowns. Those might be political events. She had said her husband was on the Pima County Board of Supervisors, despite being a veterinarian. I scrolled down because I couldn't remember his name, and then saw the post all in caps. HAPPY ANNIVERSARY TO US! MY BELOVED IAN BOUGHT ME A VINTAGE JAGUAR! YOU ARE MY LOVE FOREVER AND ALWAYS! Unlike others on Facebook who were constantly protesting their adoration of their mate, this was the only post about him, and fairly recent, about a month ago. Photo of a beautiful forest green car. What had she done to deserve that car? What had he done that made its giving advisable? See what I mean about what Facebook could provide in the way of information? Even if it only asked more questions that needed to be answered.

From there I went further down the rabbit hole to Ian Turner's account. It's hard to tell from photographs when a person is standing alone and not always the full frontal, but I'd guess that Ian was taller than Eleanore but half her size from side to side. Handsome didn't express his looks by half.

Maybe Ian didn't need a trophy wife. Love isn't always about looks. I surmised that her personality, also outsized, made her a good mate. Ian might see her as indispensable to both his profession and his possible political aspirations. I enlarged one of his photographs, this one taken with the Tucson mayor. So, a democrat and not trying to hide it. And his hair plugs were really well-plugged—if in a little too precise a line across his forehead.

Well, this was all entertaining and might be useful at some point in the future, but for now I was feeling frustrated as I bent down to massage the schnoodle who rested his chin on my foot. Where could I go to get something really useful about Dorita's murder, besides begging Max Coyote? It wasn't just curiosity, mind you. Much as I hated to admit it, I didn't think it was a coincidence that Dorita Gordino had been killed after going after the residents of the group home. I only hoped it was a more personal grievance, maybe from another pet owner in the neighborhood. And of course, being in protection mode, I wanted to make sure there was no connection to Nicki.

My cell phone buzzed on the desk beside me, and Carlo's name appeared. I debated letting it go to voicemail while the other side of the debate team argued that I'd promised to tell him the truth from now on, about everything. Phones don't give you much time to think, and I listened to his voice message. Now or never, the pro voice in my head told me.

"Hey there, how's it going?" I said as I answered.

"What's wrong?" he said.

"What makes you think something is wrong?" I said.

"Because I saw my local internet news this morning."

"Should you be looking at news while you're on a retreat? You should have left your phone here."

"Then I couldn't reach you. Don't hedge. What happened with Dorita?"

"Well, you got me there. She, um, died."

"I know she died, honey, that's usually what happens when you're murdered."

"I didn't do it!"

"That never once crossed my mind. I'm coming home."

"No! Listen, what I meant was, her death didn't have anything to do with me. I'm perfectly safe."

"What about the people in the group home?"

"Everyone is OK. All right, I'll be rigorously honest and add 'at least for the time being,' no one charged with the crime. Max is investigating. He said he'd keep me informed." OK, that right there was a bit of a lie, just a thin slice. But one way or another I'd get information.

"I'm coming home."

"Carlo. Babe. This puts us in a dilemma. You come home because you worry, and I feel like shit because you're coming home."

"And how can I stay here when someone we know has been murdered two streets away from where we live?"

Silence.

"Well?"

"Give me a sec . . . OK, what about this? You call Max and let him advise you regarding the whole deal. He and I may not be friends, but there's no reason you shouldn't be. Then I'll call you once a day. Twice, three times a day to let you know what's going on. At specific times so if I miss you by so much as a minute, and don't answer my phone when you call, you can beat a hasty retreat from your retreat. Would you be able to relax and keep letting go of your ego then?"

After another pause we negotiated the calling schedule, and Carlo repeatedly assured me he'd continue to focus on his spiritual health which would benefit me as well. We parted with murmured concerns about Al's condition (stable, I assured him), and our usual kissy noise. Then I texted Max to try to influence him about how to handle Carlo's worry. No answer. Frustrated, I logged out of Facebook and into some of my computer games, which are always relaxing because I set my opponent at "stupid." After predictably winning one game of Scrabble by my usual one hundred points and one game of Free Cell, I thought: Screw Detective Coyote. I called a friend at the medical examiner's office who I had not yet alienated. Apparently neither had I kept up with him as an acquaintance, because he told me he had retired the year before. But he said he'd call the new guy and have him get in touch with me so I could attend the autopsy.

Then I sat back and wondered if Eleanore really knew Nicki as well as I did. All of it.

EIGHT

You, Nicole Gleason, have two memories of your mother when she was alive. You don't know how old you were, but she's looking at you and laughing. Jiggling the ice in a glass of dark yellow liquid, she says, "You've got a face that a mother could love on payday." You only know what this means years later, that she was telling you that, given your strange looks, someone would only be your mother if there was money involved. Your mother laughing.

There is another memory:

Your mother very still on the living-room couch.

You touch her and cry when she doesn't wake up.

When you are hungry, you find a loaf of bread on the kitchen counter, your fingers reaching way up to claw the plastic bag.

You don't know how long you are there in the apartment with your mother but the empty bag that held the bread is on the floor.

You poop yourself. That and the pee makes your bottom itch and burn.

You are hungry, and the apartment begins to smell funny.

You rap on the inside of the door, but no one is on the other side and you give up.

You cry more. Some of the snot from your nose runs into your mouth. It tastes sweet.

Some time passes, the house gets light and dark and light and dark and light and dark.

After a while, you see other people enter the apartment, pushing your body away from the door.

Things go fast, including the beat of your heart. A rolling bed, a ride in a truck, and a smiling lady holding your hand.

Whether or not this memory is true, every year when you make a wish over the candle on your birthday cake, you wish you could nick the memory out of your brain and start clean.

You hear more when you are much older. In the hospital they have no way of knowing who you are. There's no birth certificate, no record of your mother bearing you. A DNA test confirms that was your mother on the couch. You get put into a foster home because there's no family or friend to notify, let alone take you in. The branch of Child Protective Services that places you confirms all this. You've been told that, when they asked your name, you couldn't give them one. You don't even have a name. After a brief discussion, you're legally given the name Nicole, after your foster father's grandparent. You also use that couple's last name which is Rotz. Everything is hand-me-down, even your identity, even your heritage, which happens to be Hungarian. A lot of Hungarian refugees moved to Arizona after the 1956 revolution against the Soviets.

The Rotzes, Yolanda and Andras, aren't bad. Maybe they shouldn't have given you all the details about what happened at the hospital and beyond, but they are nice. Besides the bit of money that comes from the Arizona foster-care program, they touch you sometimes (when changing your diaper or later holding your hand to cross the street, but never inappropriately). The touching saves you a little, the seed that one day will allow you to think you have a right to the space you fill in the world. As for diaper changing, Yolanda sometimes is annoyed that you still aren't using the toilet for bowel movements when you're almost four years old.

The late potty training is the first clue, but no one fully realizes you're neurologically damaged from your mother's drinking. They just think you're a little slow, a little physically uncoordinated in that you take a long time learning how to use a fork. Maybe you're a little funny looking, but nothing anyone can put their finger on, let alone ask the doctor about when you're taken for your yearly check-ups required by the foster program. He says about the diaper thing, "That's just how it is sometimes."

You go to regular classes in school because you're not diagnosed as needing special ed. There you're the butt of jokes about your name, Rotz . . . Rots . . . Nicki Rots, they'd say, and hold their nose when they passed you in the hall. You submit to all this, at least on the outside.

The experts will come later when you've really screwed up your life. No one expects much of you, just enough to shuffle you to the next grade and the next in public school. Still, you drop out after your sophomore year in high school and get a job at Walmart. This relieves your foster parents; their hope grows that you'll be OK to leave when you age out of the system at eighteen and they can afford that trip to see relatives in New York state without feeling guilty about you. No one ever wanted to adopt you.

You're proud of being able to hold down a job at Walmart, first stocking shelves, and then filling the orders of people who shop online. After just a month or so, you find one of your co-workers looking at you. His name is Vincent Gleason, and he owns his own mobile home in that park in northwest Tucson. You go out with him and, fueled by drinks on every date which makes you attractive to each other, you marry him. You don't invite the Rotzes; it was clear that they considered their job done and you never hear from them again.

At Marshall's you found a sexy little black thing to wear to bed that night, but it gets thrown on the floor by Vincent who says it's a waste of time. He hurts, but after your first gasp it's OK. Afterward you find some blood which no one ever told you about. You're afraid it will make Vincent angry, but he says no problem, that's how it's supposed to be. He takes you in his arms when he's finished. He says thank you, that was good. This is the first time you can think of that you made someone happy, and you want to do it again. Make him happy.

You have a whole place to live in now, not just a spare bedroom behind a curtain that doubles as Mrs. Rotz's craft room. Vincent's trailer is so nice, a double-wide with a couple of air-conditioning window units that keep the inside from heating up too much. And there's a space heater that can be moved into the bedroom during the winter's cold.

You get pregnant immediately. It is unclear whether your poor judgment was a result of fetal alcohol syndrome or just the unthinking acts we're all prey to in our youth. Also because you were never told how things work. Vincent wants you to abort but you resist. This is partly because you think maybe you can make another person who loves you. Also partly because you're curious about whether you can have a normal child.

You find a place near Walmart called Birth Counseling. It's not a Planned Parenthood clinic, but turns out to be a place where they encourage you not to get an abortion. They don't say you're a bad person if you get an abortion, but they show you a movie about a fetus being killed inside a womb. There are doctors there, and this is the first time when you're questioned about your biological mother. Is she still alive? No. When did she die? When you were very little. Did she drink? You don't know. This is the doctor who tells you it's likely you have this condition called fetal alcohol syndrome, FAS for short. You ask, does it mean my baby will be as dumb as I am?

By no means, the doctor says, not bothering to affirm you, all his focus on saving your fetus from death. He says you can bear a totally normal child. You don't drink, do you? You answer no, and if it wasn't altogether the truth before, it is now.

You tell all this to Vincent who has been promoted to manager of the deli department. You say you've decided to have the child and know an organization that will help.

Focused on his video game, Vincent says, "Suit yourself."

Despite his agreement, he begins to be angry with you, more impatient with your slowness than before when he would just laugh. Like maybe he really didn't mean "suit yourself." But you think, it's worth it, I can make this right. I may be damaged, but I can make a normal child. A perfect child. This is why you resisted.

What your husband appears to dislike more than you resisting him is that you've stopped drinking. It was one of the things you shared, and, now always sober, you come to terms with the fact that it was the only thing. He likes video games. You've tried to play but your hand–eye coordination is lacking due to the FAS, which makes him even more impatient and frustrates you as well.

You have no family, no friends to give a baby shower. It was another thing that Vincent liked about you, that you had no family or friends to interfere with your life together. That's how you grew up, and that's what you think is normal. He didn't discourage you from making friends; he didn't have to.

You give birth to a daughter. Because of what the doctor told you, you know what to look for. When they hand her to you, you look at her eyes and are pretty sure that they're normal eyes, just like everyone else's. It's hard to tell anything else from the baby face, but you tell yourself she's going to be just fine. Such hope, such trust.

For the first year the people from Birth Counseling provide diapers and information about free childcare services in the area so you don't have to give up your job. There had been promises of continuing to help you, but until what age, that was left unanswered. You talk to others in the break room. Some of them avoid you now because they're tired of listening to you complain. One girl said she was tired of your whining and why did you have a kid you couldn't care for?

NINE

Let's say I got into bed around nine, preparing to read Ken Bruen's latest Jack Taylor book. Ken always gave shout-outs to new authors in his stories, and finding out about his death made this reading—along with a splash of Jameson's at dinner—something of a tribute to him. I had approached the story with the absurd assumption that it would obliterate the sight of Dorita that was filling my brain.

But even Jack Taylor couldn't keep me from thinking about what Dorita's charred face had looked like. Sure she was a pain in the ass, but you have to be really angry with someone to set their face on fire and hold them down while they struggled to put it out. Who did it? And just as important, did they get what they wanted out of it? Did that deed serve their purpose, whatever it was, or was more needed? Like another death?

So the dogs barking at the back door didn't wake me up, only made my adrenalin surge a little more intensely.

Sure, I couldn't have anything to worry about, right? Or had I been asking too many people too many questions?

Stifling my paranoia, I put down the book and got out of bed. It didn't matter that I was in my sleep shirt and a pair of Carlo's boxer shorts for comfort. No bobcat would object to my attire, and my stick would take care of dispatching anything smaller. I grabbed it from the umbrella stand in the front hall and, just in case there was a prowler, didn't turn on the porch light. No sense in illuminating myself for the benefit of an attacker.

I did, however, have a pretty powerful flashlight in my left hand, which we always left on the table next to the back door. Making sure the dogs couldn't swarm around my legs and get out to get hurt, I cracked open the door just enough to ooze through while shoving them back with my left foot as surreptitiously as possible.

There was no moon tonight, and while the lights of the houses across the valley were glowing, in our yard I couldn't even see back to the fence. As my eyes adjusted just a little, the life-size statue of St. Francis loomed on the right side of the yard, while the walls of the tiny casita where I'd been spending my nights while Carlo was afraid to sleep with me, loomed on the other side. When I turned on the flashlight and swept it across the yard, standing in front of the door to the casita was the intruder.

Maybe it was just someone looking for a place to get out of the heat, which still hovered around ninety-five degrees. While pretty simple in its construction, the casita did boast a swamp cooler. No use going on full attack mode until I'd assessed the danger. Determining whether another person is a source of danger: that was the first rule. As the person held up a hand to block the beam I said, "There's nothing in there, hon, unless you think you can carry a futon back over the fence."

It was either a small woman or a very small man I saw, hand still over the face to block the light. He or she should have run at that point, hopping over the back fence the same way they'd come in. A non-threatening person would have run. Keeping that light on, I suggested it. "See, that's the second rule. If you see someone approaching on foot, your best bet is to run."

The intruder didn't take the hint. Didn't speak, didn't show any reaction at all, which could be kind of troubling. I closed the distance between me and the figure that still didn't run. Third rule: don't do something stupid. Closing the distance counts as stupid. But I wanted to get near enough so the person would hear clearly, "You might want to leave now. I called the police before I came out of the house. The sheriff's substation is just a mile away, so they'll be here any minute."

The figure said, "Fourth rule: don't make empty threats. Even if the cops arrived in the next minute I could just hop over the fence and disappear down the hill before you let them in. Plus, it's likely you didn't unlock the front door."

Someone I had trained in self-defense. I said, "Fifth rule: When you're in a stand-off and there's nowhere to run, attack first."

The woman (I could tell now it was female from the voice) ran at me, bending as she approached so I could tell her intention was to head-butt me in the stomach. I stepped out of the way and used my stick to trip her. But she caught a glimpse of the stick at the last moment and swerved, grabbing it out of my hand. I dropped the flashlight at the same time. She picked it up and shone the beam close to my face to blind me. Within a moment she poked the stick between my legs as I stepped aside to avoid the light. My heel snagged a rock behind me and I went down on my ass. Within a second moment she had straddled me.

I rocked to the left to throw her off, but she'd anticipated that and her knees gripped my sides so tightly I felt like I was being attacked by a giant Thigh Master. I nearly threw her off, but she wrenched to her own left and had me back in place, this time pinning my arms to my sides.

She held her arms wide at both ends of my stick. That acted as a counterweight to prevent me from rolling over again in either direction. Then she pressed the stick against my windpipe.

"Sixth rule: use whatever you've got," she said and pressed a little harder.

"Stop," I croaked.

She didn't stop pressing. Instead, repeating, "Use whatever you've got," she bent her head down and fastened her teeth onto the top of my right ear. If she hadn't curled her lips over her teeth she would have done some real damage.

Barely able to speak because of the stick on my throat, I repeated, "Seriously, stop."

With a final little press just to make the point, she drew the stick away and her face was close enough to mine that I could see what, for her, passed as a satisfied smile.

"Nicely done," I said, once she released my arms and sat back on my outstretched legs. I rubbed my throat and hoped there wouldn't be bruising that I'd have to explain to Carlo. "You're learning well."

She said, "Thanks, Aunt Brigid."

With my body lower than hers, I sat up just enough to push on her arms and buck my knees up simultaneously, so that she half-somersaulted over my head and onto her back where she gasped like a trout. I waited patiently until she finally got her wind back so she could hear when I said, "Seventh rule: Never let your guard down when you think you've won."

Something about my family: There were three of us kids. I'm the oldest, and have a sister in the middle named Ariel. We never heard much from Ariel because she's CIA and thinks it safer to stay out of our lives. Gemma-Kate Quinn—my attacker—is my little brother Todd's daughter. We're all in some branch of law enforcement. We came from Florida and Todd was still there working as a detective with the Fort Lauderdale Police. Mom was there too, in an assisted-living facility after Dad had died, which pleased her no end. The death, I mean, not the facility. He'd always been a bully. Gemma-Kate was out here in Tucson attending the University of Arizona as an undergraduate studying molecular biology. She intended to go on for a medical degree in neurosurgery. Psychopaths make good neurosurgeons because they're no more nervous about doing damage than is a computer tech removing software. Confidence is key.

And that was one of the most interesting things about Gemma-Kate. Oh, no doubt her superior intelligence, at least in comparison to the rest of our family, was interesting. But what had drifted down in our family's genetic make-up (sometimes I wondered about whether my own empathy was sufficient or not, but so far resisted taking any tests) came to full flower in my cute little curly-headed niece.

Maybe a little too cute. She had been getting pointers from me on self-defense because of some assaults on women who walked alone across the campus of the university after dark.

Once I'd managed to get up off the ground, rubbing my back, and limping back into the house, I put a couple of mugs in the microwave for chamomile tea. It was too late for wine for me and Gemma-Kate didn't drink. The pugs had woken up when I did and were milling about. Achilles had stayed in bed, which was one of my old bathrobes in the bedroom closet.

"Where's Carlo?" Gemma-Kate asked, taking the mug I

offered her and blowing on the tea. She moved into the living room and, so as not to spill, sat carefully in her favorite wing-back chair from the era of Carlo's first wife Jane. "Did Uncle Carlo finally leave you?"

She was being serious. Psychopaths have no sense of irony, no sense of humor at all to speak of, so I objected to her thinking Carlo wasn't hearty enough to tolerate me. As I took my own place on the camel-backed couch (same era), I said, "Hey, be nice for once. I let you nearly kill me out there."

I picked up Peg who was trying and failing to jump beside me; once up there she was able to climb my shoulder and Velcro herself behind my head as she often did with Carlo. Al sat at my feet, too weak to put his paws on the edge of the couch and panting as usual because of that damn heart condition which didn't seem to respond to medication. I picked him up, too, and let him settle along my thigh with the attachment of a bloated beige leech. The dogs reminded me of my first days with Carlo, when I was a new member of the pack, when none of them knew who I really was. So far the pugs didn't seem to care about my past. The jury was still in deliberations about Carlo.

I forced my attention away from my personal obsessions and back to Gemma-Kate who said, "Bullshit. I got you fair and square except for that last move. I can maybe give you a few points for being past your prime."

"I'd call you a smart-ass but realize you're incapable of sarcasm. Your honesty terrifies me. If anything, I might have been a little too relaxed because I'd gone to bed."

"Another lesson in not letting your guard down." She paused. "You go to bed at nine?"

"Enough already. To pretend that you actually care about my marriage, I'll tell you that Carlo and I are getting along pretty well. He's just off doing his yearly stint at losing his ego in an ashram near San Diego. What about you? Has Anthony left *you*? Someone may be using the guest bedroom but you can have the casita if you want."

"Oh, Anthony still regards me as endlessly fascinating and he hasn't finished his dissertation yet."

Anthony was the guy she'd moved in with when she shared

with him on their first date ("so tell me the most interesting thing about yourself") that she was a psychopath. While there might have been a time when I thought Gemma-Kate was trying to kill me, I discovered she didn't have that thrill-seeking trait. She just didn't feel anything much.

"Would you ever think of marrying him?"

"I don't know; mostly I just need him for sex and a place to stay. He's studying psychology so I'm pretty sure he understands what *I can never love you* means. 'Course, you can't be sure he really gets it because he's a guy. But as an added benefit, he also knows I'd never bother lying to him and wouldn't freak out if he cheated on me."

"And you wouldn't get revenge."

Gemma-Kate gave me her signature blank look that wasn't reassuring. Even psychopaths have their pride. Then she looped back, never forgetting anything. "You said someone is staying in the guest room? Who?"

"Well, not right now." I told her about the group home and the circumstances by which I discovered that someone I'd trained in self-defense had come to be there. I told her about Eleanore and Dorita. I told her about Nicki, how she'd got let out of Perryville Women's Prison a few months before with the usual seven hundred dollars.

I would have expressed my remorse for the part I played in Nicki's imprisonment, but didn't care to see the tilt of her head and the set of Gemma-Kate's mouth that would express polite interest without sympathy. She even creeped *me* out sometimes that way.

"Nimby," she said, shaking her head.

"Nimby?" I asked.

"You haven't heard of that term? It's when liberals are all over doing good for people, but when the county wants to build tiny homes for the homeless on the property a quarter-mile from theirs, they look uncomfortable, like, 'but Not In My Back Yard.' NIMBY. I tell you, Aunt Brigid, sometimes I'm glad to be an honest psychopath rather than a hypocritical do-gooder. So do you think this Dorita chick was killed because she was trying to get the group home rezoned?"

"Seems kind of extreme, wouldn't you say?"

"May I come with you to the autopsy?"

"No, you may not. Anyway, if someone else picks up the issue, at least I'll be able to give Nicole Gleason a room to stay in until she can get her act together. I'm sure Carlo won't disagree. He's always rooting for the underdog." I thought of that time when he'd let a man into the house he knew was a killer, but couldn't resist when the man said he wanted to make his confession. That's Carlo.

Mention of Carlo was the only thing, the *only* thing, that made Gemma-Kate's face soften. I couldn't tell if it was genuine affection (which she'd certainly deny), or the warmth I was certain all human beings feel when they see a puppy, even if they're a serial killer. Then I recalled that she'd once almost killed one of the pugs with a Colorado River toad just to see if the toxin was as powerful as she'd heard. I must assert here that Al lived, and Gemma-Kate always denied any ill-will toward the dog.

Maybe we were both a little too charged after our fight to end the evening. When Gemma-Kate asked to know more about Nicki Gleason, I told her. That was my third mistake.

TEN

Sometimes, when I couldn't sleep at night, my mind would once again go over the pluses and minuses of my life. Sure, working undercover for the FBI all those years, being loaned out across the country to act as bait for serial offenders, I could be proud of my unique role in a job that the FBI didn't even acknowledge existed. I was always petite, and could pass for adolescent into my thirties if the lighting was right. I caught a lot of predators, and was trained so well by a Navy SEAL named Baxter that the predators touched me, to their regret. Even after I aged out, I could pose as a child online.

But what about the good people? There was Jessica, who I was training to take my place. I lost her to a serial killer. Laura, who was alive but still having flashbacks from her abduction. Oh God, that young woman in the restaurant whose name I couldn't even remember, who I reached too late to save her? Gloria, oh God, Gloria. And Carlo, who even now I couldn't count on being totally healed from what he'd witnessed me doing.

When everything I'd done had been put on the scales at the end, would I find out I wasn't that good after all?

Then there was the testimony that got Nicole Gleason put away. I was responsible for her being on trial. I was responsible for it all.

Defense Examination of Witness

DEFENSE: Dr. Ralston, now that we've established your expertise as a pediatric neurologist, would you please describe the two photographs submitted as evidence?

DR. RALSTON: Yes. The one on the left is an example of facial features associated with fetal alcohol syndrome, or FAS.

DEFENSE: And would you please explain what that syndrome is?

DR. RALSTON: When a pregnant woman consumes large amounts of alcohol—

DEFENSE: How much, would you say?

DR. RALSTON: That's difficult to tell. All we have to go by is self-reporting, and you can imagine how untrustworthy that can be in a woman who is alcoholic.

DEFENSE: Thank you. Please go on.

DR. RALSTON: As you can see from the photo on the left, there are certain facial features which indicate FAS. [Takes pointer from defense.] Here, around the eyes, you can see epicanthal folds which aren't usual in a normal face. Along with that the top of the head is somewhat smaller, the nose shorter, and the whole face across the nasal bridge somewhat flatter than typical. In addition, here you have a somewhat underdeveloped jaw and a thin upper lip. Notably, the philtrum—

DEFENSE: And that is.

DR. RALSTON: [Pointing to his own face.] This little depression between the bottom of my nose and my upper lip? That's usually absent in a child with fetal alcohol syndrome. Of course, it's not just one facial feature that provides a diagnosis, but all the elements combined. And the degree of abnormality is on a spectrum that can go from severe, comparable to Downs, or hardly noticeable.

DEFENSE: And in the case of the defendant . . .

DR. RALSTON: A person with that degree of FAS can go through life quite under the radar, so to speak.

DEFENSE: And what do you think of the photograph on the right?

[Defense points to photograph of Nicole Gleason.]

DR. RALSTON: Fetal alcohol syndrome is apparent in the facial features.

I was humiliated on Nicki's behalf. It was like being naked so others could see the scars of your defense. But I saw the purpose.

DEFENSE: Turning to nervous system aspects. What kind of neurological problems might be associated with FAS?

DR. RALSTON: Just as with the degree of abnormality in facial features, there can be different degrees of intellectual disability ranging from severe to unnoticeable. Individuals with FAS may have other neurological deficits such as poor motor skills and hand–eye coordination. They may also have a complex pattern of behavioral and learning problems, including difficulties with memory, attention and judgment.

DEFENSE: Could you give an example of behavioral problems?

DR. RALSTON: FAS can affect the executive function.

DEFENSE: Would you please explain?

DR. RALSTON: The frontal lobe of the brain controls decisions that we make, whether to act or react, or not. In a normal person the executive function works well, for the most part, but in the case of fetal alcohol syndrome the underdevelopment of the frontal lobe—I mentioned the smaller head—can impact on decisions.

DEFENSE: Like an overreaction to what the victim—

PROSECUTION: Objection.

JUDGE: Sustained. The defendant is not the victim.

DEFENSE: Like an overreaction to what the defendant might perceive as an attack.

DR. RALSTON: Yes, that's possible.

DEFENSE: That could lead to a counterattack?

PROSECUTION: Objection. Leading the witness.

DEFENSE: Question withdrawn. Thank you, Dr. Ralston.

JUDGE: Does the prosecution wish to cross-examine?

PROSECUTION: No, Your Honor. In our mind this doesn't change the facts of the case.

JUDGE: Your turn.

PROSECUTION: The state calls to the stand Dr. Cassandra Alvarez.

I know Cassandra Alvarez. Literally wrote the book on how a person's biology, such as faulty neurological wiring, can influence criminal behavior. An excellent scientist and expert witness, as well. We'd been on both sides of a case before, and I knew she was formidable.

DR. ALVAREZ: As well as the damage that alcohol does to the developing brain, FASD has specific effects on other biological systems that have been shown to be predisposers for crime. Prenatal exposure to alcohol affects the development of the neurotransmitter systems. It seriously impairs the development of the system that produces and regulates serotonin, a very important neurotransmitter. Serotonin is a major factor in criminogenic acts. Low serotonin has been consistently associated with aggression and impulsivity, and alcohol exposure before birth results in low serotonin levels, so this mechanism alone could be related to criminal acts.

PROSECUTION: Would you please explain how FASD can be taken into account when dealing with a criminal with this problem?

DR. ALVAREZ: In the United States, Robert Harris was sentenced to death for a horrific and brutal murder. He suffered from severe FASD and was born before the syndrome was officially described, so it could not have been taken into account at the trial. Harris was sentenced to death.

PROSECUTION: But is it used as a defense today?

DR. ALVAREZ: To date, FASD is not a standalone defense. But in correlation with other factors, such as the victim suffering physical violence or psychological abuse—

PROSECUTION: By victim, do you mean the defendant or the husband she murdered?

DEFENSE: Objection.

JUDGE: Sustained. The jury is instructed to disregard that statement. The defendant is being tried for manslaughter, not murder.

PROSECUTION: Is it true that this insanity plea could only be considered as a defense in very severe cases?

DR. ALVAREZ: A finding of unfitness to stand trial, what used to be called "an insanity plea," is possible in some jurisdictions.

PROSECUTION: Would you judge the defendant to be that severely impaired? Insane?

DEFENSE: Objection. Dr. Alvarez was not the person who assessed my client.

JUDGE: Objection sustained.

PROSECUTION: Thank you, Dr. Alvarez. You may step down.

Then it was my turn.

DEFENSE: State your name.

QUINN: Brigid Quinn.

DEFENSE: And your profession?

QUINN: Retired agent for the Federal Bureau of Investigation.

DEFENSE: But you still volunteer.

QUINN: Yes, at a place called Desert Doves. It's a refuge for victims of domestic violence.

DEFENSE: And what do you do there?

QUINN: I talk to them, because I have experience with perpetrators of domestic abuse. And I also show them how to defend themselves.

DEFENSE: What kinds of defense?

QUINN: There are lots of tactics that I advise, primarily how to escape, either in the moment or for good. Then there's distraction. I tell a story about a man who was getting aggressive with his girlfriend and she tipped over his prize aquarium, allowing herself to slip out of the house while he was trying to save the fish.

DEFENSE: And if neither escape nor distraction works . . .

QUINN: I show women how to trust their strength and agility. How, if necessary, to put someone on the floor. There are rules to follow . . .

DEFENSE: And those rules are?

QUINN: Use whatever you've got. Assess your assailant. If you determine you're in danger, attack first. That kind of thing.

DEFENSE: And did you train Nicole Gleason?

QUINN: I did. She was a good student.

DEFENSE: Why did you train her?

QUINN: Because she was being physically abused by her husband.

PROSECUTION: Objection. Hearsay by the defendant.

JUDGE: I'd like to hear more.

DEFENSE: What is your experience in judging whether a woman has been abused?

QUINN: I've known many of them.

DEFENSE: How many? Dozens?

QUINN: Hundreds. They have much in common.

DEFENSE: Please explain.

QUINN: The first time I saw Nicole Gleason, when I was checking out at Walmart, I noticed a cigarette burn on her hand. She saw that I noticed it, and I discreetly gave her the card for Desert Doves. When I checked back the next day, she was wearing a bandage over the sore. Women, through fear or pride, often hide the signs of their abuse.

DEFENSE: Thank you, Ms. Quinn.

JUDGE: Does the prosecution wish to cross-examine?

PROSECUTION: Yes, Your Honor. Would you tell us again about your acquaintance with the defendant, Ms. Quinn? What did she tell you on her first visit?

QUINN: She seemed to have trouble making a decision to get out of her situation.

PROSECUTION: "Situation" meaning her marriage, I presume. But she did make that decision, didn't she? With your help?

QUINN: I encouraged her to leave, to begin divorce proceedings, to get a restraining order, things like that.

PROSECUTION: Even though that wasn't part of your job description?

QUINN: I'm not sure. Desert Doves never gave me a written job description.

PROSECUTION: And what about those physical defense strategies? What did you teach her to do?

QUINN: As I've said, I showed the defendant self-defense tactics.

PROSECUTION: What did that entail?

DEFENSE: Your Honor, we've been through this.

PROSECUTION: The court will understand that's why this is called *cross*-examination.

JUDGE: Overruled. [Nods at witness.] Please answer the question.

PROSECUTION: What kinds of self-defense tactics did you teach the defendant?

QUINN: Some moves based on martial arts, such as putting an assailant off-balance—

PROSECUTION: Sticking one's thumbs into another person's eye sockets—

DEFENSE: Objection. That didn't happen.

JUDGE: Sustained.

PROSECUTION: I'm trying to establish the kinds of tactics in which Ms. Quinn is expert. To show that Nicole Gleason was slowly being weaponized. What about driving the nasal bone into the brain with the heel of one's hand? Wouldn't you say that would take good hand–eye coordination?

QUINN: Defense strategies should always match those of the assailant. In the case of a stranger, you hit them as hard as you can before they can get the upper hand. With a known assailant, what you want to do is distract, de-escalate, disable in that order. Not kill.

PROSECUTION: Please answer the question. Wouldn't driving the nasal bone into the brain with the heel of one's hand require good hand–eye coordination?

QUINN: All defense requires hand–eye coordination, more or less.

PROSECUTION: Thank you. Did it ever occur to you that

the defendant wasn't psychologically capable of seeing the difference between defense and assault?

QUINN: That's not my expertise.

PROSECUTION: And did it ever occur to you that the defendant was seeking out your expertise with the sole intent of murdering her husband?

DEFENSE: Objection! Conjecture.

PROSECUTION: I withdraw the question.

JUDGE: Strike it from the record. And repeated instruction to the prosecution not to use the term "murder."

PROSECUTION: So when Ms. Gleason attacked Mr. Gleason with a heavy liquor bottle, was that a tactic you had taught her?

QUINN: Not precisely a liquor bottle, no.

[Laughter in the courtroom.]

JUDGE: Quiet, please. Ms. Quinn, answer the question.

QUINN: We do work with noticing what is at hand in the case of self-defense, and learning how to use it.

PROSECUTION: Like using a heavy glass bottle as a cudgel.

QUINN: If that's what it takes, yes. That would come under the rule of using what you've got.

PROSECUTION: Since you're speaking on Ms. Gleason's behalf, would you care to explain why she spray-painted the television screen without provocation?

QUINN: Without provocation? I believe it has been established there was great provocation. Mr. Gleason was so involved in playing—

DEFENSE: Objec—

QUINN: —video games that he'd left their three-year-old child in a hot car. She almost died.

PROSECUTION: We don't know this because of a medical report, do we?

QUINN: The child wasn't taken to the hospital.

PROSECUTION: So again, we only have Ms. Gleason's word

for this, after she killed her husband. Ms. Gleason was so concerned, and SO angry, that she spray-painted the television the next day for revenge. Rather than, say, moving out. As you would put it, escaping.

QUINN: [Does not comment.]

PROSECUTION: Ms. Quinn, did you train Nicole Gleason to kill?

QUINN: No.

PROSECUTION: That's all.

Did I? Train Nicole to kill because I was so angry at the husband who abused her? There comes a time in a trial when you might tell yourself you can recover but, deep inside you, resides the verdict. Maybe the jury doesn't even know it yet. But you can tell from the gleam of triumph in the prosecutor and the defeated sadness of the defender. How might it have gone without my testimony? Was I too arrogant? What could I have said? One of the half-dozen things I still think about when I'm awake in the night.

And when it was all over . . .

JUDGE: How does the jury find the defendant?

FOREMAN: We find Nicole Gleason guilty of one count of involuntary manslaughter, Your Honor.

Funny that word, manslaughter. If you break it apart, it spells man's laughter. Her child was there for the sentencing, how cruel was that? She couldn't have known what it all meant, but just the same cried, "Mommy! Mommy!" when Nicki was led from the room. It would be three years before she would see Ramona again. That's a whole lifetime for a child that young. Three years to turn "Mommy" into a stranger. It would be Eleanore Turner who brought Ramona for visits when she became Nicki's mentor.

ELEVEN

With Max telling me nothing, after Dorita's murder I began to check the Neighbors site regularly, to see if people in the neighborhood knew something I didn't. If not, I wouldn't be surprised if they made it up. That's how gossip works, it's the age-old source of disinformation.

Another incident at the group home?

What happened now?

The neighbor who was working to get the home gone was murdered the other night. I hear it was gristly.

You mean grisly. Gristly is what you get from a cheap steak.

Fuck off.

And they think someone from the home did it?

What happened exactly?

Someone set her on fire. It was bar-b-cued Doritas.

Eeeew. That's not funny. The admin is going to delete you.

And they think someone from the group home did it?

Who knows? I told you someone should light a match.

Who are we setting on fire now?

Not who, but what. Here's the address.

Hey, fire works both ways. I got your name and your development. Easy to find you.

Let the doxing begin. Whoever said to watch out for the administrator knew what he or she was talking about. This was a lot worse than that other woman who reported slipping on service-dog shit at the Safeway grocery store. I copied the thread before it was taken down and went over to the group home. Rapped on the front door and kept rapping until one of the ermines showed up. I couldn't remember if this one was Erroll or Jackson.

"OK," I said, wagging the piece of paper in his face. "Which one of you bozos made this threat?"

The ermine was bleary-eyed at two p.m. Either napping, or

drunk. If drunk, and with a computer handy, he could have been the one who posted about burning down someone's house. He took the string of posts out of my hand and squinted at it. "Small type. Let me get my glasses." I followed him into the house. "Is Nicki home?"

"She left a while ago with that weird woman."

"How's she doing?"

"I don't know. You should ask her." The place was small enough and open enough that I could see him go into the kitchen area and get his black-framed glasses off the counter. "These ones you get at the pharmacy are better than the prison-issue ones," he said, putting them on and scanning the paper he'd taken from me. "Huh, there's some really angry people out there," he said.

"Is the arsonist home?" I asked.

The question coming without warning, he answered honestly. "I'm him."

I paused to consider if he was a bed-wetter and hurt animals. That would constitute the triad that made him being a serial killer not likely, but at least possible. "Did you just threaten to find whoever threatened to burn down your house and send them a counter-threat?"

"Do I look that stupid?"

"A lot less so with the glasses," I admitted.

"Well, aren't we judgy," he said. "What do you know about me?"

"You're going to tell me, aren't you?" People love to tell stories about themselves, whether or not those stories are something to be admired.

He sat down in the armchair and hooked one leg over the arm. I took that as permission to stay a while, so I settled into the oily couch cushions without looking to see what I might be sitting in. Polite, you know?

After appearing for a moment like he was falling back asleep, he said, "Look. I got in trouble when I was sixteen, smoking dope with some friends. We were in Catalina State Park in a friend's car, that big parking lot at the trailheads. It was a dry night, before the monsoon season started, and a wind was whipping up. Rick flicked his butt out of the window and I was the one who saw it land in a patch of buffel grass and start smoking. It caught really fast and I said, "Hold on!" jumped out of the backseat and went to stomp it out. They started laughing and drove off, leaving me there with the fire going. I tried to put it out but it just went wild. I ran the mile or so in the direction of the park ranger station, and by the time I got there I could smell the smoke behind me. No one was in the station, and I didn't know what else to do, so I yelled. Finally the ranger appeared, having come out of the bathroom across the parking lot. Then he had to call the fire department. By the time they got it under control, the fire had burned about seven acres. Not too serious, as wildfires go in this part of the country, but it didn't help that I was still high when they arrested me. I was given two years which I was told was minor for starting a fire in a state park."

Arizona takes arson very seriously. It can wipe out hundreds of thousands of acres in a matter of days. I remembered more than one of them. The town of Summerhaven, at the top of Mouth Lemmon nine miles away and nine thousand feet up, was totally destroyed twenty years ago. I wasn't living here for that one, but about five summers ago there was another on the Samaniego Ridge, which was in my line of sight about four miles from our back porch. You couldn't see more than a wisp of smoke during the day, but at night you could see the red and orange and yellow flames as they crept down the slopes and canyons of the mountain in the way of lava from a volcano, going wherever there had been green. There were a lot of houses at the bottom of that mountain. People were told to evacuate. Small prop planes releasing what must have been huge buckets of some red fire retardant appeared useless. Carlo and I watched the fire grow with each successive night for twelve nights. Two years in prison was considered a light sentence.

"Why didn't you turn in your friends? The guy who actually started the fire."

He didn't answer me except with that flat stare, lips slack and lids lowered a micrometer. That barely disguised condescension that says, *Have you noticed the color of my skin?*

"I see."

"At least you didn't say you don't see color. Anyway, the prosecutor talked me into a plea deal. Hell, my public defender talked me into a plea deal. Convicted as a juvenile, which put me with relatively less violent criminals. And only two years for my family to live in shame. The only good thing is that—without anything better to do—I got my high-school diploma while I was doing my time."

"Don't you have a family to go home to?'

"I'm not welcome there. You're Black in Arizona you only get one chance to screw up."

My heart twitched a little. Oh, how I want to take care of everyone. But I can't, I just can't. Sometimes you have to leave the wounded behind. Focus. "Do you have any idea who might have made the threat on the neighborhood site, the one getting back at the person who said light a match?"

"Could be anyone. Could be someone who knows my past and is using it to make me, or all of us, look bad, to force us out of here."

"I've thought the same thing. You're right. That could be anyone."

He was a good kid. I determined to stop calling him either "ermine" or "arsonist." His name was Jackson, he said. He was a good kid.

TWELVE

I thought to take Gemma-Kate out for some lunch since I was going to be near her campus at the medical examiner's office. There was a new Mexican fusion place called Red Bird Scratch (don't ask me why) that I wanted to try. But when I forgot myself and told her why I was coming down that way, I was sorry.

"Ooh, let me come," she said again. Anyone else might have added an exclamation mark to that comment, but she said it with her usual lack of feeling, which excluded enthusiasm as much as anger.

"It's not that easy. If I knew the medical examiner maybe, but I've never met this guy. He's just letting me be present as a favor to the guy who retired."

"Take me. Say I'm studying medicine, which I intend to. I'll be doing lots of dissections myself. And if he says no, I'll wait in the lobby."

So an hour later we were both standing side by side across from Dr. Will Fressler, the new pathologist whom I recognized from the crime scene, and a frankly disgruntled Max Coyote, who couldn't do anything about my presence. We had arrived about twenty minutes into the autopsy. The external evaluation had already been done, and the Y incision exposing Dorita's internal organs completed.

"How do you burn only a face?" I asked, not being too interested in the examination of the organs. I saw again how she was so badly destroyed it looked like the bump of her nose had moved down to where her mouth should have been.

"There was a hose in the backyard. They put her face out with that, and the fire in the fire pit, too. There was still water in the bottom of it." With his finger he gently mashed some of the blackened tissue around what must have once been Dorita's cheek. "See, even though she was left out in low humidity, you can still feel some of the moisture. It pooled in the cavity."

I opened my mouth again, but Coyote answered my next question. "No fingerprints on the hose. And whatever they used as a torch wasn't left at the scene."

I could mostly tell it was her from the red hair that remained, but asked the obvious. "Are we sure it's Dorita Gordino?"

"Her father came to identify the body. We were able to keep the face covered so he didn't have to see it; he's pretty old and fragile in every sense of the word. But he did say the cross taken from the body was hers and—"

"Items of clothing aren't sufficient. Could be changed," I said softly to Gemma-Kate.

"—And," Fressler went on, "there's a surgical scar on her right wrist from a snowboarding accident when she was younger." He added, with deference to Gemma-Kate, "This is pretty gruesome. Sometimes during a person's first autopsy they tend to hyperventilate. If that happens, put your hand over your mouth and breath through it." He smiled, but looked a little desirous of the possibility of her swooning. "I don't want to have to pick you up if you pass out."

"I'm fine," Gemma-Kate said.

Did I mention Gemma-Kate is pretty cute? Fressler was as good-looking as he thought, and youngish, though still a good dozen years older than her. Plus he had that white-coat thing going for him. He conducted the autopsy like a boy waggling a frog at a girl on the playground. He couldn't know that Gemma-Kate wasn't that kind of girl. He pulled down the microphone over the table: "No rigor mortis at time of discovery at eight a.m. Attack more likely to have occurred at night to avoid notice, so time of death somewhere between ten p.m. and midnight. Overnight temperatures were in the low nineties, so rigor mortis may have eased more quickly than usual. Side note for position of body: Subject found in the backyard, curled into fetal position but with her left arm stretched over her head, the index finger of her hand pointing."

"Let me guess," I said, wanting to pre-empt foolish

suppositions before they took hold. "She was pointing at the group home across the street."

"That's not for me to say," Fressler said.

"Whoever says it is ridiculous. Straight up Inspector Poirot."

"Shall I go on?"

Max was looking at me with a keen interest at that point, and I thought I should stop talking about the group home. I said, "Sure."

Fressler leaned to examine the chest cavity more closely and then pulled out first one lung and then the other, placing them on a scale for weighing. With his scalpel he made a slit in the trachea. "There's no damage here," he said, talking to himself more than us. "Interesting."

"Why?"

"It indicates that the head was set on fire postmortem."

I felt like an annoying toddler but asked anyway. "Why?"

"If it was the fire that killed her there would be some damage, even if small, to her trachea as she took a breath for screaming."

"I'm having trouble imagining for what purpose someone would set a person's face on fire and then put it out. Especially if it was done postmortem," I said.

"Can't tell you why, it's more in the purview of a forensic psychologist; not my expertise. Whether it expresses rage is for a forensic profiler to discover, only noting."

Max said with a little impatience, "So you've got the manner of death, which I think we can say with certainty was homicide, but you can't figure out the cause?"

"I think I can. But first," Fressler took what was unmistakably the kind of pliers you get from Harbor Freight and opened the jaw. We could hear the breaking. Putting down the pliers, he chose a smaller tweezer-like instrument and poked it in the spot between the teeth. He gripped, and pulled, releasing a cloth-like substance that was black at the end and whitish in the area that might have been shoved down the throat. The blackish end of the cloth poking out was what I had mistaken for her nose. "See, it's a rag soaked with the gasoline. It could suggest that the perpetrator was trying to conceal the real cause of death."

"Which was?" Max asked in his let's-get-to-the-point voice.

Fressler smiled with satisfaction. “Extreme blunt-force trauma. The breakage of the nose, occipital ridge, zygomatic bones, and even the teeth indicates an extremely large, very heavy object. Or else one that was wielded repeatedly until all this damage could be done.”

So that’s what happened to her nose.

Max said, “Could it have been done by just one person? You’d think someone would have to hold her down while the other did the damage.”

Fressler said, “That’s hard to say. You could posit a single person hitting her so hard with, say, a mallet, that it would knock her out so the job could be finished while she was down. Could be one strong man. She doesn’t look like someone who could fight off a big attacker.”

“Someone sneaking up from behind to deliver the first blow?” Max asked.

“Nope,” Fressler said. “Cranium intact. Had to be from the front.”

“She knew the person,” I said.

“Or thought she did,” Max said.

Fressler moved to the end of the table and turned on the saw to remove the top of the cranium. The smell of the bone dust mixing with the usual formaldehyde that doubled as air freshener was pungent. Even Gemma-Kate caught her breath, but it wasn’t because she was grossed out. “Can I touch it?” she asked, looking at the exposed ridges of gray matter with her hand outstretched in anticipation.

“’fraid not,” said Fressler.

“I’m studying neurosurgery,” she said, making it sound true. I kept a straight face.

“Then I’m sure you’ll have plenty of opportunities to study this part of the anatomy. Here it’s against the rules.” He looked at Gemma-Kate’s face, which had taken on an adorably disappointed look, chin tucked so her eyes had to look up at him.

It didn’t make Fressler relent, but he wasn’t averse to putting on a show. “Actually, I usually do this later, but with the head being set on fire, I just wanted to check out a theory.”

Everybody likes to be a teacher. “Remember Pompey? A

study recently argued that some victims in the eruption of Mount Vesuvius in seventy-nine C.E. may have died when a hot ash cloud boiled their bodily fluids and caused their skulls to explode. But one article I've read says it's unlikely." He pointed to the brain matter. "I tend to agree. You'd think that setting a head on fire would boil the brain more than falling hot ashes." I thought to beg him to please stop showing off, but this was his show and I got in free. I closed my eyes and let him continue to try to impress Gemma-Kate.

With a scalpel he made a few slices at the ligaments that held the brain in place, and lifted it out of the cavity. Holding it in one hand he pointed with the scalpel in his other. "See, there's no damage at all to the frontal lobe, except where bits of the forehead are lodged. The head was on fire long enough to do some damage here to the underside of the brain. The fire must have burned upward through the soft palate. See, Gemma-Kate, the temporal lobe is badly damaged, the hypothalamus and pituitary gland all but totally gone. But the brain didn't boil. This was mentioned again in the death of the poet Percy Shelley . . ."

I looked at Max. Max looked at his watch.

Wanting to move things along myself, I said to Gemma-Kate, "The medical examiner is certainly into his work, isn't he, dear?"

"Yes, Aunt Brigid. He's positively ghoulish."

Fressler seemed to get the message and stopped trying to impress for the time being. He moved through the rest of the autopsy briskly, perfunctorily examining and weighing and recording all the organs, as if Dorita may have died from an embolism rather than the obvious cause.

I respectfully kept my mouth closed and let the man do his job, but Max was a little less patient. "Can you tell anything about the weapon that was used to crush her face?" he asked.

Fressler gazed at the face as if it had a mouth and might speak to him. Then looked a little closer. Then slipped a magnifying glass over his head, picked up a tweezer from the rolling instrument table beside him, and dug into the blackened flesh around the vicinity of what had once been the upper jaw.

Focused on the flesh, and with both hands employed, he

said to Gemma-Kate, "I don't have an assistant today. Would you please hand me that little specimen dish?"

She reached the aluminum stand near her and, when he grinned about not being able to hold it, she did. Fressler pulled several pieces of hard and soft tissue and dropped them in the dish. Then he carried the dish over to a microscope in another part of the autopsy room, created several slides, and took a look. "Want to see?" he finally said—to all of us, but letting his gaze settle on Gemma-Kate in particular.

We gathered around and took turns closing one eye and staring into the lens with the other, while all of us likely shared the feeling that he had the answer but was allowing suspense to build.

"Those pale bits. Bone?" I asked, when it was my turn.

Max and Gemma-Kate nodded.

"It's more like mineral, a rock," Fressler said with modest triumph, as if he'd anticipated our mistake. "Something crumbly like limestone, but I'm not a forensic geologist so I can't say. Wouldn't hurt to send out a sample to see if there's something more specific here."

So rock. Big deal. "Could she have fallen on her face in the graveled yard?"

"Maybe, but even the finest gravel isn't as small as these particles. And for her face to break the gravel into this size, she'd have to be dropped from an airplane." He smiled at his own little joke. "It's more as if bits broke off the murder weapon."

Again, so rock. I didn't see what could be discovered. Arizona is nothing if not rocks. Rocks of all sizes lying everywhere. "So someone used a good-sized rock to crush her face before they set it on fire. Maybe the fire was used to try to destroy that evidence." Frankly, I still didn't see what could be discovered that we didn't already know.

"Well, you can't destroy rock," Fressler said. "Though so little of the rock is identifiable in a precise way because everything was mashed together during upheavals and crashes millions of years ago. It's what you call metamorphic."

I thought of Carlo, who is an amateur geologist, muttering

when he looked at the mountains behind our house, "Metamorphic." It was said always with disdain, the way some people say "low class."

Suddenly aware that Fressler had paused his lecture and, hoping he was finished, I threw one of those prayers of thanks into the Cosmos without knowing where or whether it would land.

No such luck. He continued, "Of course, if it were pollen this would be a different issue altogether. They've been able to isolate the geographical source of pollen found at a crime scene so they could tell that a person was killed, say, in South Carolina before being transported here."

Thanks, Cosmos. Thanks a lot. I glanced at the clock on the wall while Fressler, oblivious to the fact that he was boring, continued. "And did you know that a pollen spore found on the Shroud of Turin tracked its journey to France? It's one of the ways they discovered its connection to the Knights Temp—"

"Gemma-Kate, you've got that class you have to get to," I said.

She nodded. "Right, and there's a test on polymerase chain reactions that I can't miss."

Fressler took the hint and wrapped up. "Deputy Coyote, I wouldn't wait for the results to come back from the forensic geologist. You might check the immediate vicinity around the victim's house to see if there are any rocks with tissue or blood on them. A good twenty-pound rock falling from a high enough height to at least put the victim out if not finish the job. And again, I'm no forensic psychologist, but I venture this would have been one big angry dude."

That memory of wanting to smash Dorita's head against the concrete wall came back to me yet again, with regret. No matter how great a twit she was, she didn't deserve this. Nobody does. Well OK, I'd known a few people in my time who deserved this and more. Monsters are real. But Dorita wasn't a monster. I recalled Nicki's expression when I told her about someone smashing Dorita's face. It was too personal to her own case with Vincent.

THIRTEEN

It was another summer like this one. Temperatures soared up to 112 degrees Fahrenheit by eleven in the morning. Local broadcast journalists warned us not to leave pets or children in the car. The temperature inside a car was hot enough to bake cookies on the dashboard. Some posted pix on Facebook showing this to be true. The internal temperature of a car left in the sun for fifteen minutes would reach between 180 and 200 degrees. This is more than the recommended internal temperature for a cooked turkey. All across the desert southwest, people hear these warnings on the news and shake their head in disbelief. Who would be stupid enough to leave a dog or a baby in the car? And yet it happened. Every summer there was at least one or two deaths before a concerned citizen could smash the window, or the cops could get there. Sometimes the creature survived for a while, only to die in the hospital or at the emergency veterinary office. There was a point of no return.

You've named your child Ramona, after the character in books that you got out of the school library once you finally learned to read, which took a little longer than for some other children. You might not be the sharpest tack in the box, but you love that child. Just as the doctor had told you, she's perfect. As her face develops into that of a typical toddler, it doesn't look like yours, it looks normal. And she's smart. She can sing the alphabet song with you when she's only two.

Your husband is still drinking, and he appears to have come to terms after all this time with the fact that you don't. He yells at you, sometimes, and grips your arm in frustration so that it leaves a little bruise. It was just an accident, when he tripped (did he trip?) and brushed his cigarette against your hand. It wasn't like he purposely pressed it into the skin. But it still hurt like hell. A woman at the check-out line in Walmart had seen the mark and recognized it. She gave you a calling card, something about Desert Doves for abused women. You've kept the card though you never called or went to the address on it.

So far, except for yelling when Ramona cries too much, Vincent pretends that she doesn't exist. This is better than the alternatives you've considered in the middle of the night. But you fear: might Vincent trip again and accidentally hurt Ramona?

The other thing Vincent likes besides drinking is playing video games. You've tried to play but your hand–eye coordination is lacking, likely because of the FAS, which makes him even more impatient and frustrates you as well. So he plays by himself, against the computer. This is a great distraction for him, and ensures that he'll pretty much stay out of the way while you take care of Ramona in the evenings after work. You put her in the tub first because she's a little smelly for maybe not having been changed often enough at the Gingerbread House. She still wears a diaper, but that doesn't mean she isn't smart. She just has to be potty-trained at the age of three in order to stay in day care. It's expensive, but you squeak by with your paycheck and Medicaid for Ramona's doctor appointments. She's fine, she's perfectly healthy, just the usual vaccinations and the occasional cold which all babies get.

Ramona is well past the formula and baby-food age, eating practically anything that you cook for yourself and Vincent. That's another thing, Vincent really likes not having to cook his own dinner. And Yolanda Rotz had taught you enough about cooking, both regular stuff like meatloaf, and a stew with pork, sauerkraut, and sour cream, that Vincent likes. He eats it and says, "OK, I'll let you live." This is a joke.

You've told your manager at Walmart that you can never work evenings because you have to pick up your kid at day care by five thirty (they close at six but it's a small lie). But one day the store manager begs you to stay for just an hour. There are only two check-out clerks scheduled, and one of them will be late because she had a bad battery. This is the other thing about being in the desert heat, car batteries don't last as long. So it's very likely the other clerk is telling the truth.

You have no friends or family other than Vincent. You reason that, if the clerk shows up when she says she will—and she's texted that her own husband has switched out their cars, jumped hers, and will take it to the shop the next day—you can trust Vincent just this once. If he'll agree.

Vincent is leaving as his own shift is over. He says no, he wants to get home and try out this new video game he picked up on his lunch break. He shows you the game, as if you'll see how obvious it is that he needs to play it. You agree that the fighters on the box look very mean, but that if he'll just swing by the Gingerbread House and let Ramona play on the floor until she gets home, it won't stop him from playing his game. He doesn't even have to change her diaper. Maybe put some Cheerios in a bowl for her? You promise to make macaroni and cheese with diced hot dogs for dinner, which he likes very much. He agrees, reluctantly.

Your co-worker shows up just a half-hour later and, worrying about how Ramona is faring with her father, you rush home and into the house. Vincent is there on the couch playing his new video game. You say, "Where's Ramona?" He doesn't look up from the little plastic box where his thumbs are moving. "Where's Ramona?" you say, maybe yelling. You run to the end of the trailer where her room is and don't find her. You run to the other end, to yours and Vincent's bedroom and she's not there either. The bathroom is empty. There's no place else to look. This is a trailer, after all.

"Did you pick her up?" you ask Vincent, fearing the worst, that he simply left her at the Gingerbread House.

"Yeah," he says, concentrating on killing the crowd of zombies or whatever those things are coming toward him.

There's only one other place to look. You run out of the trailer, tripping on the stairs and falling on the gravel surrounding the trailer. Later you will pick a few pieces out of your knee that got embedded, but for now you don't feel the pain. You run to Vincent's car that is parked in its usual spot. You didn't think to look inside when you got home and parked your own car. Why would you?

Through the back window of Vincent's Ford you see Ramona in her car seat. She would be old enough to open the car door but there are child safety locks on this one, and besides, she has a hard time with the latch on the car-seat strap. Her head is bent forward, too heavy for her little neck.

You run back into the house and shriek (you don't care now to keep your voice low the way Vincent likes it), "Where are your keys!" Even as you yell that, you are looking around, not seeing them, reaching into his pants pocket where you find them. You run back out to the car, open the door, and unloose the car-seat strap.

Ramona's body sags in your arms as if the heat had melted her bones. Her skin is quite dry. You put her on your shoulder and support her heavy head to rush into the house. You know you should call 9-1-1 for an ambulance but, though you are not totally clear in your head, your heart is already thinking of them taking her away from you because you don't take proper care of her. If an ambulance comes, and she lives, they'll take her away from you. If the ambulance comes and she dies, they'll take you away. This may be another bad decision, but you don't call 9-1-1.

How long has she been in the hot car? Certainly less than half an hour, right? Is she breathing? Yes, she is, and you can almost see the pulse through the thin skin of her neck. You don't want to waste time looking up on the internet what to do for a child who has been left in a hot car. Maybe like that night when Ramona had a fever and you put her in a tub of cool water to bring her temperature down? Then you set your alarm for every two hours, checked her, and put her in the tub again. You were a good mother.

You lower her little two-year-old body into the plastic tub in the bathroom and turn on the water. Because the pipes have been exposed to the sun, the water comes out very hot at first but quickly gets cooler before it touches her legs. Not altogether cold, just like with the fever, you've heard that too extreme shifts can shock the body and cause seizures.

You pray. You tell the god who doesn't care about you or your child that you'll make any sacrifice for her sake. You'll never leave her with that bastard Vincent again. Beyond that, you don't know what you'll do.

Ramona's eyelids flutter a little and then open. "Mommy." You hear that word as you've never heard it before, as life. The water is very shallow, just an inch deep or so, and you heard once that someone can drown in two inches of water and this isn't that deep so you say, "Hang on." You run to the kitchen area and get a glass, fill it with water and bring it to the bathroom. "You should drink a little something," you say. She does. She comes around. You pray more, that this isn't a little hope before she's taken away. You give her ice cream for dinner, and you don't mind when she wipes part of it up and down her arms.

Vincent has gotten to level three of his game and asks where his mac and cheese is.

A few minutes ago you didn't know what you'll do. You don't kill him yet, but now you know what you'll do.

You find the card from Desert Doves and call it during your break the following day. You wonder if the woman answering the phone, who says her name is Susan, is the woman who saw you at Walmart and gave you the card. You ask that. She says no, asks if you'd like to come by, "for a visit," she adds, which doesn't tell you very much about what they do at Desert Doves, but she's the only person you've spoken to about your personal situation since that doctor at Birth Counseling. You think now that that doctor didn't appear to be as interested in you as in urging you to have the child you were carrying, but that was OK. No one has ever been that interested in you. Why should they be? Your attention comes back to the woman on the other end of the line and you make an appointment for your day off. The Gingerbread House is closed that day, but you'll take Ramona with you.

Desert Doves is in Marana, to the west of Tucson, in one of those strip malls. While it has a small sign in the front window, there's nothing about the place that reveals what kind of business it is. You stand at the front door, and almost decide to go away, but the woman named Susan comes out to greet you. She's a middle-aged person, long hair held back with combs, comfortable with the body and face she's been given. She says hello, kneels down in front of Ramona and holds out her hand. Ramona looks up at you and when she sees you're not afraid, she takes Susan's hand. "I have a puzzle I think you'll like," Susan says. And the three of you go inside.

That's when you meet Brigid Quinn.

Brigid Quinn looks like a really, really fit older mother. With long white hair pulled back in a ponytail and just enough lines in her face to be interesting. She's wearing black yoga pants and a white T-shirt that says . . . nothing. You like her immediately because she says hello to Ramona before she reaches out, her biceps slightly prominent, and greets you with a handshake. You feel that you've failed once again because you've never learned how to shake hands properly and you know yours is too limp, but you don't know how hard you should grip. Brigid seems to sense this, seems to sense everything about you, right down to examining your face.

You talk. For the first time ever, you explain your life to someone who seems to want to know. Brigid Quinn doesn't just sit and listen so that you're not sure if she's paying attention to you. She asks questions about what you've said and then listens to the answers. Your answers make her ask more questions, on and on, as if she has nothing more interesting to do than talk with you. Finally, when she's mostly questioned out, she asks if you want to leave Vincent. After much hesitation, after nearly saying no, you say yes. But you add that you don't feel you could afford to support Ramona on your own. Brigid assures you that you can, but you can't see the reality of that. Even the best of people, like Brigid Quinn, tell you to do all kinds of things and then leave you on your own. Like the people at Birth Counseling who were supposed to help you.

So you say, wait, that's not right, that you've decided to stay with Vincent, and Brigid refers you to another person at Desert Doves who will help you get training in other skills, to at least get a better job. They even have business office clothes that you can have for free when that happens. But that's the future. For today, Brigid tells you she can train you up, to make sure that Vincent doesn't hurt Ramona, or you, ever again.

In time you learn. You get stronger, muscles appearing where they never were. Even your coordination, always a problem, improves so well you can trip Brigid without tripping yourself. You spend less time on your back on the mat and more time congratulating yourself for a well-done maneuver. With guidance, you even eat differently, more protein and less carbs, but cheap, like beans and chicken. Lots of chicken. Within six months, you see a different body in the floor-length mirror at Desert Doves. The body moves differently, claiming its space in the world as you walk through it without apology for getting in anyone's way. For self-defense, Brigid shows you how to always focus on escaping first, just making distance between yourself and whoever is trying to hurt you. But if you can't escape, you do this. And this, and this.

She tells you how you're so tall and wiry, and she shows you how to use it.

Nothing works out like that, the way you were assured in your training. You watch Vincent playing his video games night after night and you go a little crazy. So one day you pick up some red spray-paint from Walmart and, that evening, when he's finished his dinner, you spray the paint on his forty-five-inch television screen. He jumps up from the couch and comes after you. Brigid always instructed you on how to use whatever you have available to defend yourself, so you spray the paint in his face. It globs in one eye, but that's not enough to keep him from coming. Luckily, your training has made you more coordinated and you dodge out of his way so that you're now behind him. You take the empty bottle of vodka off the coffee table and hit him over the head with it. Was this part of your training? You can't remember. It's sort of unexpected. A heavy one-liter glass bottle of vodka doesn't shatter the way bottles do in video games. Then you remember what Brigid said about not trusting that you'd won the battle. So you hit him again.

Did you want him dead? Oh yes.

Did you kill him on purpose? You don't know.

During your trial for killing your husband, your defense attorney apologizes for doing what he does. He says it's necessary to paint you in the worst possible light in order to make sure you're not executed. You agree to let him cast you as mentally wanting, borderline moronic. It's not the same as being declared incompetent because of insanity, but it might as well be. You're willing to go through the public humiliation in a courtroom, but you wonder how the verdict will affect your future with Ramona. The verdict comes back as guilty, but the defense attorney was right, your sentence is lessened because you are less. The judge gives you three years in Perryville Women's Prison. Ramona will be six when you're released. Will they let you have her back, or do your "mental limitations" mean you'll never see her again? You've established that you're a good mother, it was Vincent's fault that Ramona almost died. OK, you didn't call 9-1-1 when she'd been left in the car, but you had your reasons. Fear that they might have taken her away from you.

Now they do take her away from you.

While you are in prison, you get involved with an art class and are told you have a gift for painting. Ramona can't come visit you; everyone thinks she's too little, just three years old at the time of your conviction. Plus the drive to Perryville Prison is long. But Ramona's foster parents are kind and they send lots of photographs of her. This is what you end up painting, the images of Ramona, which you stand against the glass of water used for washing the acrylic paint out of brushes in the arts and crafts room.

With each stroke of the brush, on her hair, on her cheek, you feel your fingers brushing her and you hope that somehow she can feel it, too. It takes you a few tries to get one the way you want it, the one in her flannel pajamas where she's gripping a stuffed plush river otter the fosters said they bought with money you sent. Why a river otter you don't know—you'd never seen one until now—but she seems to love it.

When you're halfway satisfied with your work (making sure her face is perfect, not flat, and the eyes normal), you send the painting to her. This was in your first year in prison, and she has turned four years old. A letter comes back that says:

Dear Mommy. Thank you for the picture of me! I love it very much and I love you! Here is my picture of us. Love, Ramona (your daughter).

Followed by many hearts all colored red, and a drawing of a big stick figure and a little stick figure. You cry at the sight of the stick fingers entwined. And look how smart she is! You couldn't have written a note like that when you were, oh, ten years old. Maybe she told the fosters what she wanted to say and the fosters wrote it out so she could copy it, but even so.

You do more paintings, and as Ramona grows older she begins to send you more paintings of herself, and of you. Some are watercolor and others are poster paints. The foster mother has come to visit you and takes pictures of you; Ramona paints her pictures based on these. It's too bad that you are wearing an orange jumpsuit in the paintings, but at least the color is very bright and happy looking. Also she captures your smile, which you made sure to wear in the photos. It makes you want to match her vibrant colors and happy smiles, so you do.

Ramona also dictates more letters to the foster mom which are sent to you, and you write letters back which are read to her until she learns to read herself. You're relieved that she learns to read at the age of five. One of your fellow inmates was a teacher. When you ask her if five is a good age to learn to read she says, oh yes, it's right on time, even a little early.

A little early! Another mile-marker of development that reassures you Ramona is normal. When you send more money that has been sent to you by Brigid Quinn, you tell the foster mom to buy books. Many books. You mention there could be a used bookstore so she can get extra because the prices are less.

The fellow inmate who worked with children is also in your art class, and is a real creative person. She even has a college degree, in theater, and directed plays for a children's theater as a side gig until she got caught messing with the kid who was playing Tom Sawyer. Now she's in her sixth year of ten for having sex with a minor. It doesn't matter, in this place, which of you is worse. You share your story with her, too, trusting her. How you got a lighter sentence than her by virtue of being a moron.

One day she tells you a story about a play for adults she directed, called *The Elephant Man*. It's a marvel, she says. She uses words like marvel a lot. They made a movie with all that Hollywood make-up to make this guy look like a monster, with a misshapen head four times the normal size, and growths the shape of melons sagging from his body. He was so malformed he couldn't even sleep lying down. But in the stage play they don't use make-up. Instead, in the opening scene the man who studied him (the Elephant Man is a historical character, see) is giving a lecture and there are ten-foot images of the man's face and naked torso. The audience is shocked by those images. And here's what happens: when you meet the character playing the Elephant Man, he's absolutely gorgeous. Beautifully proportioned, perfect musculature, handsome aspect. But that's not what you see. You are so shocked that the images have been burned into your mind. Through the whole play, you don't see a normal man, you see a monster.

When your fellow inmate finishes talking, you can tell that she has told you this for a reason. She thinks of you this way, as a monster. Probably herself, too. She immediately confirms that with, Everyone is a monster, she says, and with most people you just can't see it. It's the opposite of the Elephant Man. You and I, though, she says, may be monsters not on the outside, but deep, deep inside.

She likely meant to be kind, telling that story, assuring you that you're no worse than anyone else in the world. "But I'm not a monster, you are!" you yell at her. "Going after little kids that way!"

"I never killed anyone," she answers, shrugs, walks off, leaving you alone in the arts and crafts room, wanting to jab your eyes out with the paintbrush you're holding so you can no longer see your face in the mirror.

I'm not a monster on the outside, you tell yourself when you can't sleep that night, and for many nights after. You might look a little funny, the way your eyes are shaped, and maybe you don't always make the best decisions. You don't feel like a monster. Just slightly abnormal. Of course that's bad enough, because if you're even the tiniest bit of a monster, you might never get Ramona back. You can't control your face, but every other thing about you must be as normal as you can make it.

Nicki told me that story about the Elephant Man when I talked her into coming over for dinner.

"I remember seeing the movie they made in the eighties," I said, as she helped me clean up the remains of Stouffer's frozen lasagna coating our plates. "What do you say we confront this monster?"

Nicki agreed, and we went into my office in the casita which I had kept in service even after Carlo let me back into the bedroom. I fired up the computer and, not remembering the man's name, typed Elephant Man in the search bar. "Now I remember. His name was John Merrick, and he lived in Victorian England. That's—"

"The nineteenth century," Nicki said, to remind me I didn't have to 'splain everything.

"Sorry. Get ready, this is pretty gross." I typed "images" next to his name. Dozens of images, photographs taken during his life, appeared on the screen. I'd seen it before, but Nicki gasped and turned her face away. "Yep, you can't unsee that," I said. "But now you know to what extent you are *not* the Elephant Man. Says here he managed to grow up and joined a freak show in a circus to stay alive. A doctor found him and took him into his house. Says they thought he suffered from neurofibromatosis, but around 1986 they did a DNA analysis with a strand of his hair and decided he had something called Proteus syndrome that threw his whole musculo-skeletal system out of whack, and created those five-pound growths that looked like gigantic mushrooms growing from his face and body. They kept his skull, and that shows it wasn't just the soft tissue that was involved. His jaw looks like it protrudes a good ten inches more than normal."

I exited from the site and took Nicki's hand, which had gone cold as she continued to stare at the blank screen. I pulled her into the bathroom where we stood in front of the mirror.

"You're not a monster," I said. I bent forward and looked a little closer at my own reflection. "I, however, could use a little retinol cream."

Later I looked at the pictures of John Merrick again, and wondered what I looked like if you could see inside.

FOURTEEN

Not only could Eleanore arrange with the owner of a gallery to show Nicki's work, she could pack the showing to the proverbial rafters with her own friends. Nicki's wanting to cringe in a corner was unacceptable too. Eleanore grabbed her arm and absorbed the full force of everyone's good wishes and compliments so Nicki could benefit from them second-hand without having to respond. An eccentric. That's how Eleanore presented her. In the program and in introductions her name was Nicole.

The only people I could see missing from the gathering were the other members of the group home. Oh, what fun it would have been to see BFG and the ermines and Mr. Normal mixing with the bougie upper-middle-class folks, saying all the wrong things. Making a scene. Apparently, Eleanore had imagined the same thing and had been a killjoy about it. If I had known that in advance, I would have brought them myself to crash the party. At least Nicki would feel better with having people she recognized.

As it was, I had some time by myself to scan the faces of the guests and try to guess if any of them looked willing and able to smash Dorita's face with a concrete block and then set her on fire with a gasoline-soaked rag stuffed in her mouth. You'd think with all my experience with villains it would be easier to spot one, but they're not easy, villains. I mean, look at Gemma-Kate, with her cap of golden curls making her look like an adorable Doodle, and her perfectly symmetrical features. She could fool you.

The installation was divided into two parts. One half of the perfectly track-lighted room was called "Ramona," and the titles of the paintings were all dates—Ramona at this age and that, two for every year of her life. Nicki worked in a variety of styles and media, from her realistic watercolor years in

Perryville to the more recent impressionist oils that Eleanore had given her, and even a mixed-media collage with acrylic painted over cloth. The work looked as if she was searching for her genius. I don't say genius lightly. It was there.

The guests noticed, too. I crept around behind people to hear comments like:

"I hear she's mentally disabled."

"Incredible work for someone like that. Incredible for anyone."

"I hear she murdered her husband."

"Well, that wasn't in the program. But word is getting around."

"He probably had it coming."

"Seems like death follows her."

"You mean the junkie who was killed in the house? And the neighbor?"

I suppose, for some, there's a thrill in being associated with a villain, even a possible one. It's why people watch true-crime shows.

There were a few paintings that Nicki insisted be respectably framed and mounted as well, paintings of herself done by Ramona. With a glitter in her voice that made her appear to be on more than mere champagne, Eleanore whispered to people that those paintings were done while Nicki was in prison for killing her husband. That made the paintings more desirable than they might have been otherwise. Nicki seemed to mourn whenever a sold sticker was placed on a painting.

The other part of the showing was called Monsters. Nicki must have looked up a lot of famous freaks after I showed her John Merrick's "Elephant Man" images. He was there, of course, the torso naked to show the blobs of pale flesh growing out of him. There were also people whose hideousness was internal rather than external. Jeffrey Epstein and Ghislaine Maxwell grinned on one large canvas, their heads surrounded by a swirl of wispy children.

But most images were of what used to be termed "circus freak." There was a bearded lady in a royal purple dress from another era, her facial hair in three dimensions and hanging over the edge of the lower frame nearly down to the floor, made from what looked like orange Halloween wigs. In one of the more horrifying works in black charcoal, a geek bit the head off a chicken. Only the blood smeared around his lips and dripping to the floor was in color, and that color turquoise. The crowd loved it, though there weren't so many who wanted to buy these particular works for display in their living rooms.

After making a public and lengthy toast to Nicki's talents, and thanking everyone for being there, Eleanore seemed to be everywhere at once, with the giftedness of an Adderall-fueled society woman. At one time or another she flitted by in her chiffon butterfly gown, this one in taupe, much more refined than what I'd seen her in before. With an arm tucked firmly through Ramona's foster mother, she introduced us, the two women enthusing about each other. The woman said they had come to love Ramona so much, yet were so happy to see Nicki "making something of herself."

At one point Eleanore came up and spoke to me in conspiratorial fashion, putting us in the same helpful category. "It's going really well!" she bubbled in sync with her glass of champagne.

"I noticed you put in the program that she has fetal alcohol syndrome," I said.

"I know, I know. Maybe I made too much of it, but I figured it would make her, and therefore her work, more intriguing."

"Yeah, we took advantage of that at her trial, too," I said, rather than use the word "exploited."

She didn't get it. "This is the time of letting everything show, warts and all," she exclaimed. I tried not to let my eyes wander to the one on her chin that sprouted a single hair from the center. "I've told her to be open, that it makes her work more valuable these days. Like the man with cerebral palsy who typed a whole book with his big toe. Remember that? Would the book have been made into a movie if he could move his fingers? I think not. And see that fellow over there? He operates another gallery in Phoenix where I'm trying to place her."

In tracking the man Eleanore was pointing towards, I noticed Gemma-Kate and Anthony across the room. I'd never seen her boyfriend before tonight. Anthony was pretty good looking, tall and lean like Carlo, except he had more of a I'm-above-all-this air about him that Carlo never pretended.

As I watched them together, I noticed another man approaching. Right from the get-go he exuded the image of a man who never failed at anything and judged harshly anyone who did. A boot-strap guy. He was mostly jaw, and moved like ex-military, having fewer moveable joints than the rest of us. Two of those joints were his neck, which turned his face toward Gemma-Kate, and his elbow that allowed him to place his hand on the small of her back. At the same time, he grinned, and the rigid aspect magically disappeared. Was that the real him, or like a magician, was it misdirection? Wanting you to notice his smile so you'd ignore what was going on behind his eyes? Marking him as a typical bad boy, of course he was attractive to me, but too old to be flirting with Gemma-Kate. He bent to say something in her ear that, apparently, she didn't feel was witty enough to smile at. Anthony didn't seem to care, or took it as testament to his own taste in women.

"Who's the perv?" I asked, pointing him out.

Eleanore didn't bother to turn around and look at who I meant. Like she could guess. "Oh, that's my husband, Ian," she laughed, and bent toward me unnecessarily, as her face was already just ten inches from mine. It wasn't as large as Dorita's, but similarly aggressive. "He's a dear and totally in love with me. Don't mind him, he flirts with everyone, but he's so faithful it's dreary." She didn't offer to introduce me which belied her lack of jealousy. She didn't ask if I knew the young woman he was talking to.

I took a step back to hold on to as much personal space as I could. I could feel my back against the wall with what felt like the corner of a frame pressing against me.

She laughed again, that laugh where you wonder how you've missed the joke, and took a step forward. "No matter how big Tucson becomes, it's still a small town." Missing my nose by a few centimeters, Eleanore looked around, possibly having spent enough time with me and wondering who to descend on next. In her glancing she spotted Nicki with her back against a wall. That's not a metaphor. "Oh no, Nicki's doing that thing when she's nervous, where she rubs her forehead. People will look. Plus she's got that frowny thing around her mouth, which makes getting her Botox useless."

I looked at Nicki more carefully than I had before. "She got Botox? I thought there was something a little off about her."

"Mm, I took her to the place where I've gone for my migraines." Eleanore stared at Nicki with the critical eye of one viewing a more disappointing work of art. I stared at Eleanore, thinking how Botox would take one look at her and run screaming from the room in despair.

But I went with, "No kidding."

Eleanore said, "She's badly in need of a glass of champagne. Would you excuse me?"

For once I wouldn't let her railroad me. "Let me go," I said, without clarifying whether I meant go to Nicki or escape Eleanore. Grabbing a second glass off a passing tray, I drifted off to where Nicki was standing alone for a moment, rubbing her forehead with the heel of her hand.

With a glass of champagne in each hand, I had to give her a chin nuzzle rather than a hug, but that served the purpose of bringing her hand down from her face. "I've been wanting to give you a big hug since I arrived but you're too popular," I said. "Here, hold this. It does wonders for fitting in, even if you don't drink it." She took the glass. Nicki was nothing if not docile. Obedient. Unresistant. It made me wonder if I had taught her anything after all in my time teaching her to defend herself.

I said, "How you holding up with this crowd?"

"If anyone asks me anything, Eleanore said I should say 'yeah.' So. That's been working pretty good."

"Not bad advice, actually." I sipped a segue. "Now will you introduce me to Ramona?"

Nicki gave me a look of grateful recognition and gestured to Ramona, who happened to be gazing at her with awe from across the room. Was she shy with her mother? Turned out no. Ramona ran over and hugged her. "Mommy, lots of people came! You have so many friends!"

Nicki didn't correct her. She said, "You're proud of me, aren't you?"

Ramona's head bounced up and down. "Did you see my art work?" she asked me.

"You bet I did. I couldn't paint a picture if . . ." I started to say someone had a gun to my head but then quickly amended it, ". . . to save my life. I'm super impressed, Ramona. Also, I love your dress. Perfect for a gallery showing of your art."

"We bought it at Target," she said proudly, smoothing invisible wrinkles from the green taffeta skirt. "The one at the outlet mall. Mom and Dad said this was too important for regular clothes."

"She's smart, isn't she?" Nicki asked, her lower jaw quivering only slightly at Ramona calling her foster parents Mom and Dad.

"She certainly is. You can tell she takes after you in so many ways."

She grimaced; was she thinking of her artistic talent or her FAS? I changed the subject rather than berate her with affirmation. "Are they treating her to your liking?" I asked Nicki while gesturing to the foster parents. And then, as I did sometimes, I simplified the question because we all have bias. "Do you like them?"

Of course she understood me. "Except for having her back with me, it couldn't be better," she said. She took the slightest sip of her champagne and raised it in one of those toast gestures to a stranger, who was pointing to a collage of Siamese twins made from pink and blue gingham and a half-open zipper running between their joined bodies. Then he pointed back and forth at himself and the work in a pantomime of *I bought this*.

Toward the end of the evening, I saw Max's back. He was looking at one of the more recent paintings of Ramona and talking to Eleanore Turner's husband. I walked over and inserted myself between them so they couldn't carry on their conversation without acknowledging me.

"I didn't know you were here, Max," I said, and when he didn't look my way, put my hand out for Turner. "Hi. I'm a friend of Nicki's."

Reflex and good manners made him bend slightly at the waist, like a soldier marionette, and take my hand. "Ian Turner."

"I know. Eleanore tells me you're on the Pima County Board of Supervisors. You two are a Tucson power couple."

Turner turned his head right and left, one of those joints that apparently worked. "If there's a competition for good, I could never win," he said with what they call a "rueful grin." Lots of rue going on there. "With her mentoring," he waved his hand at the painting before us, "with all this, that damn woman is a saint with energy to spare. Did she tell you she's paying to send Ramona to Camp Genesis next month? That's where kids whose parents are in prison go for two weeks every summer."

"I did not know," I said with some grudging admiration.

"I'm not surprised. El keeps her halo in a drawer." He repeated that phrase, pleased by it, perhaps making a mental note to use it again.

When I turned back to the dwindling group of guests, I saw Nicki and Eleanore together, watching. They saw me and turned toward each other.

FIFTEEN

I stood in a pew about midway down the rows. The church of St. Philips was smallish, a petit gothic effect, with extra chapels off the sides and some ancient artistic flourishes that looked authentic.

Gemma-Kate was with me, having grown more and more interested in the Dorita Gordino case since the autopsy. That completed, Dorita's urn sat on a small table in front of the altar, alongside a framed photograph of a young woman's face. I almost didn't recognize it at first. The face was not-angry. She was actually smiling. This was a life that had something good in it. I wondered where the photograph had been kept all these years. When had she changed and why? Apparently, her hair had always been perfect, but the expression made me wish I hadn't been so judgy with her. Believer or not, I admit to having a lot of changing to do before I ultimately meet my maker, if such a thing exists.

Funerals always being about us, my thoughts turned as they always did: *who would attend mine?* Other people do that, right? It didn't take long to check off the names, and the chance they would still be alive when I went, due to old age, accident, illness, or assassination by some aggrieved perpetrator I'd put away. Mom, if she was still around; Todd, the youngest in our family, who had been thinking of retiring from the police force. And of course, Gemma-Kate, his daughter. Gemma-Kate would probably attend if she didn't have something better to do. Then there was Ariel, the middle child, who was God-knew-where. She worked for the CIA (am I repeating myself again?) and told us long ago that it was better if she wasn't involved with the family, that it could put us in danger. That was ironic, considering that I'd been in pretty much a constant state of danger for most of my life. Except for Carlo, I didn't have any other people. No friends in Arizona. I'd tried but it didn't go so well.

There were some people from the neighborhood in attendance, either from curiosity, genuine caring, or guilt because they thought signing her petition got her killed. Dorita's parents sat in the first pew, old and frail; what more needs to be said? When we had walked by them on the way to our seats, I noted the father looked grieved, but the mother's eyes had the stare of someone who's politely bored and thinking about what flavor of cubed Jello would be served at the assisted-living facility. There was a younger man, much younger than Dorita, I think, who introduced himself as her brother coming from Oregon to attend the funeral and take care of . . . I think he started to say his parents, until he glanced at them and might have been met with a glare from his father which made him change course to say he'd be "taking care of Dorita's estate." That sounded a little antiseptic for a eulogy, but he recovered and went on for a decent length of time about what a great woman Dorita was, so civic-minded, such a professional—a realtor, he said, which I remembered seeing on her Facebook page.

Always adding an extra layer of sadness, these eulogies, when delivered to a group no larger than twenty; and a half-dozen of those were only there to help out with food for the reception.

Service ended, the urn was carried out ceremoniously for deposit in a niche of the columbarium that her parents had purchased for themselves. I turned to leave the church and spotted Eleanore and Nicki half a dozen pews behind us.

There was a flash moment when you can trust your instincts or let them rest. Eleanore looked . . . what was it, carefully blank? She was nowhere near as effervescent as she was when we first met, even less so from her hyper-hostessing function at the gallery. Of course, this was a funeral. But it was more than respectful somberness. There was something in the tightness of her jaw that sought to control not only herself, or Nicki, but the whole world. Nicki startled when she saw me. Both those expressions made me wonder.

My attention shifted. Behind them, way at the back, Max Coyote—dressed in civilian clothes—watched us all like a vengeful ghost. Investigators looking for a perpetrator do that. Too bad we weren't on the best of terms, or I would have told him what I saw in Eleanore's demeanor. Then I thought about protecting Nicki from suspicion, and figured maybe it was best after all if I kept my perceptions to myself.

I saw Max duck out the door at the back of the church, apparently not having seen anyone he hadn't already interviewed, if only I knew. I followed him at as much of a trot as I could manage without calling attention to myself or appearing disrespectful. Got him before he could draw his left leg into the driver's seat of his unmarked car. I pinned the leg against the inside of the door with my own and he fell short of punching me in the stomach.

"See anyone interesting?" I asked.

"Nope," he said.

"Max, I bet you're at a standstill in this case, and you're getting some heat for it, am I right?"

He did not corroborate or deny my guess, which pretty much counts as corroboration, except that he reluctantly added, "Waiting on forensics."

I wasn't sure what he was talking about. There didn't seem to be much that Dr. Fressler had found. "You know we've always worked well together, right? If only you'll let me in, maybe I can help, do a little investigating on the side that you wouldn't be able to."

"Why?" he asked, interested in spite of himself.

"Maybe because Dorita was a nicer person than I thought. Maybe if I'd been different, took her grievances more seriously, she would still be alive."

Max almost laughed with a brief softening memory. "You always think that. If only you'd done this or that, someone would still be alive. And you're the only one who could have saved them."

It was true, but this conversation wasn't about that. "Just let me see the police report. Look at the body cam. Listen to the nine-one-one call from the burglary. Stuff like that."

"Do you think the burglar was somehow connected to Dorita Gordino's murder?"

I didn't dare answer that.

Max turned the key and the air conditioning on immediately

after. "This won't get cold until the car is running. It's one hundred and sixty degrees in here."

I heard myself pleading, "What have you got, Max?" Of course I meant, *What have you got on Nicki*, but I couldn't say that.

He just said, "You going to let my leg go or do I have to arrest you for assaulting a deputy?"

"I know, I know. The heat makes you cranky." I let go of his leg. "Would you just consider letting me help you?"

Without answering, Max closed his door and backed out of the parking spot.

When I turned from watching Max drive away, I saw that Gemma-Kate had followed me out and hovered close to where she could observe me trying to will Max into cooperating.

"I need to go to the reception," I said, seeing the others head in the direction of the parish hall.

"Oh God, spaghetti casseroles?" Gemma-Kate said. "Kill me now."

"We're Episcopalian, not Lutheran. We do quiche. Plus you don't have to eat anything," I said.

The Daughters of the King—sort of a women's auxiliary function of the Episcopal Church, from the days when women did all the cooking, serving, and cleaning up; they still do. There were no quiches but the casseroles weren't bad, and there were some salads too that got Gemma-Kate's approval. Too much food for too few people.

I pretended to speak to the rector (the name they give for the head minister at Episcopal churches), angling him so I could watch Eleanore and Nicki over his shoulder.

"Lovely church," I said. "Did Dorita attend often?"

He gave me one of those blank-eyed looks clergy reserve for a woman whose marital status is in doubt, to make sure he couldn't be suspected of flirting. "It's Dorita's parents who are members of the church," he said. "There's a bus that brings them from their assisted-living facility every Sunday. Mrs. Gordino has Alzheimer's." He put his mouth in a pout that implied a small regret. "Dorita went to a different church. I think we were a little too liberal for her, so . . ."

"Excuse me," I said, patting his hand, and going to the drink table where Eleanore was getting a cup of coffee. From the shaking of her hand, I would think she shouldn't be having any more amphetamines, let alone caffeine, but who am I to say? Some spilled over her wrist and I couldn't tell if her hissed, "Stupid!" was directed at that. I hoped she wasn't saying it to Nicki, who had put some food on her plate and was using her fork to push it around.

"Nicki. Eleanore. Hi. I didn't expect to see you here."

"Nor I you," Eleanore said, putting her cup down on the table with two hands when her one hand wobbled alarmingly and the coffee sloshed again over her well-manicured nails. I had to admit her hands weren't as ugly as her face.

From our meeting at the group home following Dorita's murder, I had known she knew who the woman was, but hadn't expected they were close enough to warrant attendance at her funeral. "So how do you know Dorita? Were you very close?"

"Oh no. Not close at all." She seemed to think better of that answer and added, "But she was so good to Ian and I when we were looking for a house in Oro Valley, that Desert Crest area, you know?"

"Personally, I do not know. But I've heard you can become very intimate, forge strong and life-long bonds over the buying and selling of property."

I watched for Eleanore's reaction to that. If she thought about how maybe I was being sarcastic, her eyes narrowed but she didn't say. Maybe she wasn't as much a clueless butterfly as I'd supposed. When she didn't respond, I turned to Nicki, who was shrinking from us both in a realization that our conversation was way out of her league. When we'd spoken in the house, first reconnected, she was the Nicki I'd known after we'd worked together for some months.

Now she was the Nicki I saw when she first walked into Desert Doves.

That was about six months before she killed her husband. Nicole Gleason was terrified that her husband would find out she had come to a place that helped abused women. She refused to go through the general intake process, and instead asked to see me. I came out of the workout room when I'd finished my self-defense class, introduced myself, and reached to shake hands. That was the first tell I could use. Her hand was obedient to her will, what she had of it. It could extend but it couldn't grip. It shrank back when her palm met mine. This was a woman who sought to disappear. Without letting her know all I knew of her in that moment, I smiled and took her back into the classroom slash gym. We sat on a couple of those plastic chairs you can hose sweat and vomit off of.

I began with some small talk that Arizonans always use—the dry heat; how late the rains were this summer. Where she'd been born. Apparently that last question wasn't exactly a no-brainer for her. Her chin ducked and her eyes slid to the side in thought. "No one ever asked me that," she said. "I don't actually know."

By this point I could see her respiration had dropped, so probably her heart wasn't pounding the way it likely had been when she first walked through the door. It was time to move on to why. "Did your husband make that cigarette burn on your hand?" I asked.

"Oh that. That was just an accident. I saw a program about second-hand smoke on TV and asked if he might smoke outside the house."

"And did he agree?"

"Well, he gave me some argument about how they had it all wrong, and how I shouldn't listen to scientists because you couldn't trust them. How what I actually knew you could 'smack up a gnat's ass with a butter paddle.'"

"How witty," I said, "in a hillbilly elegy kind of way. That's a lot of words to get to 'stupid.'"

Nicki grimaced involuntarily and I made a mental note to never use that word in her presence again. Those were the days before she was exposed to irony. "Well, he was joking," she said.

"But the burn?"

"While he was talking, he was waving his hands around and the cigarette brushed against me. My fault."

So there we were, Nicki painstakingly crafting the narrative for why she shouldn't be in a refuge for abused women. The usual. "So you don't have any reason for being here?"

Her eyes begged me to understand without her having to admit to anything.

I'd jumped too soon. This time I gave her a softball question, easier to answer. "Is that your child playing with Susan?" I wondered if she knew how important that question was to the rest of what we might accomplish.

Nicki's face softened momentarily and I felt my heart break. That has happened so often, sometimes I think my heart wishes it had a different person. "What's her name? How old is she?"

"She's almost three. Her name is Ramona."

"And you work at Walmart."

"Yes." Only a little defensive as all working mothers are, she added, "Usually she's in day care at the Gingerbread House.

"So she's safe."

Whether it was instinctive or reasoned, Nicki knew exactly what I meant by safe. Safe from the husband who had caused that burn. The features of her face seemed to inhibit the expression of emotion. A bit frozen. She nodded, but it was half-lie.

"How long were you in the system?"

"I don't know."

"You mean from a very young age?"

"I guess so."

She seemed to relax again, no longer punctuating her sentences with those deep draws of air into her lungs before she spoke. So I ventured, "And where are you supposed to be right now?"

"I told my boss I had a doctor's appointment. See, no one knows I'm here." She said that as a plea, and I reassured her that no one ever would.

With questions like that, weaving and looping so I could find out something like the true story that she was unwilling to share, Nicki didn't check off all the boxes, but enough of them. She revealed how her husband Vincent worked at Walmart with her, drank with the manager, changed their bank accounts after they married so her check would go straight into his account, gave her an allowance and made her account for what she spent on clothes, diapers, baby formula. No family or friends beyond the casual superficiality of co-workers. It was all there, the control, the pain, the classic psychological and physical abuse.

"Do you rent or own?"

"Own."

"Is your name on the deed to your house?"

"I don't know. It's not really a *house* house. It's more of a trailer."

"Do you want to leave him?" I finally asked, when I finally thought she could take it.

"I don't see how I could, with Ramona and all," she said.

"I, we here could help you," I said. "You can do anything. No, don't look away. Stay with me, Nicole. I swear to you, you have more options than you think."

That's when she finally began crying, a good sign. Very soon after that, when she came back to Desert Doves, I handed her a ten-pound free weight and we got started on some basic strength training. When she told me she didn't dare keep weights at home where Vincent might wonder what she was doing with them, I told her never mind, a nice big rock in the yard would do just as well. Arizona does not lack rocks. A few visits after that (I never asked what excuses she gave him for where she was going), we launched into basic self-defense.

Now, at the funeral, I wondered what the hell was happening with Nicki? She had that same look now when she wanted me to know what Vincent was doing but didn't want to have to tell me. If I could talk to her, what would she say? The way she drew back when Eleanore put her hand on her forearm told me this wasn't the time.

"We should go," Eleanore said. "You have to check in with your parole officer, remember?"

Nicki looked down at her plate as if remembering came hard. Eleanore took it and tossed it in the large bin at the end of the food table. "That's garbage. I'll take you out for a real lunch after," she said, her big smile again in control, making the visit to the parole officer just a girls' day out.

SIXTEEN

It wasn't until we were in the car and driving back to my place that Gemma-Kate told me Dr. Will Fressler had called her.

"Not surprising," I said, thinking of the medical examiner flirting with her. "Are you going out with him?"

"I already did, last night," she said. "Will—"

"Will, is it?"

"He took me to dinner at El Conquistador, figuring I'd be impressed. Anthony was a little miffed, and not like I felt I needed to explain, but I told him I'm interested in this case. Haven't worked a case with you since that Beaufort guy."

The name still made me shudder, not because I feared him, but because I almost lost Carlo because of him. "We don't 'work cases together,'" I said, lifting my index fingers from the steering wheel to provide the air quotes. "I promised your father I wouldn't let you get involved. I didn't tell him it wasn't for your sake, but the life of the suspect."

Gemma-Kate never took offense when I brought up her psychopathy. "You never thanked me for putting acid in that eye-drop bottle. I probably saved yours and Carlo's lives."

When I didn't respond she changed the subject back. "I guess I shouldn't have noticed, not being involved, but did it strike you that those two women were acting strangely?"

"It did." I paused, waiting to hear what the ME had told her at dinner. She made me ask. "What happened?"

"Over the appetizer, Fressler regaled me with a case from when he was with the Miami Medical Examiner's Office. I think he just wanted to introduce the topic of sex to see how I'd react. About some woman who claimed rape on the beach and when she went to the emergency room at the hospital, the forensic nurse sure enough found sand in her vagina. Only the jury decided she could have put it there herself. They thought he should have done some DNA testing."

I didn't encourage her. "You know I mean did he give you any useful information."

The corners of Gemma-Kate's mouth turned up in that facsimile of a smile. "He didn't give me anything very interesting. Remember that grit he found embedded in the face? Will said he sent those little crumbles to a forensic geologist at the university. She told him it wasn't rock."

"What else could it be?"

"Concrete."

"Isn't that rock?"

"Not really." Gemma-Kate not only told me what Fressler said, she repeated his words verbatim. She has what's called eidetic memory, never forgets anything. "It contains rock, but concrete isn't just one thing. There are several components that make it up, the way metamorphic rock is an amalgamation of minerals smashed together over time. You have the binder, which is typically cement, a fine powder made by heating limestone and clay at high temperatures and grinding the resulting rock-like substance—"

I wanted Gemma-Kate to stop talking and just move on, but I knew her and knew she had to spit out the whole thing. I could never tell if it was a matter of that eidetic memory, a compulsion due to her neuro-wiring, or if she was just showing off. I fiddled with the car's air-conditioning vents while waiting for her to spend herself.

"—then you add a coarse aggregate, like small gravel, and a fine aggregate like sand. The third component of course is water, which allows the material to be molded and hardens as it dries." Even Gemma-Kate grew bored with the recitation. "I managed to stop him when he was about to launch into a history of cement from ancient times. You know, concrete and cement aren't the same thing—"

I lifted my hands in surrender. Good thing the car was stopped in front of her apartment when I did so. "I'm begging you," I said.

"Anyway, he's sticking with the cause of death being from massive head trauma. But he's revised the murder weapon to be specifically something like a concrete block dropped on her face from a level of at least three feet."

Even I found that disturbing, and I'm not easily disturbed. I'd once investigated a trucker who got his rocks off on mummified bodies, surprisingly easy to produce in the dry southwest. "So that's why all the bones in her face were smashed. A concrete block must weigh twenty pounds, and dropped from some height . . . one and done."

"Or maybe once on her forehead to knock her out, and then boom, once on her face when she was on the ground," Gemma-Kate said with some relish. "So he thought maybe the fire was set postmortem, hoping it would conceal the real cause of death."

"That's not very smart," I said. "Is it possible there are murderers who have never watched *CSI* and know about what they find out at autopsies?"

Gemma-Kate shrugged. "Sounds like we're developing a profile."

"We are not doing anything," I repeated. "Your father would kill me if he found out I was letting you get involved in something dangerous."

"Again."

"Get out of the car," I said.

When I got home and waited about the amount of time it might take for Nicki to report in to her parole officer and then go out for lunch with Eleanore, I texted Nicki to ask if I could come over. She didn't respond. That wasn't a red flag or anything, I could just have the timing wrong. It didn't mean she was avoiding me. Right?

Still, eight hours later, when she still hadn't texted me back, I headed over to the group home. There was no harm in stopping by, just my typical early evening walk when the temperature was safely under one hundred. Between Eleanore and me, plus her parole officer, there were a number of people who were keeping an eye on her. I didn't know about the others, but I knew my motive was clear.

At least one of my motives. Instead of walking up to the front door, I skirted around the side of the house to check on the pile of concrete blocks I'd seen on my first visit. Sure enough, they'd been piled up into a chest-high (my chest, I mean, about forty-eight inches off the ground) wall extending out from the adobe wall. Behind the wall were the garbage bins, one for trash and one for recycling. I ran my finger over the cement between the blocks. It was dry.

Alfred Hitchcock used to have a show on TV in the fifties, with mystery stories. A classic one had an elderly kind of matron (she must have been all of forty in those days) kill her husband with a frozen leg of lamb. When the detectives come to question her, she invited them to dinner, serving the murder weapon. It's never established whether the husband had it coming or not.

With this memory in mind, I happened to look up at a window that overlooked this side of the house and saw the fellow I'd first identified as Big Fuckin' Guy looking out at me. What was his name again? Henry. I waved. He didn't wave back. So I walked back around to the front of the house and knocked on the door. It took a couple of similar knocks before Henry finally answered.

"I was just admiring your new wall. Did you do all the work yourself?"

"I did."

He was a lot less friendly than when I first met him. "Nice bit of home improvement. And it's not even your home."

He narrowed his eyes in that expression that showed a suspicion of a meaning under my words. I guess he decided there was no harm in telling the truth. "Well, you know, it's something to do. We've taken your advice to shape up. No fights, at least in the front yard. And that wall was planned before—"

"—Dorita Gordino was killed."

He didn't feel it necessary to nod or refute that.

I put my foot up on the door jamb, as if expecting to be invited in. "I'm actually looking for Nicki. Is she in?"

He looked down at my foot, and paused a little too long before answering. The house wasn't that big. He would have known. "No."

"Could you tell her I stopped by?"

He gave the slightest nod, leaving me with the impression he knew he was giving off a Reacheresque vibe, with nearly enough body to go with it. Either he was a reader or they had cable. Funny all the things you can tell from a few words.

I was pretty sure Nicki was in the house, and didn't think Henry would have lied without instructions. So I waited until ten p.m., when Basha's was near to closing, and got inside with a minute to spare. I ran down the cereal aisle and up the special fluids aisle. Down the canned vegetables aisle and up the plastic bags and aluminum foil aisle, wanting to look like I was desperately trying to find the hoisin sauce or something. I finally spotted Nicki bringing out a cart stacked with canned soup.

"Great!" I said, loudly enough to be heard by a manager who might be coming to kick me out. I pretended to examine the soup. "I need split pea with bacon." With her head cocked in a what-the-fuck way, Nicki handed me a can. I looked at it and backed away. "No, that's not bacon, that's ham. My husband hates split pea with ham."

"Please go away," she said, not quite in a whisper. "I'm working."

"You realize you don't need to work here after you sold all those paintings."

"I need to keep a steady job in order to get Ramona back. Eleanore says the art is promising, but you never know." She handed me another can of soup, and this time I took it.

"I just wanted to see how you are," I said. "You didn't answer my texts all day."

"I was, I was sleeping," she said. "Had to get some sleep in with the funeral and all before work."

I gave her that one seeing as how she worked nights. "But you've been different for some days, Nicki. Seems like you'd started trusting me again and then at the funeral . . ." I let that sit for a moment to gauge her reaction before asking, "What's up with you?"

"Nothing!" Nicki said. It was too big a nothing for nothing.

"I call bullshit," I said, and barreled in there while there was an opening. "Is it something to do with Eleanore? Or Dorita's murder? Or both? Do you realize you're in trouble?"

Nicki was restocking some cans of Progresso soup on the top shelf and one slipped from her hand onto the floor. The metal bent from hitting a shelf on the way down, and she picked it up and put it at the back of the row.

"Yes, I realize I'm in trouble. How stupid do you think I am?"

"Nicki . . ."

"Everything is fine. Just fine," she insisted.

"It really isn't. How is Ramona, by the way? When did you see her last? Since the gallery?"

I brought up Ramona on purpose and that was enough to get a truthful reaction from her. Her mouth opened as her head drew back. "Want to know something? OK, there's this. They were at the house."

"The cops, you mean?"

She nodded. "Some guy was going over that new wall that Henry built."

"Interesting."

She nodded and it wasn't friendly. "Let me ask you something. Why are they interested in the wall?"

"Beats me," I said. I didn't tell her I'd found out about how Dorita was killed with a concrete block, and the closest blocks, before they went into the wall, had been across the street at the group home that she was threatening to shut down. She didn't need any more to worry about, and besides, her question about why they were interested in the wall didn't sound like something a guilty person would say. It was promising, I thought. Then I thought, why did I need to hear her say something that indicated innocence?

Nicki said, "And about Eleanore, if you're so interested in her. Eleanore has a lawyer lined up for me in case I need one. She's paying for him. And you know what else? She has contacts with the Department of Child Safety and they agreed to let her be a witness so I can see Ramona at her house. So don't you say anything bad about her. She . . . she's the only friend I have."

"I know lots of good criminal defense lawyers," I said. Even I thought that was kind of pathetic.

"Ma'am," a voice said behind me. "The store is closing. Did you need to make a purchase?" I turned to the fellow behind me who was wearing the outfit of a Mormon missionary kid with a badge that said, Manager. At his age he needed that badge.

I didn't want Nicki to lose her job, it was too important for her. *Call me*, I mouthed, put the can back on the shelf, and left without it because I don't like pea soup and I don't like anybody who does. It looks like it was already eaten before I got to it.

Nicki didn't give me much to go on, but the inspection of the wall by a forensic technician was something. And I didn't need her to find out more.

Getting shut out by both Max and Nicki, I checked the Neighbors site to see if anyone had heard something I missed. Even if they were just conjecturing it could be useful. With all humility, you never know where good thinking will come from, not necessarily from me.

Anybody know whether garbage pick-up will be delayed a day because of Labor Day holiday?

Check the company website that picks yours up. How are we supposed to know

Scrolling.

There was a date and time for a special session of the homeowners' association to get information on events surrounding the group home and what to do about it. That followed by:

I found out there are five registered sex offenders living in Catalina.

(Lots of angry face emojis and a couple of wow ones.)

Who are they? Are they living in that group home on Randolph?

Now don't go jumping to conclusions.

Why not? Who else will protect our children from molesters? That home is close to where the school bus stops!

That sounded like something Dorita would say. I'd think she was posting anonymously if she wasn't dead. Or maybe that's just how misinformation goes viral. I don't participate in the foolishness. Then I thought, what the hell. I typed, thinking maybe this time facts would win:

The group home doesn't have any residents who were convicted of sexual offenses.

Maybe they're lying. Ever think of that?

And conspiracy theory in two moves. All it took was a question that couldn't be answered, such as "Why is there so much violent crime in Tucson?" Anything after that isn't heard. I gave up as the pile-on predictably proceeded with slimy phrases like "educate yourself." I would have checked further to see who the people were who were part of this conversation, especially the one suggesting there were sex offenders in the group home, but the chain disappeared. The administrator had taken it down as they did when things got too heated, too political. I had learned not to be reactive unless I thought there would be a benefit. And delicious outrage did not count. The only piece of information that was revealing here was the meeting date and time of the homeowners' association.

Still with questions about Eleanore and why her altruism was so focused on Nicole Gleason, I went back to Facebook. This time I checked out her friend list. That might be interesting. Among her four hundred and sixteen "friends" she counted Dorita. Like she said at the funeral, her realtor. If that was true. Had Eleanore agreed or disagreed with Dorita on the ousting of the group home? Once she had Nicki out of there, maybe she couldn't care less what happened to the rest of the residents. Was there another motive for engineering the success of Nicki's gallery showings? As I scanned her posts, there were no mentions of Dorita's death, no sentimental mentions of a life passing.

When I was with the FBI, I had a close friend named David Weiss, who was a forensic psychologist. I learned a lot from him, some about the strain of psychopathy that may run in the Quinn family at different points on the spectrum. It's not altogether a bad thing. A lack of empathy allows a person to perform better under conditions that would completely derail a high-empathy soul. Like finding that clue at the scene of the triple axe murder that leads you to the killer. Getting upset and throwing up is a waste of time in situations like that.

But where I fall on the empathy spectrum is not the point I'm getting at here. Like I said, I learned a lot from David, and one of those things was "apophenia." Apophenia is the wiring in our brains that makes us see patterns. The face of Jesus in a slice of burnt toast is the classic example. That's visual apophenia, but the brain doesn't stop there. Causing us to see patterns where they don't exist is the basis for all propaganda. Two things happening in close conjunction is called correlation. Propaganda occurs when someone claims that two things are not only in proximity, but that, without evidence or logic, one thing has *caused* the other. Those who manipulate us, from marketers to politicians to media pundits use this tactic, that correlation is causation.

Wait. The way David Weiss got me to understand the difference between correlation and causation is the story of the grasshopper:

A scientist is doing an experiment. He puts a grasshopper on the table and says, "Grasshopper, jump!" The grasshopper does, and the scientist measures the distance. Then he pulls one leg off the grasshopper and says, "Grasshopper jump!" The grasshopper gives it a go, but doesn't get quite as far as he did the first time. With each successive leg that the scientist removes, the grasshopper jumps a smaller and smaller distance until, with the last leg removed, the insect doesn't move at all. No matter how many times and how loudly the scientist says, "Grasshopper, jump!" the poor creature just sits there. So the scientist records his finding:

Grasshopper with no legs cannot hear.

Correlation is not causation.

Actually, that's not the point I'm getting at either. I used to be able to focus more than I do now. I don't know whether it's retirement, spending too much time with a philosopher husband, or, heaven forbid, the cognitive decline of an aging brain. Sometimes it feels like my entire mind is a piece of lace when my intention is to collect rain.

OK, here it is, what I was thinking before I got sidetracked:

Eleanore is mentoring a formerly incarcerated woman, who was in prison for killing her husband.

Eleanore may be supremely altruistic. Or not. Why is she so involved with Nicki's life? With her child?

For the benefit of Nicki?

For the control of Nicki?

If so, why?

No matter which question I asked, Nicki's name appeared. And one of the questions must be: What was I willing to do to save her? I didn't like thinking of the answer to that. I had approached Max on two separate occasions—once at the crime scene and once at Dorita's funeral—but he wasn't about to share information. I only had one card left to play.

SEVENTEEN

Max was in his little office at the Pima County Substation when I showed up. I could see him through those blinds they put up to give you privacy when you need it. Despite Max being a relatively good poker player, I've known him a long time and could tell by the look on his face that he regretted those blinds were open.

"I have an appointment," I said as I walked past the receptionist, knowing that I had to do this quickly or I'd lose my nerve.

"I told you no," Max said, when I sat down in the chair across from his desk.

"What did the ALS find on the wall?" That stands for alternative light source, an ultraviolet kind that makes semen and blood glow.

Satisfaction washed across his face and he could not stop himself. "Blood. Only on one block, second row. No DNA test yet, but type AB positive, same as Dorita Gordino. I'm liking Nicole Gleason."

"Why Nicki? Could have been one of the others."

"There's more."

"What more?"

Max sat back in his chair and folded his hands over his stomach, as if his belt buckle was a good poker hand.

"How about this," I said, taking a deep breath and speaking before I could think about why I should not. I couldn't force myself to be more specific, but I promised myself I'd get there eventually. "How about if I have some information you don't have yet, you let me help?"

I knew he wouldn't be able to resist calling my bluff. Like I said, we'd played poker. I knew his tells and I'm sure he knew mine. But his unblinking stare told me that this time he couldn't figure out why my jaw was set as tightly as it was when I had nothing but a pair of threes. That was doubt and reluctance showing, not a royal flush. "OK, let me have it." Max had been expecting me to give him information about Nicki. Surprised despite himself, now he sat back in his chair and laced his fingers over his ample belly.

That's because I told him I'd be willing to make a confession. The only thing I didn't provide is what crime, because he had a pretty good guess.

You probably don't remember that time when I was in the Canada del Oro wash underneath the bridge, collecting rocks. Nothing better to do as I was retired. It was April and the heat wasn't so bad. But I sweated anyway when I saw Gerald Snesil approach me. In his stained undershirt, thin nylon shorts, his long greasy hair, and most tellingly a prominent boner, it didn't take someone with my criminal experience to know he wasn't looking for directions. The white van with the covered windows that he had parked on the dirt road running along the wash gave me to think it would be something bad.

I could have outrun him, probably, got up the side of the wash to the street and hailed a passing car, but I was stupid. I didn't want to just let him get away. I wanted to see how bad this man was and do something so that he would never hurt anyone again. I played the weak old lady card and let him drag me into the van. Before he shut the door on semi-darkness, I was able to spot a plastic sheet draping the floor, spotted with what I imagined to be blood. There was something else there, too. A Barbie lunch box. I guessed he had a taste for women of all ages, not just old ones like me. That was all I needed to know about the man. For his part, he didn't know that the walking stick I carried wasn't just for hiking. It had a blade at the end of it, the same one that I used to sever the lizard's tail at the group home. When, with his back to the closed door of the van, he cornered me, I fought back. He managed to land some blows that drew blood because it was hard to see, but I managed to jab him in his femoral artery. Like everyone else in that situation, he tried to stop the spurting with his hands. Like everyone else, it didn't do much good.

That was my last chance to call emergency services. I should have done it, I know, even if I could have stopped him from bleeding out. But if he'd lived to go to trial, there was no guarantee they'd find evidence of his killing anyone, what with his blood squirting out over the rest I thought I'd seen. Worse than that, everyone, and by that I mean Carlo, would know the kind of woman I am. I adored Carlo, we had just married after too brief a courtship. I was still trying to hide from him that I was capable of killing with such efficiency, or such coldness, something he would find out in time, anyway. If that truth came out, I'd have a hard time keeping my other truths a secret. Then I knew what would happen because it had happened before with another man I loved. Carlo would leave me, too. I was certain of it. That's my only, and admittedly boneheaded, justification, especially in light of the fact that Carlo found out what I'd done anyway and I nearly lost him. It was the first close call of several.

Plus, I hadn't had the time for a more reasoned approach. What do you do with a dead guy in a van when you promised to be home for lunch and your husband might be coming to look for you? So I staged the scene to make it look like the van had tipped into the wash. Someone who lived a little way up the hill found the van some days after that and called local law enforcement.

Max Coyote found Snesil's decomposing remains, and I can't remember whether with the condition of the body they were able to see the jab in his thigh. Apart from that, the forensic team had a field day collecting DNA and blood samples not only from him, but several other victims which they used to determine what happened to a half-dozen missing women and girls. I guessed they probably got some of my DNA too, because I hadn't come out of the fight without a wound or two. I'd been wrong about his blood ruining the evidence. Whoops.

They could run most of the DNA specimens against that of missing persons. But I couldn't help thinking that a DNA specimen of mine had been sitting at the medical examiner's office for some years now, due to a typical backlog and lack of an exemplar. That is, I'd never given a sample of my own DNA to provide a match to me. For all that time, I'd occasionally think of that specimen, and worry in the middle of a sleepless night about being asked for a swab inside my cheek.

Now I was volunteering to tell the truth. I could see the national headlines now: "Retired FBI Agent Arrested for Murder." Former colleagues would shake their heads on CNN and comment that they weren't surprised, Brigid Quinn was always a loose cannon. She had been implicated in all kinds of shady doings, skirting justice. Coyote would run for Pima County Sheriff. Carlo would finally dump me—regretfully, but finally.

"So prove it," Max said. "How do I know that you're not just lying to me in order to get involved with the Gordino investigation?"

While one Brigid was at the back of my brain screaming, "YOU IDIOT! WHAT ARE YOU DOING?" the Brigid at the front part of my brain said calmly, "Because I know things that were never released to the media, things you never told me."

"Like?"

"No. First we follow the evidence in Nicki's case. Agreed?"

I watched him consider. He said, "Maybe you're faking it. We were talking at that time. There are things I might have told you that were kept from the public. Cop talk is hard to resist."

"Nope, I'm sure you didn't tell me everything." I thought about that Barbie lunch box I saw when I was in the van. The punctured femoral artery that made Snesil bleed out. "You'll have to trust me on that."

I watched him waffle. "What's your motivation in all this? Why do you care so much about Nicole Gleason that you'd be willing to go to prison for her?"

Because there are things more important than love, I thought, thinking of Carlo before anything else, and how the real me was better than the lie. *Honor. Duty. Bringing Nicki and Ramona together for good.* Could Max understand any of that, or was he too young?

I said, "Because I'm old and tired. And maybe because some lives are worth preserving more than others. I was the one who encouraged Nicki to defend herself from her husband. And though I didn't want to, I ended up providing testimony against her and got her sent to prison. Max, I'm beginning to think I'm not all that after all." And that there was the truth.

"What about Carlo?" Max asked. "What will this do to him?"

"Look. Don't make me think about this anymore," I said. "Take the deal or not."

Max had to let a little more out of his system that he must have been storing up. "I'll agree with you about not being all that," he said. "You're always so cocksure of yourself. Always the one to throw the final punch, have the last word. You played me."

For once I kept quiet, no defense. After showing I could take a little criticism, I said, "C'mon, let me have one last go. If Nicki is the killer, I'll turn myself in. Remember how you and Carlo used to play poker? Let's make the game more interesting."

Max didn't have to respond that if Nicki knew how to bash someone in the head once, she might have been motivated and able to do it again. I could see the extra light in his eyes. That made it even more important that I clear her name, before I got called to testify against her again. With a long release of air that sank him deeper into his chair, Max said, "I'll take that bet."

"OK. Let's start from the beginning. Show me what else you got about that incident with the burglar."

And we were working together again.

He said, "For one thing, the burglar had one thousand dollars in cash in his pocket when he died. Why look for drugs in that house when he had money to buy them? Nicole Gleason was the only person there with him. We interviewed her repeatedly, but I think she's holding something back. I think they may have been in cahoots. And that makes her the only one of the people in the group home who could be linked to both the burglar and Dorita Gordino."

I hoped I hadn't made a huge mistake.

"Got anything else?"

Without further discussion, he got up and took me to listen to the 9-1-1 call and see the body-cam video of the SWAT team shooting the burglar at the group home.

I recognized Nicki's voice on the audio recording:

"Nine-one-one, what's your emergency?"

"There . . . there's a man in the house. Help!"

"Where are you?"

"I'm in the bathroom."

"Give me your address. Don't disconnect."

"Three-seven-six West Shepherd Street. He's got a gun."

"Lock the door. Sending help immediately. Stay quiet."

A gasp.

"Are you OK?"

Sounds of struggle, woman screaming. No further communication.

Max looked at me. "Here's more. There's a problem with the timing. According to the time stamp on this tape, she called the police five minutes before she came out of the bathroom. We know that because she left the line open, and we could hear when she confronted the burglar. That's curious," he said. "Any brilliant conclusions?"

"Not so far," I said. "What about the body cam?"

He moved to a video screen and showed the SWAT guy's body camera panning across the yard of the house I knew as the group home. With two other officers, he moved around the sides of the house to make sure no one else lay in wait for them. You could hear the bull horn in the front yard, saying things like, "Come out with your hands up," and "Let the woman go." After a spare few seconds, the SWAT team moved through the front door and flowed down the halls of the house. Things moved fast from there. A woman's voice calling and one SWAT guy rushing the door from where the voice came. The sound of gunfire. The body cam moving up to where the burglar had slumped over, blood everywhere. Kicking a pistol out of the man's hand. A voice behind him saying, "Thank God he has a gun, Jim," which would have meant that with the pistol, the officer wouldn't be put on administrative leave until internal affairs cleared him for killing an unarmed man. Leaning close to the dying guy, whose lips were moving around the blood. Something soft and garbled.

"What?" I asked.

Max backed up a second, then played it again.

"I still can't understand what he's saying."

Max backed up again and turned the dial to maximum volume.

"I didn't put in for this shit," the dying man said.

Max turned off the video. "That's what we got. I can show you the written report, too. So, any ideas, big important FBI hotshot?"

I shook my head, the blood draining from it already as I regretted I'd promised to confess to Snesil's death. "Nothing immediately. Except what do you think he meant by, 'I didn't put in for this shit'?"

Max's turn to shake his head, but he mentioned my husband because he really had learned some philosophy from him. "Carlo might say it was an existential thing, about how life is cruel."

I felt unsettled by my thoughts because Max was right, there was something about the sequence of events that didn't make Nicki look real good. Besides reporting someone in the house some minutes before she could have known, Nicki also said he had a gun before she opened the bathroom door. It made it look like she knew there was a stranger in the house well before she opened the bathroom door, and that she knew he had a gun. How did she know this? Second, and I didn't mention this to Max, when she was describing the events to Eleanore and me, she said the front door must have been left unlocked. It was always locked, but not that day, she said.

That last little item was easy to corroborate. Later in the day I stopped by the house, walked up the front path, and tried the door. Locked. One of the little guys, Not-Jackson, spotted me out the front window and opened the door. "You always try to get in other people's houses like that?" he asked.

"Just checking. You always lock the door whether someone is home or not?"

"Damn straight," he said. "Since we moved in, there've been so many threats from people in the neighborhood that we agreed to be extra careful about it. The door is never unlocked even if we're out working in the yard."

So it could have been left unlocked, but highly unlikely. And what a coincidence that it would have happened on the day of the burglary. Nicki knew a stranger was in the house. Was Royce DeWitt really a stranger, or not? Like I said, I kept this to myself, not showing my cards.

EIGHTEEN

"So have you lost your ego yet?" I asked Carlo that night when he called from the ashram. He knew I could kid him about his retreats. With his tendency to quote others so that no one would suspect him of original thought, he'd once said, "Where there is the most diplomacy there is the least love." That.

"I try, but it keeps coming back. I probably feed it too much. How're you?"

Oh, that question. What to answer? What to not? "No suspense here. I'm telling you upfront that I'm in no danger."

"That's nice."

I told him what was going on with Nicki Gleason, and how there was a bit of trouble in the neighborhood due to the group home.

"You told me about that before I left. Is there any news on who might have killed Dorita?"

"Nada." I decided not to give Carlo the details until he came home and I was honest about it. "I'm not going into it right now, but I wanted to ask you if you knew anything about Eleanore Turner. She seems to be prominent and you've been around here longer than I have."

"The Turners. They're a power couple, if there is such a thing in Tucson. In the news lately, organizing turning cargo containers into tiny homes for kids who have aged out of the foster program and have nowhere to go. The husband got the zoning approved and the wife is getting the funding."

"That sounds like a good thing."

"I haven't decided yet. They're spending nearly half a million on seven dwellings which comes to sixty-five thousand per. I think you can buy a new single-wide mobile home for half that."

"You think they're raking off some of the contributions?"

"Not enough information to make that conjecture. Anyway, what about the Turners?"

"The wife is mentoring Nicki."

"I remember you told me."

Made me wonder again if I was beginning to repeat myself more often, that aging thing. "I know. I'm trying to find out more about her."

"Why?"

"I ran into her after the gallery thing . . . she was with Nicki . . . at Dorita's funeral . . . something was off."

"Do I want to know in what way?"

"No, you don't, it's too boring. I do hear that Nicki isn't her first mentee. Is that how you'd put it?"

"Sounds right to me. Listen, give Deacon Leslie MacKenzie a call. She works for the diocese in the prison ministry. She might be able to tell you what she knows."

"OK. Love you." It was easier to say over the phone.

"Love you too."

First thing in the morning I looked up Deacon MacKenzie's contact information on the Diocese of Arizona website and told her I was married to Carlo DiForenza. She cooed, sounding remarkably like a pigeon. That's what all women do when they hear his name. An acquaintance once told me if I died suddenly there would be twenty casseroles on the front porch by sundown.

"How is our dear reverend?" the deacon asked.

"Fine. He's fine. What I'm calling about is that . . ." I paused, not wanting to raise any suspicions, good or bad, that might get back to Eleanore with an e. "I'm thinking of mentoring a formerly incarcerated woman myself, and Carlo . . ." I emphasized the name to remind her of the connection, ". . . said you could let me know how to get involved."

She didn't coo this time but she did twitter a bit. Still gave me an image of someone with feathers and a full bosom. "That would be lovely!" she said. "I'm sure we could get you someone in short order with you being married to Father Carlo and all. But there's a little application you have to fill out and we do a background check."

"That would be fine." I gave her my email address so she could send it. "Eleanore Turner told me it's very rewarding. That she's done it"—I wracked my brain to see if this was an acceptable lie—"a time before Nicki?"

"Oh yes, several times. And all the women said she's just lovely. A huge help with getting them back into the world."

Somehow I couldn't envision felons sprinkling the word "lovely" about in unison, but that could just be MacKenzie channeling them through her own perspective. Sometimes all you have to do is be quiet for a moment, and I was. It worked.

"There was Laretta Gonzalez, and Beth Vivarito . . ." she appeared to be thinking and I didn't stop her, ". . .you know, Georgette Seamon was the only one who didn't work out."

"Why's that?"

"Why? It wasn't anything bad, I just think Eleanore came to the conclusion that Georgette didn't need her so much after all. Something like that. Why do you want to know?"

"Just, you know, trying to find the good and bad, ins and outs, ups and downs . . ." I tried the quiet again but this time it didn't get me anything. We were both quiet. I finally gave in. "Do you know where Georgette Seamon is now? Whether she's getting along OK on her own?"

"Last I heard, she moved in with her family in Green Valley."

"Do you remember what she was in prison for?"

"How could I forget?" That twitter again, this time sounding like a bird of mystery. "But if you talk to her, she can tell you that herself."

"Can you help me get in touch with her?" I asked.

Another piece of quiet. "Well, I shouldn't . . . but seeing as how you're Father Carlo's wife . . ." she took a minute to look it up and gave me her number. "I think this is her cell phone, so even if she moved it should still be good."

"You've been exceptionally kind," I said, trying my best to sound like a volunteering kind of clergy spouse rather than someone suckering a naïve deacon. I even answered her final twitter with one of my own before disconnecting.

Followed immediately by a call to Georgette Seamon while the phone was still warm. She was cheerful, she was upbeat, she agreed to meet me for coffee on the U of A campus the next day. That way I wouldn't have to drive all the way down to Green Valley. Very accommodating.

"You're taking classes?" I asked.

"Yeah. Working on a degree in molecular biology."

The irony of someone studying what amounted to DNA analysis while having a last name that sounded like semen wasn't lost on me, but to engage her I said, "My niece is doing that too. Do you know her? Gemma-Kate Quinn?"

"It's a really big school," she said.

We met the next day at a café on the corner of the main drag that ended at the old stone entrance to the main campus. When I'd asked her who I should look for she said, "Tattoos." Now these days that might not be considered very helpful, but she wasn't kidding, she might have been auditioning for one of those movie rolls, the gal with a shaved head thing and inked to her eyeballs, but her ponytail was almost as long as mine.

"You like cats," I commented, pulling up a chair at her table and examining not only the tats of kittens chasing each other around her upper arm, but also the claw marks on her hands. And chest. And legs.

"It's my brand," she said. "Did Deacon MacKenzie tell you what I was in for?"

"No, but she told me I'd enjoy hearing the story. And then she giggled."

The corner of Georgette's mouth twerked up in an *I am not amused* way. "Prison can be so funny when you're not the one there."

"When did you get out?"

"About six months ago. I still have two years of probation."

Enough small talk. "A friend of mine was at Perryville round the same time as you. Nicole Gleason."

"Nicki!" Georgette said. "I took art lessons from her. She's really nice. Doing OK?"

I rocked my head back and forth in a comme-si, comme-ça way. "She's in a group home. You can imagine how that might be."

"That sucks," Georgette said. "I'm lucky to have a pretty big family and they took me in when I got out." She tried to hide the fact that she was looking at her phone that was face up on the table beside her. "So what can I help you with?"

"Deacon MacKenzie tells me that you signed up for a mentor. The same one as Nicki did, only earlier."

"Yeah. That probably wasn't the best move. I was feeling unsure of myself, afraid of how it would be to navigate the world once I got out. It didn't last long; I can't even remember the woman's name."

"Eleanore Turner."

"That's right. Big woman with a big personality. She was a little intimidating, to tell you the truth. And when we got together she hovered a lot. Wanted to know all about me. Where I'd come from, how badly I needed her."

"So you were the one to cut off the relationship?"

Georgette thought a moment. "Let's see, how did that go? We exchanged a few letters while I was still in, and then she did this big thing where she brought flowers and took me out for lunch. To the Ritz-Carlton at Dove Mountain! My mom and sister had been at the prison the day I left Perryville, but Eleanore was right there after. She was all-in. What my mom would call gung-ho." Her mouth at the corner twitched again and I surmised that gung-ho wasn't altogether a compliment. "She started telling me how we'd go shopping for a new wardrobe, and how she had connections to help me find a job. When I told her I wanted to go back to school, she said she could help there, too."

"Like pay your tuition kind of help?"

Georgette nodded. "That. Get me into a dormitory. Connections, you know? I told her I'd be fine, that Dad owned a breakfast lunch place in Green Valley that did a good business, and I could live with my folks."

"You made it clear you didn't intend to freeload. So what happened?"

"I'm not sure. It seemed like by the end of that lunch she started . . . I don't know, drawing away? You get to know how to read people when you're in prison. Sometimes it's a matter of survival. That was the last time I met her."

"With no explanation?"

Georgette thought. "Oh, now I remember. Deacon MacKenzie called me and told me that I was in such good shape emotionally and financially that Eleanore didn't think I needed help all that much. She was more into unfortunate women who'd been convicted of worse things than me."

She looked at her phone again and pushed back her chair a bit, making the move to be gone.

I said, "OK, but before you go, you really need to tell me what you did that got you sent to prison. You don't seem like a lost soul to me either. You're smart."

Georgette crossed her forearms, making it look like the cats tattooed there were cuddling.

"I *am* smart. The only mistake I made was getting caught." She told me how she had seen a news program about how people with beloved pets were getting them cloned when they died so they could keep them forever. "I could do that," she said. "And I wouldn't even have to do the actual cloning myself. The more I looked into it, the more I could explain to clients, with complete honesty, that just because you clone an animal doesn't mean it's an identical match. Animals have so many genes that one dog or cat can look quite different, and have differences in behavior, too. There was no guarantee. I showed them pictures of litters born to purebred dogs and how between the puppies there were significant differences. They bought it, and paid me ten grand to give them back their pet. I spent part of that money, not on actual cloning, which I knew nothing about, but in researching available pets across the country to find one that was a close enough match, and driving to bring them to their new owner. Long-haired dachshunds, papillons, shar-peis. The Rhodesian ridgeback was a little hard to find. Pit bulls were easy; I never knew why there are so many of them."

"But did you get some of the original pet's DNA? You must have had to do that to make it look legitimate."

"Right. I had them send me a bit of fur. Told them seriously that it had to be pulled out with tweezers to get the roots. Before they cremated the animal. Did cats too, did I mention?

That was easier than dogs because most people don't have purebred cats. It's just a mixed bag."

"You said you got caught. How?"

"Someone from Houston was suspicious, reported me. Had kept a little of the fur from the original dog. There was a sting operation; can you imagine the FBI messing with me when there are real criminals out there? They had a DNA test done against the new dog I provided."

"So why are you studying molecular biology? Seems like it would have left you with a bad feeling."

"Are you kidding? I made a couple hundred thousand dollars before they got onto me. Just think what would happen if my business was legitimate? This time I'll provide proof."

Georgette grabbed her backpack from where it was hooked over a corner of her chair and flicked an index finger at her coffee cup. "I have to go. You got this, right?"

I took out my wallet. She would get along just fine.

And I . . . I would have to let what she'd told me simmer for a while. There wasn't anything useful, but then you never know when one piece of information bumps up against another piece of information you don't yet know and voilà, it's a clue. For now, I just sat back with my diluted ice coffee, signing the check that the waitress brought me and adding my usual large tip out of gratitude that I never had to do that job.

I looked at the glass sitting before me, picked up the straw and examined its invisible evidence, still thinking of Georgette, DNA, and how it was everywhere.

Oh, Nicki, I hope you're as innocent as I think you are.

NINETEEN

I wondered how much I had to share with Max in order to get useful information back. He knew me as well as I knew him. So I tried to get the first questions in when I stopped by his office. He was just leaving, but stopped to talk. The way he eyed me, I felt like a wildebeest on the Serengeti. He was already anticipating bringing me down.

I asked, "Have you interviewed all the felons? And what about talking to their parole officers? Anybody immediately lawyered up? Is there anyone in the neighborhood you'd like me to talk to?"

Max nodded with each question but only answered one. "Gleason's mentor has retained a defense attorney for her. Not that that means anything, right?"

When he wasn't able to read anything in my face, he said randomly, as if he just thought of it when indeed we had discussed it before, "What if we're missing a link? What if there's a connection between the burglar who was killed on the premises and Dorita's murder? Something tied to the group home?"

There was only one person in the vicinity of both deaths, and that person was Nicki. What I didn't agree to is that Nicki had a motive, though not a terribly strong one. No stronger than anyone else in the group home who had a bone to pick with Dorita. Unless . . . if she got kicked out because of rezoning, where would she go? Would she have a harder time getting Ramona back from foster care? Sure, she could move in with Carlo and me, but would DCS give us Ramona? Thoughts go fast, and hardly a moment had passed before I said out loud, "A connection between the dead burglar and Dorita—that's a reach, isn't it, especially since the burglar was killed by the police? It could be just as likely that someone followed Dorita home from the Elk Club. She always went on Friday night, and her body was found in the morning."

"How do you know that?"

"When you mentioned it at the crime scene, I stopped by there and asked around."

"I checked," Max said. "She didn't go to the Elk Club that night."

"So someone she'd met there on a prior night. Or what about what she did for a living. Real estate, was it?"

Max nodded.

"Maybe it was someone who was upset by the house she sold them? Maybe it was a lemon."

"Now you're being ridiculous."

"Sometimes one ridiculous suggestion makes a person think of one that makes sense. I do it all the time." I did not add that linking the dead burglar with Dorita was one of those ridiculous ideas that could make ultimate sense. It seemed to be sticking in both our heads.

But that encounter, between the burglar and Nicki, that was random, right? Right? Remembering that Dorita was in real estate, when I got home I went to the computer and checked out Dorita's professional background. Turns out she had sold some houses in Catalina and surrounding places like Oro Valley and Saddlebrooke through Sloan Realty, but nothing that would win her any awards or a write-up in *Realtor's Weekly*, let alone real money. I went through the part of my closet that I think of as the costume wardrobe, and chose a desert chic outfit that would make my looking for a home in the Foothills—a ritzy part of town—believable. My Kia Forte wasn't much, but I could bluff, and went to Sloan Realty about seven miles south on Oracle.

"Hi," I said to the receptionist, who put down her copy of *Anna Karenina*. (Everyone in Tucson under thirty is getting a degree.) "I'm looking for a realtor a friend recommended to me. Dorita Gordino. Could I make an appointment?"

The receptionist stood, asked me to have a seat, and went down a hall where I heard her knock, and enter.

Came back following a woman in a hot black pant suit (and by hot I don't mean sexy; it was over a hundred and ten degrees outside). She was one of those real-estate agents, probably a broker, who was too much. Too much hair, too much make-up, too much jewelry. Foundation applied with a spackling knife. Hula-hoop earrings. You could hear her charm bracelet jingling as she walked. A smile that was only teeth. One of those rare times the word "brassy" comes to mind. Both she and the receptionist looked as if their curiosity was balanced by their wariness. Maybe they'd gotten word that the sheriff was interviewing everyone remotely connected to Dorita. Maybe Max had already been here and withheld the information for some reason.

The receptionist took her seat at the front desk, looking happy that she was close enough to hear as she covered her face with the book so we'd think she was reading. The woman put out her hand. "I'm Marge Sloan." I stood, shook, and acted like I wasn't sure what would happen next. Whether she'd give me Dorita's card or what. Instead, she sat down in the chair next to the one I'd risen from. I sat down again, looking properly curious.

"I'm Greta Kissinger," I said, cobbling together a couple names at random and repeating what I'd told the receptionist. "Looking for a new home, and got a recommendation for Dorita Gordino." I remembered Eleanore telling me Dorita had sold her a home once, but I didn't say she was the one who gave me the referral. If you're going to lie, it's better to use as few details as possible, and only those most necessary to your purpose. That's how you can tell someone is lying, if they're spilling all those extraneous details that are easily checked.

"I'm so sorry to share this information, but Dorita isn't . . . here. As a matter of fact, she hasn't been with this firm for over a year." Marge paused, and then took the dive. "As a matter of fact, she's . . . deceased."

"Oh my word!" I said, surprised but not swooning. That would have been overacting. I leaned forward in my chair. "How?"

Well, of course, that was something Marge didn't want to deal with, or did she? With the expression of someone sharing church gossip, *I'm only telling you this because we're all so concerned*, she said, "We were horrified to find out that Dorita was killed."

"How?" I said again. That seemed to be getting me somewhere.

A little more than a whisper, "She was murdered. At her home."

I fell back in the chair, not too upset because I wasn't supposed to have known her. Figured one more time I could get away with, "Golly. How did it happen?"

Marge lifted both hands and danced her fingers in the air to dismiss the subject. "It was awful," she said, and stopped, trying to figure out a respectful enough segue to business. "But you know, I could help you with any of your housing needs. We have some lovely homes, did you say Saddlebrooke? The Foothills?" She swallowed, as if that last location gave her a Pavlovian response.

"I'd like that very much," I said. "But one last thing, you said Dorita hadn't worked here for a whole year—"

"Over a year," Marge said, fingering her charm bracelet as if it was a talisman that would distance herself as far as possible from the woman and the crime. She was getting a tad impatient at this point but hung on to the bait for the business.

I asked, "Did she quit the business altogether?"

"Ah, no. She told me that she was going to work exclusively with a developer. That new area, about ninety homes, around the Black Horse Ranch subdivision?"

"Sounds like a good way to go, having ninety listings dumped in your lap."

"You've heard about it?" Marge took her lips between her teeth in an unconscious expression of wondering how I knew that piece of information and what it indicated about me. Was I a rival realtor?

I nodded and made my eyes as clueless as possible. "I thought I saw something about it on the Neighbors social media site. Some people are afraid of areas being overbuilt, losing their country charm."

She gave a trusting nod, having nothing to lose at this point.

"You've got that right. But time marches on, and you can't fight progress. After a respectful amount of time has elapsed, I'm going to contact the developer myself, see if I can take over sales."

"And you don't think that's at all . . . risky?"

Marge put on the brakes. You can't be a successful realtor without a gift for reading people. "Why, you think someone killed Dorita because of ties to the development?" She frowned. "And are you really interested in buying a home? Or are you with the newspaper?"

I saw that behind the make-up was no fool and decided to drop the act. "Actually no. I'm a private investigator and grateful for any information you've given me. I'm sorry I wasn't forthcoming about that. Good perception on your part."

Marge gave an exaggerated pout that told me my flattery beat my trickery. "I've been in the business a long time and I can spot a serious buyer. I was interviewing you, too. Is your name really Greta Kissinger?"

"No," I said. "It's Brigid Quinn. My turn?"

"Sure, now that I know what's up, fire away."

"What company is doing the development? Someone around here or maybe a foreign investor?"

"When Dorita quit she said the developer's name. Someone local. I remembered because that's my business, and like I said, I thought I'd make them an offer to do their selling. I have a longer list of clients than Dorita had. Come to think of it, I'm not sure why they hired her."

I needed to wrangle Marge back from her plans to step into that gap. "And the name is?"

"Oh, sorry. Phone Home Enterprises. Sort of cute, with the slogan Find Your Place on the Planet. They haven't been around a long time and that's the only development they're currently involved in, not like some of these companies with the cookie-cutter homes. These are all distinct designs, at least on the outside. But I sure wouldn't have put all my eggs in that basket, if you know what I mean. Then, Dorita was always kind of impulsive, risk-taking behavior if you know what I mean."

Interesting perspective. I said, "Risk-taking? When I talked to her it seemed like she was always coming in hot about something, neighbors not sweeping their gravel off the sidewalk or getting signatures for a petition. But I don't think any of that was particularly risky."

When investigating, never underestimate the value of gossip. Marge brushed her long full hair back from her shoulder. I was amazed that her charm bracelet didn't get caught. "Well, she never made a secret about her drugs, or her gambling . . . or her men."

I shifted my tone to match her conspiratorial one, adding a dash of, "She gave me the impression of being a good Christian woman. Were there that many men?"

"Well, I'm not saying that I'm opposed to living fully," Marge said, sliding a large ring up and down her index finger. "I'm not a prude. But I do draw the line at married men."

"Did she ever name one?" My memory banks flashed across the neighborhood: Jake the Jehovah's Witness, others, Carlo? I laughed to myself. Someone or someones at the Elk Club.

"No, it was all in-nu-endo." Marge dragged the word out like it was somehow suggestive, like it told a whole story by itself.

Something to consider, a jealous lover or some such. I'd work on that later. But for now I thought I'd gotten everything from Marge that I could get, except, "The development Dorita was selling. What's the location?"

"You know that subdivision that's cut in half with the two parts having the same name, Dark Sky Vista? It's in the area between them."

Just west of the group home. Was that why Dorita was so keen to have it rezoned after the burglar was killed in it? Was it hurting her sales? If so, this could be the connection between the death of the burglar and Dorita's murder that Max had suggested.

TWENTY

Along with other things getting in the way, you gotta eat. The forest green vintage Jaguar in the parking lot of It's Greek to Me was as flashy as its photo on Facebook had been. Eleanore was not. I was there to pick up a salad with gyro meat, treating myself to things that Carlo wasn't fond of while he was gone. As I stood at the take-out counter and looked around, I spotted Eleanore in a far corner of the eat-in part of the restaurant. That part of the place was kind of cute—vivid blue walls and white pillars, colors of the Greek flag, the only tablecloths in a thirty-mile radius, and a fake fresco on the ceiling depicting some random god surrounded by cherubs.

Eleanore sat with her back turned, facing a wall painting of a bright white building on a beach overlooking what was supposed to be the Mediterranean. A good place to sit if you didn't want anyone you knew to catch you day drinking by yourself. She was far enough away from her own neighborhood, so that was a pretty safe bet. I guessed she'd just been doing something with Nicki to make her feel better and didn't want to drink in front of her.

The funny thing is I don't know how I recognized her from the back or the front. Eleanore was wearing a T-shirt with a neck that had stretched out, looking like something you'd sleep in rather than wear out in public, and not even then if you were Eleanore Turner. The shoulders under the shirt slumped forward, and her whole spine bowed in a perfect arc with her sagging head. It was a good opportunity to find out why.

After I had paid for my salad, I carried the Styrofoam container to the back of the restaurant.

"Eleanore, hi," I began.

Her head jerked in my direction as one who has either been in deep thought or suddenly frightened. I couldn't tell which it was. But the every-which-way of her hair, and the dumplings under her eyes rimmed with a darker shadow showed that if she had been in deep thought, the thoughts were awful. I didn't think this was about Nicki. This was personal to her.

She looked like hell. She tried to sit up straighter and force the corners of her mouth into her standard smile, but the corners twitched with the effort like those of a politician being asked the one question they could not answer. None of it worked. She was smaller than I'd seen her in our last several encounters. Some giant thumb pressing down on her for too long and she could no longer resist. I sat down across from her, not looking at what I now noticed was an empty wine glass and nothing else in front of her. "I was coming in to pick up a salad," I said unnecessarily, pointing at said salad as Exhibit A. "I should have known you were in here. I can't imagine too many of those cars in Tucson, let alone Catalina."

Eleanore giggled. Even if giggling was part of her repertoire, I could still tell this one had a cringey edge to it. I felt she was begging me to leave her alone but of course I could not.

I lied about having seen the picture of her new car because I was stalking her on Facebook, saying instead that I'd noticed her getting into it after the gallery showing.

"When did you get it?" I asked.

Her eyes flared, still consumed with her own thoughts rather than small talk with someone who was almost a stranger.

"The car," I helped. "It's gorgeous. I love vintage cars."

"Oh, Ian bought it for me just about a month ago." At least her story matched the one on social media. She raised her wrist to show me an elegantly classic watch, the face surrounded by a ring of emeralds. "He got me this at the same time. So much prettier than a smart watch, right?"

I said what one woman typically says to another at a time like this. "He must adore you."

"Oh yes. He also finds me useful." Here she giggled again, but it was more like a single high-pitched "ha!" than an actual laugh. Just kidding, the ha said. It was followed by fingertips to her lips and a furrow in her brow, perhaps a note to self that she had to be more careful about what she said. Was that furrow *I've had too much wine* and *shut up with oversharing*?

She scrambled to suit her comment to her image. "I shouldn't be that way. Ian is such a good man; did you know he's on the Pima County Board of Supervisors? And thinking of running for mayor of Oro Valley. I just say I'm useful because I'm the extrovert. I know how to navigate the social scene."

Was my imagination running away with me? I don't think so. Some might say I was reading too much into her expression, but maybe because of my background, for the first time I began to get vibes that no matter how independent and brash Eleanore presented herself, I might be talking to a victim of domestic abuse. Certainly psychological rather than physical, but abuse none the less. I flashed back to the gallery when she blew off any hints of him being unfaithful. Not that they were a bit . . . mismatched . . . in looks, heaven forbid I should think something as sexist as that. But did Eleanore protest too much?

I sensed upfront that directly asking her "are you OK?" would only make her withdraw further, like out of the restaurant altogether. Whether her presence here had to do with embarrassment, guilt, some insurmountable challenge to her marriage, or just an inordinate fondness for white wine, I could not tell. I motioned to a waiter, pointed to Eleanore's glass and then to myself. He slid over to the table to confirm. "Could I have a glass of that? And another for my friend?" He nodded and returned with two glasses less than a minute later, removing the one which was her first, or second, or third. She looked at the glass wistfully, but kept her hands in her lap, under the tablecloth. I realized they had been there since I sat down. I took an opportunity to look her dead in the eye to make her focus on me; she was focused, but only just.

"The thing you and I have in common is Nicki Gleason," I said, coming in at an angle and addressing my own feelings rather than hers. "I'm worried about her being suspect in Dorita's murder. You make one stupid mistake and spend the rest of your life being the one everyone suspects, right?"

Eleanore didn't agree that this was what had brought her low, but she didn't deny it either. "Poor kid. It's like if she didn't have bad luck she'd have no luck at all." That high-pitched "ha" again. "Did she tell you I've gotten her a good defense lawyer just to be on the safe side?"

I didn't say that Max Coyote knew this also. "She did. But overall I get the sense that she's holding back with me. She doesn't share her feelings the way she did when we first reconnected. I'm glad someone will be there to advise her. She's not good at sticking up for herself."

Eleanore's eyes flashed and I couldn't tell if what I said was a good or bad thing. She couldn't stand letting the wine sit there anymore, and when she lifted the glass it wobbled the way her coffee had at Dorita's funeral so she had to two-hand it. She tried to hide her palms, but failed altogether, so I could see the skin looked reddened, almost raw, like someone had taken a file to them. Eczema? Some odd form of spousal abuse? Could I have Eleanore all wrong, that her sympathy for Nicki was genuine because they were both victims? Like I've said, life is complicated, all kinds of things happening on top of other things.

That's why I added, "At least I can do something, a little pro bono investigating. I'm going to call the Department of Child Safety and make sure Ramona is doing OK. When I asked Nicki about her all I got was a 'fine' that I wasn't sure I could trust. Have you heard anything about Ramona? Let's see, she was at the gallery event. And maybe Nicki said something at Dorita's funeral?"

That hit a nerve. Eleanore began slightly but definitely rocking back and forward in her chair like an elderly patient in a mental health hospital. "You know, I can't," she finally said, leaning back as if I was coming at her. "I've got problems of my own and I just can't." There she was again, teetering on the edge of truth. As if even *that* was more than she wanted to say, she stood, grabbed a purse that had been slung over the back of her chair and left, stumbling once, her shoulder hitting one of the plaster pillars as she made her way to the front door.

I had no chance to suggest maybe she shouldn't be driving and I could take her home. In just that moment I actually felt sorry for her. For a tough broad I can be a real pushover sometimes. I made a mental note to check into the Turner finances when I got home. There's the phrase "money talks," as in, with enough you can have anything you want. But I see it differently. You can tell so much about people from the money they have, how they got it, how they use it. And the more a person has, the more it tells you about them.

Urban terrorists should talk to each other, coordinate to avoid duplication of effort. A bomb threat was called into the Golder Ranch Fire Department the following afternoon. The bomb threat was easy to deal with. The residents of the group home were evacuated and the house searched but the police found nothing.

Then, at 11:20 p.m., two Molotov cocktails were tossed at the home in a drive-by attack. One fell harmlessly by the concrete wall and burned itself out. The second went through the kitchen window on the same side of the house. It must have fallen near the gas stove because it gutted the kitchen, including the drywall on the back of the house. Both of the little guys (I won't call them ermines again) must have been in the vicinity at the time. They were taken to the hospital where Not-Jackson was treated for minor injuries and released.

Jackson died.

I knew Jackson. When I first saw him with Erroll (now I remember, that's the other guy's name), he was trying to fit in, taking his cues from the white guy. I thought he was a young jerk. But when it was just the two of us, him talking without resentment about how he took the fall for the boys who set the fire in the state park, he was thoughtful. He'd learned much about the friends one keeps, about consequences, about injustice. If you're curious, you spend a little bit of the right kind of time with someone and you know them. They become a real person. I'm certain he could have done something real fine.

It was on the local news the next morning. Social media began their usual conspiracy theories:

Drive-by bombs, my ass. They were probably making them and they accidentally went off.

Could it have been one of those false flags?

You mean did they bomb their own house on purpose? To take suspicion off?

As usual, in the style of TV commentators, all those pesky question marks would fall away. A question would become a statement on its way to being fact. And it would spread like an infection forever because there's no vaccine for lies. Jackson was a good kid. Doing time for a crime he was innocent of. And even if he wasn't innocent, he was still a good kid.

I typed under the name BQuinn,

You can ram your false flag up your ass sideways, motherfuckers!

Knowing that I could do no good that way except to stoke the fire of my own rage, and collect some laughy faces that would only anger me more, I deleted it. Contented myself with yelling the satisfying fricative at my computer. "Motherfuckers!"

Achilles ran into the room and fell at my feet, rolling onto his back and whimpering. I don't know what that was about, but likely it had something to do with how he lost one of his hind legs. I leaned over and rubbed his belly gently. "I'm sorry, kiddo. Mommy's not mad at you. Mommy's mad at the rest of the world."

Having tamped down my rage for the sake of Achilles, I woke in the night with the anger hardening my gut, and finally gave up on falling back to sleep. I wandered out into the living room, and found Al standing, panting, like he couldn't get comfortable. I got down on the floor with him, and he finally settled, tucked into the curve of my arm. Dogs don't care whether you're innocent. We both fell asleep that way. My lower back and the hip I was resting on were sore in the morning.

TWENTY-ONE

The lack of sleep and residual anger were not good for attending the HOA meeting. I was already cranky going into it and hoped I didn't say something I'd regret. I had told Gemma-Kate about the special homeowners' association meeting called to discuss solutions to the problem of the group home, so when I arrived at the club house I wasn't surprised to see her there. I *was* surprised at part of the reason when I pointed at the pad and pen in her lap.

"What's that about?" I whispered.

"Anthony has gotten really interested in this business, says it has to do with his dissertation. Something to do with mob-thought. He wanted to come with me but he's prepping for a seminar."

Multiple conversations around me. Every seat was taken and a few people standing at the back of the room. I scanned the faces in the crowd, fairly certain that one of these talking turds had launched the bomb that resulted in Jackson's death. The room was awash with different gradations of light beige, from skin tone to shirts and pants. It was as if the desert had been brought inside for the evening, minus some of the more radically chartreuse cactus flowers. There were a dozen baseball caps which stood out because they were darker hued, several declaring a branch of the military or tired political slogan.

I didn't recognize the HOA president. I had found through Max that Dorita had been a member before she was murdered, a well-known and particularly caring member of the community, taking casseroles to the home-bound, even the ones who weren't likely to need a realtor in the foreseeable future. So the group was fully prepared to express its shock and grievance, not all of it performative. Probably some of those people on the Neighbors site were here for the entertainment value. Not much going on in Catalina. I would have made a quip about the mob scene in *Young Frankenstein* but have found that satire doesn't play well in most large groups. Besides, it would have been bravado. I was concerned about Nicki and the others. Jackson's death and my reaction to it the night before had taken some of the steam out of me.

The president, the picture of a well-trimmed-and-tanned golfer hovering somewhere around seventy years old, with a button-down collar on beige shirt, introduced himself as Cary Worthington. A little elderly woman in a beige dress sitting to my left whispered to me with some awe, "He used to be a CEO."

"Wow," I whispered back, thinking PIP, my term for a "Previously Important Person."

"Have we met?" she asked.

"I don't think so," I said, staring at Worthington as he rose from his chair at the table facing the audience. The room was small enough so he didn't need a microphone, but he was one of those people whose voice was bigger than his body and I had the sense he wouldn't need a microphone anyway.

Worthington explained that, after what he sensitively called Dorita's "passing," he had spoken to the appropriate official in the State Capitol office in Phoenix. With apparent distaste at having to use the phrase, especially for the likes of himself, he said he had been given "the run-around" concerning rezoning the group home property to eliminate formerly incarcerated people from the neighborhood.

The audience grumbled in unison. One edgy man behind me startled me a little by leaning forward and shouting, "Shut it down! Shut it down!" When I turned around, I saw his wife put a tentative hand over his, a gesture that I suspected was not rare. He sat back, looking a little embarrassed that he'd brought his best three-word slogan and no one else had picked up on it. I wanted to tell him maybe he'd just offered it a little too soon in the proceedings and should have waited for the grievances to build naturally, but he'd quieted down.

Worthington turned the show over to Max Coyote who was also sitting at the table with the other four leaders of the HOA, looking like he knew he didn't belong here. He stood and said the investigation into the murder of Dorita Gordino and also that of Jackson Donofrio was ongoing, and, preempting expectations, for that reason he couldn't offer a whole lot of information regarding evidence and suspects. There were indecipherable murmurs, some possibly taking offense that the two murders were getting equal attention.

"False flag. One of them is a goddamn murderer," someone across the room called out too quickly for me to see who it was, link them to the social media posts. Luckily, Max had a better vantage point.

"That may be true in the legal sense," Max said, knowing they meant, not Jackson, but Nicki. "But that was four years ago, the parolee has served time. And we're not going to accuse anyone of anything without due process."

"Due process . . . did Dorita Gordino have due process?"

I wished I had stood at the back of the room so I could see who was saying these stupid things. But they came by it honestly. The U.S. immigration head had recently said the same thing.

Max sighed, attempting patience, but you could hear the *cry bullshit* in his voice as he tried to explain. "Due process is what a suspect is afforded. The rule of law called habeas corpus that says you can't judge someone without a hearing. It has nothing to do with victim's rights, with Ms. Gordino."

"Get them out! Get them out!" interrupted the man sitting behind me, going for a second round of stirring up the crowd as he'd done before.

"Shut up, George," said Worthington. "Let the deputy talk."

"Who cares about legal sense?" another man chimed in. "What about common sense?"

Murmurs around me indicated that the group liked the sound of that, whether it made any sense at all or not, so the man continued, "I've lived in this town for forty years" (*oh oh, here we go*, I thought), "and it used to be a peaceful place. Cattle roamed freely. You know those cattle guards on Wilds and Oracle? Those used to be necessary to keep the cows from getting hit on route 77. Now what do you have?"

No dead cows? I thought but stayed quiet. I reminded myself I was keeping a low profile.

Worthington said, "Hank, maybe let the deputy tell us what he came here to tell us?"

But the small crowd clearly wanted to hear more from Hank, and he knew it. "So now we got drug dealers breaking into our homes. Illegals swarming from the southern border. Forming gangs so it's not safe on the streets at night. And now a house full of ex-cons that the state won't do anything about. And you know what I found out?"

The silent group got silenter. Whoever this guy was, he was good at group hypnosis.

"I found out that one of them, the woman, is a certified moron. She's the one who got put away for killing her husband, and she's the one who killed Dorita."

I would have wanted to ask him when he saw an "illegal" lately, let alone a swarm, but maybe later. Higher priority was keeping attention away from Nicki and I felt powerless to do it myself. For now, I just sent all my will to Max, who stood waiting for an opening. Max would calm them down, I thought, and if not that, I thanked whatever gods there were that Nicki wasn't listening to this. I was glad she was safe at home. My home. All the felons had moved in that morning after the bombing. That was another reason for me to keep a low profile at this meeting.

"Deputy Coyote is here to tell us about what we're dealing with," the HOA president said. I would have corrected him with not "what" but "who," that these were people rather than things, but you have to choose your verbal battles or get called woke.

All edging towards the front of their seats, attention turned to Max with the avidity of an audience at a true crime show. Nothing this thrilling had ever happened in the Black Horse Ranch subdivision before.

"Look," he started, with the verbal tic that has become endemic these days. "These people may seem threatening, but when you get to know them a little—"

A woman somewhere behind me interrupted, "You sound like you're defending them." And to the HOA president, "Are we going for rezoning or what?"

The president held up his index finger with the confidence

of someone for whom that finger has worked in the past. "Let's listen to Deputy Coyote, shall we?"

A little less aggressively, a woman in front and to my right said, "What did they do?" as if she actually wanted to know.

Max was ready for this. He checked his notes repeatedly, though he didn't read them word for word. "We've got Henry Brandon, who was in the Florence penitentiary for five years, having set up a fake business that purported to mend and restore vintage jewelry. He took deliveries from all over the world, having the jewelry sent to ever-changing post office boxes. He actually did mend some of the items but then 'lost' them in their return. After a time these items began showing up at pawn shops and flea markets, and he was finally tracked down to an address in Mesa. Convicted of mail fraud."

"That's BFG!" I whispered to Gemma-Kate, and then translated, "Big Fuckin' Guy. He's about six-four with hands the size of capons. Who'd think he could fix little pieces of jewelry?" I was about to say, "I once saw him lift three concrete blocks at one time," but I stopped.

"Next there's Erroll Garcia."

"Goddamn illegal," came a mutter, but I couldn't tell from who.

"He's second generation," Max pointed out.

"So his grandfather was illegal. They should get rid of birthright citizenship."

Max backed out of that round-about. "He got caught stealing from mailboxes where people are still writing checks to pay their bills. None of the checks he diverted to his own account by using a technique that could change the 'to' entry were enormous. But a hundred dollars here, fifty dollars there, twenty dollars in a grandkid's birthday card, it added up. Word to the wise, you should take envelopes with checks in them to the post office, don't put them in your mailbox with the flag up. It tells people like Mr. Garcia where to look."

"No wonder crime is on the rise, these wetbacks," muttered the same mutterer.

Max Coyote's father came from the Tohono O'odham Tribe. Often being told to "go back where he came from," despite his people having been living in this land for centuries before the white man arrived, he couldn't help but offer a defense of those who looked a little like himself. "Statistically, undocumented people commit fewer crimes than citizens. That's partly because they're eager to keep under the radar and not take chances with law enforcement."

This time there was only a ripple of grunt, showing that Coyote's words did not fully enter the consciousness of the mutterer; that the same objection would be repeated at another opportunity.

When it appeared that Max wouldn't be interrupted again, he went on.

"Jackson Donofrio was convicted of arson and served four years. Tried as an adult though he was only sixteen at the time. Arizona takes arson seriously."

"I should say so," said one of those steely older ladies in front of me who only pretended to be frail when it served her purpose, much like me. "Now I think there's someone you have to worry about. Who's to say he won't start burning down our houses?"

Her husband, whose head had been nodding through most of the meeting, muttered, "He's the one who died, honey."

She nodded her approval.

Though nothing was said by the rest of the crowd, nothing needed to be said. Nobody took a crotchety old woman seriously, right? The mood of the room was more of the silence of the charcoal in a grill slowly glowing as it caught fire, turning the black coal into the grey ash left behind by a mob.

You could tell Coyote was getting tired of the rising tension in the room and was torn between wanting to lunge at the woman and wanting to defuse the situation. A muscle above his jaw tightened. "That's correct. Jackson Donofrio is dead, killed in the bombing of the home." With a glance designed to pin the old woman to her chair, he added, "And we take all threats seriously, doesn't matter who makes them or who is threatened."

"He was the Black one. That Donofrio guy," I heard, so softly that even the person speaking must know it was superfluous information.

Max didn't even try to go there. "Let me just finish, OK? Only two more to go. You want to hear it or not?"

More grunts.

"Tyler Wrobleski. Convicted of computer hacking for profit—"

"My computer was hacked!" a man's voice wailed. "He set up a Facebook account in my name."

Max barely hid a *you're too stupid to live* kind of look. Again, playing poker with him had enabled me to read his most subtle expressions, and I knew he was running out of diplomacy.

"Wrobleski had a sophisticated tactic to use a remote access trojan, or what you might call a spider, to invade computers and access their browsing history and emails, etc., for the purpose of sending scam messages. You know, like click here if you want your computer protected, or fake warnings like telling you to call a number if you don't want the IRS to take your house. Wrobleski is—was—more of a hacker for hire."

Most of the crowd was lulled by the computer jargon which must have sounded like *blah blah blah blah*. It wouldn't have surprised me to learn that Max put Wrobleski toward the end as a crowd control tactic. And then he dropped the hammer.

"Finally, Nicole Gleason." Max hesitated. You could tell he didn't want to fan the flames of the attendees and was searching for how to put Nicki's crime in context. Context being, of course, she killed her husband and what do you do with that little piece of information?

This was the main event in the arena and this time the crowd didn't wait. "We already know who Nicole Gleason is," someone called out.

"Who's Nicole Gleason?" a soft voice spoke. It was getting harder and harder to pinpoint who was speaking, or even from where in the room the voices were coming. Like they were slowly merging into a single voice. That was never a good thing.

The first voice spoke again. "I just said. A retard who killed her husband by smashing him over the head with a liquor bottle. Do we really want someone who did that living next door? Someone who doesn't have the brains to tell right from wrong and has anger management issues to boot? I don't understand."

Funny how people think *I don't understand* is a valid argument instead of an admission of ignorance.

I sat there thinking about the part I'd played in getting Nicki convicted; how I could have spoken up more in her defense but told myself she got the best outcome that could be had. Was I going to just sit here and do the same thing? Gemma-Kate appeared to feel some seismic tremor coming off me, because she gripped my arm in a stay-put gesture. What could I do, after all? Decry anyone calling Nicki a "retard?" Tell the story of how she was abused, her daughter nearly killed by her husband, and attacked the night that she finally fought back? How her defense played up her fetal alcohol syndrome, invoking the sympathy of the jury so that she'd get a lighter sentence? No one wanted to listen to the truth at that time, so why would they listen to me now? Could I convince them of anything? Oh, to be able to make a speech so compelling, so full of compassion, that I could turn the bias of a crowd. I wished I was as articulate as Carlo. If he was here, he might be able to do it. I'd heard his sermons and they were great. But I could not. It wasn't cowardice that was holding me back, God knows. Physically I could probably whip this whole crowd's collective butt. But verbally? Rising from my seat to give that whole group a good dressing-down and convince them in the style of "Mr. Smith Goes to Washington," to follow their better angels? No, I'm just no good at that Frank Capra kind of thing.

Max and I locked gazes as the buzz grew around the room, the snap and crackle of the blaze beginning to catch. Outrage looking for a reason. "Hold on there," he said. Sort of lame, but I told you I'm not good at this either so I shouldn't judge.

Emboldened by the support in the room, the man who had spoken at some length before stood up. At least that's what you'd say. Even standing, he barely cleared five foot three, but felt the force of the crowd behind him, a growing wind behind his back. "I'm a retired Detroit cop. Instead of telling us to hold on, how about you tell us how your investigation is going into Dorita's murder."

Max tried to speak but the little man was on a roll.

"Tell us. Is that Gleason woman a suspect? She's at least what you'd call 'a person of interest,' right? Have you interrogated her? Did you find out she's not as retarded as she lets on?" It was bound to happen. There it was again, the string of questions that people had learned from watching propaganda news commentators. You don't have to go to all the trouble of using logic or finding facts. Asking a question rather than providing an answer does a lot more damage more effectively because all people have to do is keep asking the question until everyone believes it's not a question at all, but a truth. Guilt by inquiry.

God knows, Max tried. "The investigation is ongoing," he started. "We're following a number of leads that I'm not at liberty to share. But I promise you, we will find the person or persons who killed Dorita and bring them to justice." This time he left Jackson out, seeing how it had sparked more outrage than it was worth.

He had a commanding enough voice and stature to subdue the group so that it would likely not turn into a mob. But I'm glad I hadn't taken the chance of that eventuality. All the people in the group home, not just Nicki, were in danger, and that danger definitely wasn't coming from anyone formerly incarcerated.

The crowd was beginning to go elsewhere with that thought. "Whatever happened to the petition we signed? Who's got that petition? Last I heard about sixteen people signed it."

The woman next to me who'd been impressed by Worthington's professional background said, "Oh my God, I signed it! What if they're targeting all of us?"

Whisk a couple dozen people, stir in some paranoia and the smallest dash of reality, ask a question to light the stove, and you've got a dish to turn your stomach. I met Max's eyes and could tell he was thinking the same. Nothing to be done here that he couldn't do, and I was doubly glad I'd decided to travel under the radar. I got up and left Gemma-Kate still sitting there. Who knew, maybe she was feeling pretty good, seeing how people were more like her—though plus hysteria and minus critical thinking skills—than anyone would expect.

When I was headed toward the back of the room I glimpsed a movement, but there was no one in the hall leading to the main door.

TWENTY-TWO

I had not known that Max would be attending the meeting, and that was surely what prevented a mob from forming and attacking immediately the group home, at least with rocks through the windows, and at worst with a repeat of the explosion that killed Jackson. Like I said, I was so concerned that, straight after hearing about the bombing, I had discreetly brought all the felons over to my house.

I walked in the front door, patting myself on the back for doing what Dorita said I would not do. Bringing someone into my home to protect them, I mean, whether it applied to asylum seekers on the run or ex-felons in danger from a mob. This act had repercussions, I discovered, as the smell of curry hit me.

Mr. Normal, who I now knew as Tyler, offered me a plate. "Got lunch. Want some lamb vindaloo?" he asked. "We also had some Kentucky Fried Chicken delivered in case you don't like exotic food."

I felt in my bag for my wallet to confirm I'd had my credit card with me. He had enough experience to know what I was doing. "I ordered off your computer," he said. "I didn't see that you had a DoorDash account, so I set one up for Grubhub. I hope I didn't duplicate something, but you can always cancel after a month."

I tried to give him the benefit of the doubt by asking, "I didn't realize I left my computer on?"

He scratched an unshaven cheek, smiled without apology and without admitting that he had hacked me. "Uh, no."

I took the plate, added some palak paneer and grabbed a piece of naan bread. I love Indian food and intended to chow down so complaints about the intrusion into my computer accounts would fall flat. I took a can of Budweiser off the counter, too.

Now we were all on the back porch, sitting around on the patio furniture and taking advantage of a rare afternoon with temperatures dipping precipitously into the low nineties. A bucket of fried chicken sat in the middle of the large rectangular table that I had bought when I thought there was a chance of making friends. I watched Henry eye the bucket of chicken with some regret that he hadn't asked for one of his own. I didn't see Al, but Achilles and Peg were outside too, getting accustomed to hand-feeding and so looking furtively at each other when the company slipped them bits of lamb next to their chairs. But otherwise the guests were pretty polite, almost uncomfortable at being out of their group home bubble together. What the hell, I thought. People are people.

They were friends too. Henry raised his beer and said, "This is kind of like a wake, isn't it? To Jackson. The Black bro always gets it in the movies."

We all followed suit, raising our beer cans after that succinct eulogy. "Did they reach his family?" I asked.

Tyler answered that one. "The hospital called the house, told me politely as they could that the family 'didn't wish to claim the body,' and was there anyone else?"

Erroll, who had been silent so far, said, "Fuck family," crushed his empty can, and shut up again except for quietly crying.

Tyler said, "I told them we'd take him. How much does cremation cost these days?"

They looked at me. "I'll take care of it," I said, figuring they had set me up and that was fine.

Nicki was pretty quiet but, that piece of business done, she asked, "How was the meeting?"

"It was all rezoning issues," I said. "Really boring." They all knew I was lying, of course, or at least not being totally truthful. Again, prison survival making it imperative that you learn how to read people. So I gave them what I thought was safe.

"Lots of questions. About who ya'll are, what you were in for, like that," I said by way of a casual mention.

Tyler was the most on the ball and didn't hesitate to throw

it in my face. "So are they going to come after Nicki for killing that woman across the street? Did that come up? And are they even going to investigate who killed Jackson, or is that not important?" He tilted his head, observing me like a specimen who would reveal all the secrets with a little patience.

I was so focused on picking and choosing what to tell them and what not, what had happened at the HOA meeting, minus my reasons for not sticking up for Nicki, I saw them look over my shoulder before I heard the back door shut.

Turning around, "Carlo!" I said, with pleasure both at the sight of his face and relief that he would interrupt our conversation. "I thought you were coming home tomorrow!"

I started to rise to give him a proper hug, but he beat me to it, bending over to kiss me on my forehead, too much of a traditional gent to kiss his wife on the lips in public. At some point in recent years he'd shaved his goatee, so I could feel the prickles of what was probably a two-day growth. Probably that long since he'd had a shower, too. Guys retreat differently than women. No one at the table seemed to notice his sloppiness, or if they did they were more polite than some people I know. And of course he fitted right in. Carlo always fits in. He grabbed a clean paper plate off the table. "I haven't had anything since early breakfast, is this for anyone?" he asked.

Without knowing who this man was, the others greeted him with all the camaraderie of an old friend. I introduced them all to Carlo and explained how he'd been away at a spiritual retreat in San Diego and didn't know everything that was going on. They nodded politely as if they knew exactly what it would be like to attend a spiritual retreat in San Diego.

"He's a priest," Nicki whispered loudly with a stained-glass voice. The others nodded respectfully both at Carlo's vocation and Nicki's insider knowledge. As for the group, "Brigid was just telling us what happened at the HOA meeting today," Mr. Normal . . . Tyler . . . said.

Without comment, Carlo nodded his interest as he munched on a chicken thigh, and I got the focus turned back on me. I continued to relate the events at the HOA meeting, leaving out the sensational parts that would just get them worked up and worried, like the guy chanting slogans and the threats. And the accusations. I thought. "There were some pretty harsh suggestions," I finally decided.

"Like what, shooting us?" the Not-Jackson mail thief asked. (I should call him Erroll.) "We've all heard that *pop pop* sound coming from the Catalina gun club in the early mornings. And wondered if they were using our faces as targets." He sniffed the air for that slightly acrid smell of gunpowder, with hints of sulfur and dirt, as if he really was a wild animal and knew a predator when he smelled it.

"It was all pretty vague . . ." I paused, pretending to pick at the rest of my basmati rice to show just how insignificant I considered the meeting. Then I gave them a slim summary, the report on the progress of the state investigation into trouble at the group home that might warrant rezoning, and Max's report on the investigation of Dorita's murder. "They ended up letting off some steam but otherwise not resolving anything. You know, a typical HOA meeting." I reached for the bucket of chicken as a feint but found it empty. I avoided looking at Carlo, who was licking his lips and looking appropriately remorseful for not leaving any chicken in the bucket. Usually well-mannered to a fault, he must have been pretty hungry.

"Am I leaving anything out that you can see?" I asked, knowing damn well that I'd left out the accusations and slurs thrown Nicki's way. She didn't have to know that.

Tyler guessed. "Did they say anything about Nicki? That sheriff's deputy has seemed more interested in her than the rest of us. We can all vouch for her."

I looked around at the men nodding, and back at Tyler. He'd been in the Marines, I remembered. It was their code, "never leave a man behind," and it didn't just apply to the battlefield. These guys would defend Nicki in all ways, maybe even lie for her. But one of them had not, I reminded myself. One of them told Max she'd had a fight with Dorita.

Nicki raised her hand. She actually raised her hand, the dear thing. "What about the Turners? Was Eleanore there? She said she's been worried about me being safe."

There it was. Anyone who would think of Nicki as being

less than intelligent should have their own head examined. "Well, she lives in Oro Valley so she might not have gotten the notice about a Black Horse Ranch meeting," I said, hoping to reassure her.

"I texted her after you told me," Nicki said. I could see some emotion play across her face which was as expressive as anyone's. *Still yearning for a mother*, I thought.

"That's what was missing, then," I said. "Eleanore. And what about her husband. Do you know him at all?"

"He's really nice. And is totally devoted to his wife. He just bought her a new car, a vintage Jaguar."

Henry whistled his appreciation. As with his work in jewelry, the man must like nice things.

I asked Nicki, "How did Eleanore react when you told her about the bombing of your home?"

"She texted back, 'Oh no!' She said she was really *really* worried about me, and that she'd make sure Ramona was OK."

But Eleanore didn't offer to come get Nicki, I thought. *Nicki was on her own now as much as ever.*

Nicki took the little pad and pen out of her purse that she always kept to remind her of things, wrote a few words on it and passed the paper over to me. Before I could read it, Erroll interrupted. "Does anybody else smell that?"

"What?" We all lifted our noses and a couple of them did pick up on something, like the smell of the dry desert after a rain. Only this wasn't rain.

"There's a fire," he said, not concerned with prolonging the suspense.

"This time of year, before the monsoon rains come, there's always a fire somewhere," Henry said, wiping up some chicken tikka masala with a piece of naan bread long after the rest of us were full.

Erroll shook his head. "Well, this one is closer than usual."

At the same time Nicki said, "I think something is wrong with your dog."

TWENTY-THREE

Life isn't like a story where there's one big problem to solve, a murder or what-not. Life is bunches of things happening all at once, good and bad, collateral damages on top of collateral blessings. You can be distracted by a wedding at the same time as an election at the same time as a killing. With me it was a houseful of people with problems, Carlo coming home to it, wondering if Nicki was worth saving at the expense of my own freedom—and now it was Al.

With his in-bred smashed nose that had him snoring on our bed for as long as I'd lived in this house, Al had always been less than active. Lung problems set in and he began panting one winter evening when the temperatures were too chilly and he'd done nothing but lie around all day. That night that I slept on the floor with him wasn't the first.

Recently it had happened more often. Not wanting to wake Carlo who slept like that log that eludes the rest of us, I would carry Al to the living room and sit with him on the couch while he struggled to catch his breath. He'd stand up. Lie down. Sit. And then do it all again in that order. Make little airy sounds that sounded like gentle crying.

Now he was doing it on the back porch in the middle of the afternoon.

Help me.

Carlo jumped up from his chair and we were out the door within ten minutes. We knew where the emergency vet was, with Achilles having had a run-in with a cholla cactus about six months before. Usually jittery in the car, I knew Al wasn't doing well when he made no fuss about being in the back seat. Now he didn't even try to change positions as he had on the couch. But he kept panting.

Where we live is at least a half-hour from practically everywhere, but on a hot Saturday afternoon there was a little less traffic. I slipped under some lights as they turned red, and I wasn't stopped going ten miles over the speed limit. We made it to Veterinary Emergency Services in twenty minutes.

It was a free-standing building next to a strip mall at the corner of Ina and Oracle. As we walked through the front doors we found a large area with four people, all women. To me they looked like angels in scrubs with their arms out to receive our boy. One of them, who introduced herself as Dr. Cohen, had taken the trouble to apply outrageously large false eyelashes. You had to respect that.

They put Al on an examining table while Carlo and I stood hovering and trying to be out of the way at the same time. I would never have thought that Al's eyes could bug out any more than they usually did, but it was different now. The whites showed, and put me in mind of watching a film of a deer being attacked by a wolf. Yet I had the sense it was his physical distress and not the bustling women that made him look that way.

One gave him an injection that we were told was a sedative while another rigged him to oxygen and a third shaved a bit of fur from his leg, prepping him for an IV.

"He's been on meds for a while," Carlo said. "Congestive heart failure."

Dr. Cohen took a look through a portable ultrasound, and nodded. She turned to us. "There's a chance he'll respond to some heart medication. Maybe, and just maybe, you'll have him for a few more months. But if you want to call this end-of-life," she said that so delicately, "I would support your decision."

The sedative was working a little to calm Al down, but only just. I looked at Carlo. "He's yours and Jane's," I said. "He and Peg are all you have left of her."

"Pull the plug," he said through his teeth, more gruffly than I'd ever heard him speak before. That was when I began to cry. And then Carlo began to cry. It was the first time we'd been that way, neither of us being strong for the other. We didn't touch. It was too much for sobbing into each other's arms in front of these kind strangers. Too histrionic. I grabbed a tissue from a convenient box nearby and didn't care how loudly I blew my nose. Some women have a single tear flow gorgeously from each eye. Me, I'm a nose crier. "I'm going out to the car to get my coffee," I said.

They tried to help us. "We have a private room with coffee if you two want to be alone and talk about your decision," Dr. Cohen said.

"I'm going to the car to get my coffee," I repeated, and stepped out the front door.

I'll never know why I did that. The things you do at significant moments. When I came back inside, Carlo had at least temporarily gotten a grip, as had I. One of the assistants lifted Al and carried him through the open bay. We passed by cages, one with a one-eyed husky and another with a preposterously small, depressed kitten. I stared at that kitten before continuing. The world is horrible.

The room was too tiny for all of us but we managed. A small low couch sat against one wall.

The nurse put Al on his side on a table that was covered with a gray fluffy. By this time he was at last still, the sedative having finally done its job.

"Dr. Cohen will be here shortly," the nurse said, and left. Sure enough, within a moment she entered, one hand holding four syringes. She put one in his IV port. "This is propranolol," she said. "It will slow his heart." That was all I heard; she may have said what the other drugs were as she administered them one by one but I wasn't listening. I was looking at Carlo's and my right hands, both resting on Al's side that wasn't heaving anymore. Maybe needing to think about something more bearable, I noticed how his fawn-colored fur matched the color of my hand. Then I felt his ribs and that brought the next wave of hurting.

"He's gone now," Dr. Cohen said. She gathered up the syringes and pointed to a button attached to the wall behind us. "You stay as long as you like. Just press that button when you want us back."

Gemma-Kate was the closest I came to having a child and you already know she's hardly warm and cuddly. Al, on the other hand, with his snoring that I actually loved hearing at night and his sloppy kisses and zest for Cheddar cheese, was someone I loved. Al was the only creature I'd known besides Carlo who could make me cry. Carlo took his hand off Al's side and put it on mine. I felt a healing go through me, a renewal of something like love, or even better than love in sharing this painful moment with him. Carlo and I had both gotten into our sixties without ever having a child. I won't say that losing a pet is the same as losing a child, I won't say that. But, if you've never had children, this is as close as it gets.

"I wish I'd named him something better than Al," Carlo whispered. "Alfred, maybe. Even Fredo. Fredo would have been good."

"He always responded to the name Al in a very positive way," I said uselessly, trying oddly to control the feelings in the room, feeling something close to alarm when Carlo bent to kiss Al's hip without caring who saw.

Now Carlo was crying again. I knew it was partly for Al and partly for Jane. But his hand on mine told me that at least some of the crying was for us, what we'd had and what we'd come near to losing.

Now to understand the full grace of what was happening in that moment, why I'm telling this part of the story, I have to tell you how the pugs came to be in the first place:

I'd been jealous of Carlo's first wife Jane off and on during my marriage, especially after stumbling on the book in his library that she had written about criminal justice. I discovered then that Jane was intellectually brilliant and matched Carlo in brains, spirituality, and moral activism. They met while she was in prison ministry, and he left the priesthood for her.

As for the pugs, Jane had given them to him while the treatment for her breast cancer was failing. She told him he'd need someone to look after when he would no longer be looking after her. Carlo's disinterest in the pugs was shown by him neglecting to name them. He blurted out the names Al and Peg when one of them had to go to an emergency vet like this one.

And here's the main thing I learned: How I would never have dreamed that something Jane did would make Carlo and me suddenly close, back together in a way we hadn't been since we first married. You just never know. And even then you never know. If I believed in God this would be the sort of god I believed in. Someone like Jane. Thank you, Jane.

While we stood there over Al's body, Carlo's cell chimed, the first notes of "Joyful Joyful We Adore Thee." He pulled it out of his shirt pocket and looked. "It's Max," he said.

"Answer it!" I said.

He did and handed it to me. "He wants to talk to you."

Without letting Max get a word in, assuming what he was going to say, I said, "Listen, it's crazy. We're at the emergency vet. They had to put Al . . ." I couldn't bring myself to say "down," it was such an ugly word for it, so decided on, "to sleep. The felons are all safe at the house, but someone thinks someone maybe started a fire. We could smell it. Was it at the home? Some person or persons who were at that meeting and decided to finish the job?"

Understanding my meaning, Max told me that yes, there was a fire, but no, it wasn't at the group home. Someone had snuck onto the new development beyond it and started a fire in one of the garages that didn't have the door on yet, but that it was under control. "I can vouch for the gang," I said. "I smelled the fire when we were all of us out on the back porch."

"But listen, Brigid."

"How much damage?" I asked.

"Like I said, it was in the garage of a home being built."

"So someone or someones from the HOA meeting with an alternate gripe, right?"

Max said, "I'm seeing more comments on Neighbors that it was a false flag so yes, we think it's one of the people at the HOA meeting. Brigid—"

"All I can say, it wasn't Jackson Donofrio," I said, in a cruel joke. I wouldn't let anyone forget him. "Like I said, everyone else has been at the house all day. The only thing you could charge them with is hacking my computer to order a food delivery. But I'm not pressing charges because I ate some."

"Great, but if you'll stop talking for a second, I'll tell you why I'm calling." He told me he was at the hospital, the closest one about five miles from our house. But it wasn't anything to do with the HOA meeting or its aftermath, except in one way.

Gemma-Kate was in the emergency room at Oro Valley Hospital. So far, that only meant she likely wasn't dead yet. It was about four p.m.

Without asking another question I disconnected, with maximum brevity told Carlo where I was going and why, that I'd drop him off at home which was near Oro Valley Hospital, and no, I'll go alone yes, I can keep my mind on my driving, just stay with the guests and don't let them on my computer, got in the car, came back into the vet hospital where I'd left my keys in the room where Al had died, got the keys, got in the car again, and took off.

Gemma-Kate had just been moved to a private room, and Max was with her. Once I'd confirmed she was coherent, I turned on him.

"Why didn't you call me sooner?" I lashed out.

"I just got here. The fire had my attention at first, so you're lucky I was assigned to investigate the assault rather than someone who didn't know her because she didn't have any ID on her. Otherwise, who knows when you might have been contacted? Plus you hardly let me get a word in when I did call."

"Why didn't you have your driver's license?" I turned on her with an accusation, as if the attack was all her fault, that it wouldn't have happened if she'd been able to present appropriate identification to her attacker. Ironic, in retrospect, how close I was to the truth. My question reminded me of how when I came home with a bloody knee, Dad would say how did that happen and I would say I was running and he would yell why were you running. But never mind that.

"It's expired. I left it at home," she mumbled. Then, "Can I get a little sympathy? I hurt all over."

"You can still talk, right?" Max asked. "It's real important that we get all possible information from you so we won't lose any time catching this guy." He turned on his recorder and opened a pad at the same time. I sat at the foot of the bed and listened.

TWENTY-FOUR

Have you ever gone to the movies alone? Sometimes I like to do this because Carlo isn't terribly fond of horror films. Or thrillers. Or suspense. Or conflict. Or anything with a plot, actually. OK, what he really likes is travel documentaries and original stagings of Gilbert & Sullivan operettas. But the point I'm trying to make is that I go to the movies myself a lot. He offers to come with me, but I'm co-dependent, and if he was sitting next to me I'd spend the whole movie wondering if he was bored.

Gemma-Kate shared this trait with me, going to movies alone. Sometimes I went with her, but when she asked after the HOA meeting if I wanted to go to the Oro Valley Marketplace Theater down on Tangerine to see the latest *Saw* movie, I declined. Not only do I have my limits for horror (as in no torture, no animals or children harmed), I also had to get back to the house where everyone from the group home had probably by now discovered the liquor cabinet. That actually intrigued her, thinking of having a good talk over martinis with actual criminals. I discouraged her, saying they would probably go home shortly. So she was on her own.

Another thing to regret.

Second question if you answered yes to "have you ever gone to the movies alone?" Did you ever find yourself the only person in the theater so you sit in the row right behind the metal railing so you can put your feet up on it? And then, just when the lights dimmed, you had the sense of another person entering the theater and going up the stairs to sit in a row somewhere behind you?

What do you do? Tell yourself that it's paranoid to think that no one else but you goes to the movies by themselves. Tell yourself that the other person didn't sit in the row with you because he (it's always a he) was being courteous. Then you ignore that feeling on the back of your neck and settle into the twenty minutes of previews, so that by the time the feature film comes on you've forgotten you're not alone.

Though groggy from the painkillers, Gemma-Kate described all this to Max and me from her bed in a private room. I let Max take the lead with questions for his police report. It made the interview formal. GK and I would have time later to go more in-depth, maybe about things I didn't want Max to know.

Medical Report: Contusions on torso and neck. Broken tibia. Fractured sternum. Mild concussion.

Police Report: The victim had gone to the Oro Valley Marketplace Theater at one twenty p.m. to see a matinee of *Alien: Romulus*. She bought a large popcorn. She was the sole customer in the small theater and sat in the first row above the center aisle. Just as the film was beginning, she noticed a second person, who in her peripheral vision she judged to be a tall, thin man, enter the theater and go up the stairs to a row somewhere behind her. She did not turn around as she reports she would have, to spot where he was and get a good look at him, because she was distracted by a preview for a new M. Night Shyamalan movie.

About fifteen minutes into the feature film, the victim was startled to feel a cord wrapped quickly around her neck. Before it could tighten, she reacted by throwing her bag of popcorn over her head, reaching her thumbs under the cord, and pulling on it. The assailant may have been surprised by her sudden move and the popcorn and eased his hold on the cord. The victim, who has had some martial arts training unbeknownst to the assailant, turned in her chair, pressed her feet against the railing, and launched herself over the back of her chair at her attacker. Though much taller than her, he (she still assumes it was a male) slipped on what was later identified as some soda that had been spilled on the floor. They both went down on the narrow space between the rows, the victim apparently breaking her arm in the fall.

The attacker seemed to sense the victim's incapacity and put his hands around her neck, preparing to choke her. The marks are apparent on her throat.

As he bent toward her, she wrenched her upper body at him to get her face closer to his, and bit it. She wasn't sure in the darkness on the floor, but she thinks it was his lower right cheek. She recalls feeling his jawbone under her teeth. (Sketch available here.)

Too panicked to finish what he came to do, the man jumped up and ran over her body to the emergency exit. This set off the alarms so that the victim's screams for help were not immediately heard. Also the fracture in her sternum caused by the assailant stepping on her chest kept her from calling out very loudly. About eleven minutes elapsed before a passing worker heard her cries over the sound of the movie, accompanied by her left palm striking the back of the seat next to where she was lying. Once her body was found, an ambulance was called and the victim delivered to the emergency room of the hospital where the interview has occurred.

The assailant was able to escape without his probable wound being seen as the emergency exit leads to an alleyway where there is little traffic. No one saw him.

Upon a search for evidence at the theater, the cord allegedly intended to strangle the victim was found wedged between the back of her seat and the bottom, which automatically folds up onto the back. Bloodstains on the victim's clothing, assumed to be from the bite, will be analyzed for DNA along with the cord.

The theater staff reports no other ticket being sold for that showing of the movie. It is conjectured that the assailant may have bought a ticket for a different, earlier movie, and hid in the restroom. No credit card receipt, indicating cash payment. Interviews of theater staff and investigation ongoing.

"He stepped on your chest!" I said when Max appeared to be finished with the report. "No wonder it cracked your sternum; you don't have near enough padding there. Didn't I tell you to get a Victoria's Secret bra? The kind with extra padding?"

Gemma-Kate made a slashing sound with her good arm to indicate this was not the time to make her laugh. "I can just see the commercials. 'This bra could save your life.' He was running over me, but at the point of contact I grabbed his ankle and pushed, and I think that kept him from coming down on me as hard as he might have. He sort of tripped over me." After all her description to Max, her voice was breathy when she added, "When were you going to tell me I should always get a good look at everyone around me?"

"Well, that was my next thing." I turned to Max. "I don't go for that theory of him buying a ticket for an earlier movie and then hiding in the bathroom. How would he know she was going to be there and what movie she would see?"

Max nodded. "I was just blue-skying. So what do you think?"

I thought. "Maybe he arrived at the same time, following her to the theater and buying a ticket for a different movie. He watched which theater she went into and, taking advantage of the fact that mid-afternoon theater is as empty as a church on Monday, he was able to get into her theater once the lights had dimmed and the feature began. He got lucky that she was totally alone, otherwise he might have waited for a better opportunity. He didn't make a move until the feature had begun to make sure no one else came in a little late to witness what he was doing. It was smart, really, smarter than accosting her outside where there are more potential witnesses or even a camera." I thought about the tall and lean description, and cursed my mind for letting that thought into it. I would have stayed silent, but Max got there, "You're sure it was a man?"

"I guess so," Gemma-Kate breathed. "Yeah, pretty sure."

Not good enough. Max looked at me and his eyes told me he knew what I was thinking.

Max said, "Gemma-Kate, is there anyone you know who might have some . . . disagreement with you? An argument at school? Politics? Otherwise there's the possibility you just got unlucky."

"I can't think of anyone. I don't have any enemies that I know of. Or friends for that matter. Except for Anthony."

"Who's Anthony?"

"My roommate."

Max frowned, the way he does when he's found a person of interest. "You getting on all right with him?"

"Far as I can tell."

Max made another note on his pad.

"Don't bother him," she said.

"I will bother him," I said.

"Can I go home?" Gemma-Kate asked.

I spoke up. "I talked to the doctor; they're going to keep you overnight to make sure there's no internal bleeding and that your concussion isn't more severe than they think. I'll come get you tomorrow and bring you to the house." Mental note to stop at Walmart and get a lot more bed sheets. I said to Max, "It sounds like we're agreed this wasn't some random attack."

"Could be random. But we don't know, if it wasn't random, what the motive might have been."

Max stepped up to my glance and I was grateful for him no matter how adversarial we were. "I'll make sure she's got security," he said.

"Not that stupid guy, OK? The one who didn't call for back-up and went into a house alone and got himself accidentally shot?"

"He's not even with the department anymore. Don't worry, Brigid. No matter what's between you and me, I'll always take care of your family like it's my own," he said. Then added with faux solemnity, "Even when you're not around."

That deserved a fuck-you because he was hinting about my upcoming on-record confession of killing the serial rapist. He was getting a little too much enjoyment out of the possibility of seeing me behind bars. *Schadenfreude*, Carlo would say.

I stroked the tips of Gemma-Kate's fingers emerging from the cast on her broken arm. Even with the morphine, that made her roll her eyes, so I pulled away. Talked to Max instead. "I'll stay with her until someone shows up."

"Not necessary," Gemma-Kate wheezed. "You go."

"Right. This is how you end up when you've been attacked. What would you do now if someone got to you? Have I taught you nothing?"

She closed her eyes, likely to pretend that she was dozing off rather than answer that question.

I stepped outside her room as Max turned to go. "Do you think this had anything to do with the HOA meeting?" I asked. "One of the people in the room who saw her?"

"I can't make an immediate connection, but you know how they say there's no coincidence."

"Maybe whoever it was saw her with me. Maybe I'm the threat."

Max tilted his head in that *maybe yes maybe no* gesture. "It's not always about you, Quinn. I got a half-dozen possibilities in mind. We'll follow that line of inquiry along with any others."

"Good. And also, does it strike you as odd that the fire in that garage could have been started immediately following the meeting? Like who has a few incendiary devices—let alone Molotov cocktails—in the trunk of their car? The fires weren't a spontaneous reaction. Whoever it was had it preplanned. The same person who exploded the group home, sounds like."

Max nodded this time, giving that more credence than an assailant going after Gemma-Kate because she was sitting next to me. "Unless it's a copycat," he said. "Or a conspiracy." He lifted his hands as if to block any more thought. "Man, what a mess."

When he left, already having been on the phone to assign someone to security at her door within an hour, I went back to Gemma-Kate's bedside and pinched her undamaged leg.

"Ow!" she yelped, clearly overreacting.

"I knew you weren't asleep," I said. "Now tell me. Are you still sure that your attacker was male?"

"It wasn't Nicki, OK? That's what you're asking, right?"

"No. She was at the house when it happened."

"It was a man. That morphine is making my mouth dry," she added.

I thought while I poured her some water from that terrible little plastic jug they give patients. "OK, what about that guy you're living with. Could he be nuts?"

"Anthony? He's a nothing."

"How would you describe him?"

"He didn't do it."

"How are you sure?"

"Anthony has a beard. I would have felt it when I bit his face."

"You can shave a beard. What's his last name?"

"I don't know."

"You're living with a guy and you don't know his last name? I call that bullshit."

"Really. I don't know. It never seemed relevant."

"I'll find out. Does he know you're here?"

"I don't even have my cell phone so how would he know? Where is it?"

I went to the side table and picked up the large plastic bag with a string tie that had all her clothes and an over-the-shoulder tote and sunglasses in it. The phone wasn't in the tote.

"I can't find yours. Here," I said, fishing out my own phone and reaching it in her direction. "Call him now."

"Now?" she asked.

"Now," I said.

With one arm in a cast, she tried to take the phone but fumbled it. I took it back and made her give me his number saying I'd give it to her when I connected so she could talk to him. Only I didn't give it back. And now I had his number.

"Hey!" she objected.

"Not as smart as all that, are you, missy."

I left, still going through my brain files of all the people who might have attacked Gemma-Kate. Somebody tall and lean, given the angles of the attack and her recollection of the event. I mentally scanned everyone at the HOA meeting and came up with a couple of maybes. Of the felons, Henry could have easily killed her. Erroll was too short. Tyler only average. Nicki was the right height and had the strength and dexterity to take on someone who'd been trained in self-defense. Had all the felons stayed at the house the way I claimed while I was at the vet?

The HOA meeting, the fire, Al's death, Gemma-Kate's attack. It was a long day.

TWENTY-FIVE

I got back to the house around ten p.m. and made my way through sleeping men who seemed to be more than comfortable sharing couch pillows on the floor. The light on my phone picked up only the gleam of Peg's bulgy eyes the size of gigantic blueberries, which noted my arrival with minimal interest. She had lifted her head from where it rested on Henry's foot. I didn't turn on any lights but assumed that Nicki was somewhere among the bodies. The place still reeked of masala sauce, garlic naan bread, and deep fat fried chicken. I turned down the air conditioning to seventy to balance that and the heat and Indian food scent rising from the skin of the sleepers. They didn't seem to have a care. I couldn't bring myself to look in the kitchen. Some things are better saved for morning. Like dirty dishes and finding alternative housing for your overnight guests.

If Carlo wasn't asleep when I undressed and got into bed and pulled just the sheet over me, he was pretending to be. Have you ever noticed how nearly impossible it is to act as if you've been asleep? I've never seen an actor give a credible performance. He gave a fake yawn, rolled in my direction and kindly didn't mention that I hadn't brushed my teeth. Poor guy, he comes home early from a retreat to find his house filled with felons, his dog dying, and his wife running off.

Knowing that he was waiting to hear what had happened, I told him what I knew about Gemma-Kate's attack and that both Max and I would be investigating. I told him I'd be going out again in the morning and would he please tell the felons (I know it's a slur but shorthand is a little easier, OK?) they could stay at our place until other arrangements were made. As I would have expected, Carlo didn't bat an eye at the thought of them all crowding into our home. Of course, this was in the dark, so if he batted an eye I might have missed it. Then I fell asleep and I hope he did too.

Gemma-Kate had said Anthony was a morning person, so I got up around seven to contact him. Without daylight savings time (we don't do that in Arizona), the sun had been on full blast since five thirty, so I could get a clearer picture of the slumber party than I had the night before. Maneuvering around the bodies again, I made my way into the kitchen, careful not to land on an outstretched hand but stepping into something on my way that gooshed up through my toes. "Shit," I said quietly, but it wasn't. I heel-walked into the guest bathroom and hopped into the tub to wash off what looked like dog vomit. That vindaloo must not have agreed.

After that, I cleaned the remaining puke off the floor, made a large pot of coffee, poured a to-go cup, sipped it until it was cool enough to drink down, and eyed the still-open Styrofoam containers with their west Asian residues of green and reddish brown respectively, the empty KFC bucket, and dishes that had been politely put in the sink if not rinsed. Achilles preferred to stay asleep spooned in Tyler's arms, but Peg stared at me, possibly resentful that she wouldn't be able to eat her own puke for breakfast. Of course, pugs always look nothing if not resentful.

I left a note to Carlo suggesting he take everyone out to the Sunnyside Up Cafe, because there were only a couple of stale muffins in the fridge. Either that or Tyler could hack my computer again and have something delivered. Then, on my phone, I contacted Anthony with the number Gemma-Kate had provided. I texted,

I'm using my aunt's phone. Where are you?

The reply came quickly. At home of course. Why?

I've got some information you won't want to miss. Re mob at group home.

Cool. I have appointment with DA around nine. See you here around ten?

See you.

I kept my words to a minimum so he wouldn't guess that it wasn't Gemma-Kate he was texting with. As a Ph.D. psych candidate, he might have some feel for linguistics.

I called the hospital and got a hold of Gemma-Kate on her room landline. "How you doing this morning?"

"Everything hurts."

"That's to be expected. What's a DA?" I asked, coming up with only District Attorney and figuring that couldn't be the case.

"Doctoral advisor. What did you tell him?" Gemma-Kate asked.

"That you were in a little accident but you were OK and that I was there with you."

"What did he say?" She sounded more curious than hopeful.

"He said OK and let him know if you need anything."

That was kind of true. He hadn't seemed to care where Gemma-Kate had been all night. If I'd told him Gemma-Kate had been the victim of an attempted homicide, I didn't get the feeling there would be an "OMG how bad is it?" Of course, Gemma-Kate wouldn't react that way to him either. But more on that later.

I knew the address because I'd been there once or twice to pick Gemma-Kate up for something, but had never been inside. The place was a dump. To be precise, half of it was a dump, the other half was tidy to the point of compulsion. When I had knocked at the door Anthony opened it with an annoyed look of *why are you knocking, you have a key.*

The first thing I noticed was that he was tall and lean, the only description Gemma-Kate had for her assailant in the dark theater. Tall and lean was easy to tell as he wasn't wearing a shirt. Even though his torso was as fish-belly white as most Arizonans who stay out of the sun, I still felt a little flutter in my nether regions, and realized how much I looked forward to cuddling with Carlo, how much I had missed him. When all this was over and we didn't have guests to hear us . . .

The second thing I noticed is that he had a red beard to match his hair and, I couldn't help but imagine, his groin.

"Hi," I said, trying not to blush. A psychologist would note it. "I'm Gemma-Kate's aunt, the one who contacted you. Brigid Quinn. She's been in an accident. May I come in?"

Anthony's scowl settled in and I assumed he didn't like the fact that he'd been tricked.

"I apologize for tricking you into seeing me. The truth is that there's going to be an investigation because we think it was an attempted homicide. I wanted to talk to you before the cops do."

Now he was interested. He was quick to open the door to let me in, which was the first possible sign that he hadn't been the attacker. That was when I assessed the selective dumpishness of the place. Of course, it was spare and shabby and not very inviting; that's just the nature of off-campus housing unless a kid comes from real money. Obviously, Anthony did not and I knew Gemma-Kate wasn't rolling in it either. The only way she could get in-state tuition was by claiming my address.

I looked at the piles of paper spread like a large deck of cards on the dining-room table, the kind of arrangement where you'd see things from an archeological dig perspective with the strata telling different stories. A glass top desk in the living room was the opposite, laptop closed, books neatly set between gargoyle bookends, and two pens side by side lined up perfectly perpendicular to the edge of the desk.

"Let me guess, the dining-room table is Gemma-Kate's study area."

Anthony nodded.

"How do you tolerate it?"

"I try not to look at it."

I took a seat on the end of the couch that wasn't piled with books. Anthony looked like he resented this, but what could he do? With an elaborate sigh he disappeared for a minute into another room and came back wearing a T-shirt that said "Minds are like parachutes. Just because you've lost yours doesn't mean you can borrow mine." He sat in the office chair by the neat desk and swiveled it toward me, making me feel like a patient.

I took an extra look at his face, with that bushy red beard surrounding full lips, the whole picture making me think of bagpipes. Gemma-Kate had mentioned using him for sex. What was that like? What kind of sex would Gemma-Kate enjoy? Could it be something with role-playing? Could it be a pretend attack in a movie theater that went seriously awry? Why would she lie about it if it was an accident? Would it get Anthony in trouble if anyone knew that happened? Did she lie about biting a beardless face to throw off suspicion? Was she protecting him?

When I finally emerged from my stream of consciousness, I saw Anthony examining me.

"Gemma-Kate tells me you're studying psychology," I said, hoping to put him at ease by talking about himself. Big mistake, it worked. He was clearly more interested in telling me about his dissertation than hearing how his girlfriend was.

"I'm currently working on my doctoral dissertation. Are you familiar with the nineteenth-century book, *Extraordinary Popular Delusions and the Madness of Crowds*?"

"Sounds fascinating," I said, trying not to look at the clock on the kitchen wall.

"It is. It covered topics ranging from the witchcraft scare in the American colonies to the mania for tulips in the eighteen hundreds. With that book as a starting point, I'm showing a progression to our current time, the manipulation of the masses via social media, and the algorithms that drive political propaganda. You know, the modern mob. Actually, that's what I'm calling it, *The Modern Mob: Incitement to Violence in the Age of Social Media*." His pause invited my affirmation.

"Great title," I said.

He blushed becomingly. "Like I said, right now it's just a dissertation, but someday I hope to turn it into a book. It's the kind of thing that Routledge would love."

I thought maybe now I could turn the topic away from publishing to something I cared about. "Gemma-Kate says you're fascinated by her psychopathy."

You could tell how we both took that for granted. "Absolutely. Of course, I'm very fond of her, but being able to live with a psychopath has lent a whole new dimension to my studies."

"Of course," I said.

"The general public only encounters them in the likes of Hannibal Lecter and Tom Ripley. Or real-life serial killers like Wayne Gacy. They don't realize that just because someone lacks empathy doesn't mean they kill without compunction."

"Of course not," I said. Apparently knowing even a little about me didn't stop a psychologist from mansplaining. I didn't bother to tell my part in catching Wayne Gacy.

He went on, telling me everything I already knew about my niece. If you were writing a book, you'd call it idiot dialogue. "Gemma-Kate doesn't seem to need the thrill of hurting someone, and doesn't seem to miss feeling strong emotions like love. Of course, she's never told me if she would kill out of some expediency, say if someone were thwarting her desire . . ." When he lingered on that word and stared at me I wondered if he was seeking corroboration or possibly some anecdote of a time she'd done just that.

"You could thwart her desire and find out," I suggested.

Anthony didn't get an appreciative twinkle in his eye, let alone smile. Psychologists often don't get irony, or if they do, see it as pathology. Given that and the insensitive message on his T-shirt about people losing their mind, he was also making me wonder where he himself was on the empathy spectrum.

"I have yet to find out whether it's genetic, vis-à-vis real psychopathy or more environmental, i.e., some sort of abuse or neglect as a child, resulting in sociopathy." He pinned me with his stare, still hoping I could provide some information that Gemma-Kate had not.

"So you say you've been at an appointment with your dissertation advisor."

Now he twinkled. "You sound like a detective on one of those crime shows. You say that someone may be getting in touch with me. Am I a suspect in trying to kill my own girlfriend? How about telling me what you think I did."

"Gemma-Kate went to the movies by herself."

"She does that often."

"Someone entered the otherwise empty theater, came up behind her and tried to strangle her with a rope. She managed to get out of the choke, turned around and launched herself at the assailant. They went down on the floor, where he tried again to choke her but she bit his face. He ran over her to get out of the theater and she called for help." I left out a few key details because that's what you do.

He nodded. "Oddly, that sounds like something Gemma-Kate would do."

"Why, you into hypoxia play?"

He gave his head a cursory shake, showing that he knew exactly what that was. For someone even approaching the status of lover, he didn't seem to be affected all that much.

I said, "Anthony, she's in the hospital with a broken arm, contusions where the assailant stepped on her body, and a concussion. Do you care?"

"Of course I care. But this isn't that scene where I go to the hospital and wet Gemma-Kate's hand with my tears. This is where you try to find out if you can pin something on me. If that's the case, you'd have to establish my motive. That's what you'd try to figure out, right?"

Anthony was as smart as a Ph.D. candidate. "You got me," I said, shaking my head with duly feigned admiration. I paused as if to let that sink in. "But maybe it wasn't any heinous intent. Maybe just a little role-playing that got out of control?" I said, hearkening back to my earlier train of thought.

There's some that might have squirmed at that suggestion. Not Anthony. "That's silly. If we'd wanted to do that we'd have gone to the Loft Cinema on Speedway, it's much closer."

I hadn't said which theater Gemma-Kate was attacked in, and I didn't say now. Let Max do that so Anthony wouldn't be warned in advance. But I was the one who was threatened when he asked, "So what did you think of what Gemma-Kate did?"

I was too taken off guard to bluff, unusual for me. "What?"

"Oh boy, do you mean she didn't tell you?"

"You better spill it now, kid, because it sounds personal."

"GK thought it would be fun to see if she could do some investigating about . . . who was that woman who got her face smashed?"

"Dorita Gordino."

"That's it. Not a name you forget easily."

"But you did. And Gemma-Kate did this because—"

"With your being on Nicki's side, she didn't think you could do it honestly. So she decided to interview some of the people surrounding Nicki, but as you."

"You mean . . ."

"She said she was Brigid Quinn, a private investigator working with local law enforcement."

I'm gonna kill that kid, I thought, then chuckled in a that's-our-Gemma-Kate way and said, "She didn't tell me a thing yet. Did she tell you who she talked to and what she found out?"

"Not sure I can remember. Give me a minute." Anthony went for another cup of coffee and brought me one too, without my asking. Black. "Let me see, she said that some people knew you, like everyone in the group home, so she couldn't go there. Neighbors likewise. I think she went to Dorita's church and spoke to the pastor. He put her on to a couple of people she knew pretty well there . . . I'm not even sure I should be telling you this, I mean if GK hasn't already said anything, she must have had a reason, right?"

I guess the edge found its way back into my voice as I said, "You bet she had a reason. Go on."

Anthony did a little verbal tap dancing. "Well, I guess since she got herself into some trouble, if her attacker wasn't just some random rapist or whatever, this is a good time for you to know. So anyway, GK got several names from the church and then from Dorita's business as a real-estate broker."

"You know what these names are?"

Anthony sipped his coffee. "The only one I can remember is because she's both a member of the church and connected to Dorita through business. Turner, I think was the name. Oh, now I remember. She was the one who set up that gallery event for the woman who killed her husband."

"Eleanore Turner," I said. "Gemma-Kate wouldn't try to interview Eleanore Turner because Eleanore and I had already met."

"Did Gemma-Kate know that? Did she see you talking at the gallery, maybe?"

"Well, if she didn't, Eleanore would certainly set her straight when Gemma-Kate tried to pose as me. Trust me, Eleanore wouldn't be shy."

"Well, I'm certain she said she went to the Turner house. That's all I remember. You'll have to ask her."

TWENTY-SIX

When I got back to the hospital, the security guard properly asked me for ID and admitted I was on the list of those who could visit Gemma-Kate. How could they know I was the one who'd want to beat her up? But I didn't.

She knew what was going on from the moment she saw my beating-up face, though.

"Anthony," she said.

I managed to keep from shouting so the security guard standing outside the door wouldn't be alerted. "You idiot. If you ever *ever* pull a stunt like that again . . . You're really smart, aren't you, Gemma-Kate. You're so smart you think you can go around playing private investigator and there won't be any repercussions."

"What repercussions?" she asked. The painkillers were still working to take her edge off some, and made her sound too contented to be defensive. "Are you saying Ian Turner was the one who attacked me in the theater? Really, Aunt Brigid, isn't that a little too obvious?"

"So it was the husband you spoke with?" Eleanore's husband was a long shot, true, but he could have told Eleanore that Brigid Quinn had been at the house, and then Eleanore told someone else and so on until word reached the attacker. "Now tell me. Everything. Before I break your other arm."

"Well, first I talked to the foster parents where Ramona was living."

"Was?"

"Is. Is living. They told me that they were on their way to the Grand Canyon. They were pretty excited. I've never been to the Grand Canyon."

I held an index finger in front of her eyes. "Focus," I said. "Was Ramona going with them?"

"The wife told me child safety had arranged for Ramona to stay with another foster so they could have some time to themselves. She said it's called respite care and people do it all the time. Did you know about that?"

"When was this?"

"Just a few days ago."

"Who's the respite care foster?"

"I didn't ask them that precisely. But the wife said she knew them, and Ramona was happy to go, so I knew it was all good. I would have told you if I thought there was something suspicious going on."

"Who was the agent who arranged for the respite care?"

"I didn't ask them that."

"So you decided on your own that there was nothing suspicious. You idiot. That's the trouble with smart people—they think everyone is dumber than they are."

"The corollary to the Dunning-Kruger effect," Gemma-Kate said thoughtfully, as if none of this had to do with real people suffering real pain. I stared at her, sorry for thinking I could bring her into a normal world. Into anyone's world. She went on to explain while I was stunned into silence. Gemma-Kate may have known I was not interested, but she was never inhibited by another person's lack of interest. "The Dunning-Kruger effect is what they call it when stupid people don't know they're stupid. So you're saying that with me I'm too smart to know when other people are smart. Interesting."

I was inclined to scream, but that would only interest her all the more. Also, I knew that I wouldn't get any more information out of her if I did. "When were you planning to tell me this?"

"I was going to tell you. There was just a lot going on with that HOA meeting and the bombing and all."

"Who else did you see?"

"When I heard that Ramona was with different fosters, I went to see Nicki, to make sure she'd been told. I'm pretty sure DCS is supposed to inform the parent of any changes. See? I didn't take anything for granted."

"Nicki didn't mention this to me, that you'd been to see her. Now *that's* suspicious."

"Maybe she didn't want you to know."

"Why wouldn't she?"

Gemma-Kate took a deep breath which must have hurt. Her thumb wandered to a little button that would release some morphine before continuing. "I can tell you Nicki looked pretty nervous when I questioned her about Ramona's whereabouts. When I asked about that mentor of hers, she looked even more nervous. That's when I went to see Eleanore Turner."

"I know about that already."

"But you don't know everything."

"Why not?"

"You couldn't, because I didn't tell Anthony everything."

"So what did Eleanore say?"

"She wasn't there. I talked to her husband, Ian. I met him at the gallery but hadn't told him my name. I wasn't sure if he knew you, so I told him I was Brigid Quinn."

"You didn't."

Gemma-Kate gave me what was for her an unusually goofy smile. "I thought it would be fun to pose as you, and confuse him."

Round and round and round, getting every small detail out of Gemma-Kate was making me tired and I was conscious of a faint ticking clock in my head. I think, after my initial annoyance with her, she was getting to enjoy the process. She waited for my next question. Her pupils were beginning to dilate and I had to get some answers fast before I lost her altogether. "What did he say?"

"That Eleanore was out with Nicki."

"Only you'd just been with Nicki, and Eleanore—"

"Wasn't there." Then he said he remembered meeting me at the gallery show that Eleanore set up for Nicki, and he was really friendly. He invited me in for a drink."

"Did you tell him you don't drink?"

"I can fake it when I want something. I sat down in the living room. It sure wasn't decorated for Tucson; all kinds of Asian art and furnishings. These huge Foo dogs. I'm not an art connoisseur by any means, but I would guess everything in the house was expensive. When he brought two drinks back from the kitchen, I asked why Asia just as a conversation starter, and he told me it was mostly inherited from Eleanore's parents who did business in China after Nixon opened trade relations with them. Oh, I didn't mention he'd put on a kimono-style of robe over his bathing trunks."

I sat on the bed because I'd run out of pacing room. That was when I realized I'd been pacing. "He was only wearing swim trunks when you arrived?"

"Speedos," Gemma-Kate nodded with a small grimace. "He said he didn't much care for the décor and what did I think? I said, well, Ian, I'm a libertarian, so I think everyone should decorate how they want. He said that was very diplomatic. You know, Aunt Brigid, I'd assume from his mention of inheriting those Chinese furnishings that at least some of their money comes from her side."

"Not a bad assumption," I said.

"Ian was standing up during this part of the conversation, and encouraged me to take a sip of the drink to see if I liked it before he sat down."

With all the fascination of watching an impending train wreck, I asked, "Did you?"

"Like I said, I can fake it. But you know, was there something in it? That's what you're thinking, right?"

"Could be."

"I thought he's probably not the murderer, only a rapist, and that could be interesting too." Her eyes and thoughts drifted off momentarily.

I was dumbstruck, and while I was trying to process all the ramifications, she added, "Humans are so interesting. So yes, I drank it." Gemma-Kate half-suppressed a giggle. "Do you see now why I didn't tell you everything right away?"

"Oh yeah. The Asian décor alone is shocking."

Gemma-Kate ignored the sarcasm. "When I came to—apparently it was a very light dose of whatever it was—my underwear was down around my knees and Turner himself was sprawled back on a nearby loveseat with a smile and ruffled kimono." She frowned. "Have I mentioned the child?"

"What child?"

"The one in the pool."

"Ramona. You saw Ramona."

"Not sure. It was a Ramona-sized child on the patio. She'd been swimming."

"Was it Ramona or not? You saw her at the gallery."

"This one had wet hair. And she didn't have a dress on. They kind of all look alike."

Turner had been in the pool alone with a child. Turner was a sexual predator. I felt my teeth gritting and tried to grab onto some kind of reality so I wouldn't feel like I was talking to the Mad Hatter. Gemma-Kate's thumb snuck over to the morphine button. Whether or not it was time for a dose, I grabbed the thumb and asked, "Did Turner say who the child was?"

"He said something about watching her. For a friend of the family, I think."

I leaned over the bed and grabbed both sides of her head between my hands. "You knew Ian Turner was a sexual predator, and you didn't think to inform someone he'd sexually assaulted you in front of a child—because you thought it would be interesting?"

"Give me a little credit; he had rolled down the shutters so she couldn't see inside, and she didn't drown."

"Good God." I squeezed her head harder, and for just a moment thought that feeling her skull give way would be satisfying. "You left a child in the care of a sexual predator and didn't tell anyone."

"Ow," Gemma-Kate said. "You're hurting me!"

Her eyes shifted and I turned my head to see the security guard standing at the door, hand not quite on his sidearm, but damn close. "Everything OK here?" he asked.

With my right hand I tapped the side of her cheek gently. "She's fine, officer." I added, with as friendly a grin as I could muster given my adrenalin surge, "Her pain meds are just wearing off."

He appeared doubtful until Gemma-Kate said, "It's OK, just family stuff."

When he was gone, Gemma-Kate asked if I wanted to hear the rest or did I want to keep being all judgmental.

"There's more?" I said dully.

"You have to understand that the underwear situation was as bad as it got," Gemma-Kate began.

With the threat of security coming in the room again, I managed to keep my voice low. "He drugged you, then tried to humiliate you and show you what he could have done. What happened then?"

"Let go of my head and I'll tell you."

I dropped my hands to my side and began pacing again.

"So thinking I had the goods on him for sexual assault though not rape, I started asking him the questions you're likely interested in. Who was the child? And more pointedly, why did he lie about Eleanore being out with Nicki when I'd just been with Nicki? He said, but still calmly, he didn't much care having people show up on his doorstep asking questions, especially if they had no right to ask questions. I didn't respond to that, didn't go on the defensive. I just took my good old time pulling up my underwear while staring at him.

"'Why are you here?' he asked, rather than answering any of my questions.

"I told him I was only fifteen. He said 'nice try;' he hadn't actually done anything while I was out. That he only did what he did to teach me a lesson. Then he waved the wallet he'd taken from my purse and tossed it at my feet." Gemma-Kate shook her head in appreciation of his cleverness. "He said, 'You're not who you said you are.' That appeared to be a question. 'You've got the license,' I said.

"He said, 'All that tells me is your name is Gemma-Kate Quinn and that you're a little girl who thinks she's smarter than anyone else.'"

I said, "He got that right. Maybe he didn't tell Eleanore about your visit after all. Maybe he's become suspicious of her? Maybe he doesn't say anything to Eleanore because he's stopped trusting her."

"Speaking of Eleanore, here's something interesting. He

got all righteously angry at my asking any questions about her. He guessed you and I were connected because of the last name and my questions, said to tell Brigid Quinn that his wife had a drinking problem and was spending some time at Miraval."

"How fucking noble of him to keep that confidence. Days later you get attacked in a movie theater."

"See why I was hesitant to tell you what I know? I knew you'd be disappointed with me."

Gemma-Kate's flaw was that, despite being so smart, she often missed understanding human motivation. "Disappointed. I had to get the truth from your boyfriend. Does he know you were willing to risk being raped by Turner in order to get information?"

"I can't remember if I told him. When we were at the gallery, did you tell Eleanore who I was?"

"I can't remember, maybe not. Damn, I used to be better with these details. But two things: Whether he knew who you really were or not, he'd still see you as a threat. And two, he could ask Eleanore about you."

"If she's still alive. We only have his word that she's in rehab."

They keep the temperature in hospitals low, to avoid infection, they say. I had a chill. "Don't be so dramatic."

"Then maybe she's in a conspiracy with someone . . . or someones," she said.

I stared out the hospital window at the top of an adjacent roof where an American flag was waving in a strong breeze. My mind wanted to dwell there rather than discover yet another strand in this already complex web. And that led me to, "Where was the child at this point? After what he said was a non-rape?"

Gemma-Kate thought, apparently not having thought about it at the time. "Can't say for sure. When I came to, he got off the couch and opened the blinds over the glass door that led to the back patio. I could see out to the pool and there was no one out there. Wait. I recall hearing water running. Maybe she was taking a bath."

Gemma-Kate was not disturbed, still thinking logically as

she changed the subject. "Re. the movie-theater attack; in this case, yes, correlation might just be causation."

I wished I didn't love this creature as much as I did. I loved her the way someone loves tigers. Fascinating and beautiful animals, but you had to be cautious around them.

TWENTY-SEVEN

No matter how many times I went over the details with Gemma-Kate, questioning her did not get me any closer to finding out why Ian had been alone watching a child who might have been Ramona. There was a gap of several days between that and me seeing Eleanore at the Greek restaurant. Was she in rehab? Miraval was a lead. I hoped it might get me closer to finding Eleanore, who would confirm that child at the house when Gemma-Kate went to visit was Ramona, and would know where Ramona was now.

Finding Ramona was as critical at this juncture as clearing Nicki.

I called Miraval from the hospital parking lot. Only Miraval doesn't share their guest list, and the man I talked to refused to tell me whether she was there. I hung up, went home, waited three hours, and then recognized a different voice at the reservation desk. I made an appointment for a month of rehab under the name Eleanore Turner. The woman this time didn't tell me that was impossible, that she was already there. Eleanore wasn't at Miraval. I didn't know why yet; I didn't even know all the what. And if a guy gives someone a roofie, whether or not he follows through, he's a predatory jerk, but that doesn't make him complicit in his wife's shenanigans.

My only hesitation in calling Max to share information was how much Nicki could be implicated in all this. Whether I was helping get her charged with a crime, either as perpetrator or accessory, and, if that was the case, how I could be throwing away my own freedom for nothing.

Me aside, who else could be hurt, and how long did I have before a more successful attack? I don't know how long I was mentally down Eleanore Turner's rabbit hole, but there was something stinky there, something carrion-like. Was the sainthood that Ian claimed for her a cover? Were they both hiding a darker side?

I couldn't go to Nicki with my questions. About whether the child at the Turner house was her daughter Ramona. I hadn't seen her myself and Gemma-Kate hadn't identified her. Plus I was losing track of how many days had elapsed since Gemma-Kate had been there. What was the chain of events? Because what if I'm seeing links where there are none? How would Nicki feel about that? What if it's not Ramona? Even that wouldn't matter, Nicki would set me straight. Or, what if the child at the Turner house is Ramona, but Nicki doesn't know that Eleanore has her? If she knew, how would she feel? That would depend on whether Nicki still trusted Eleanore, whether the trust was warranted or not. If she thought Eleanore had Ramona, and she trusted her mentor, Nicki wouldn't be keeping it a secret from me.

I was getting tired of just questions, and so far they all led to a final one: Now what to do? When you're drowning in that many questions, there's nothing better than a nice stake-out. Gives you time to think. It would have been simpler to do a stake-out if it wasn't summer. Ramona, if that child in the Turner house was Ramona, wasn't in school, so I couldn't follow a bus or car and wait for her to emerge. I knew better than to make contact with Ramona personally—that could get me and possibly Nicki in a whole lot of trouble, legally. A photograph would have to do.

I wanted to help Nicki, to prove that she hadn't had anything to do with Dorita's killing, nor with Eleanore, though she had plenty of motive and I knew she was capable. But I also didn't want heatstroke. So I watched the weather report, which you can rely on none of the time, but it's the only game in town.

While the summer temperatures are brutal, July also brings the promise of the monsoons, which is desert hyperbole for rain. Then through mid-September is the time when nature becomes a drama queen, with black clouds rolling down the sides of the mountains, and fifty-mile-an-hour wind gusts called microbursts. At that time, right before the rain and golf-ball-sized hailstones, before the streets flood and stupid people who think they can drive through them have to be rescued from their cars, before the thunder makes your fillings vibrate and you can smell ozone from the lightning, the temperature drops thirty degrees in one minute. There were two days that week when the local meteorologist estimated a 60 percent chance of that happening. No one would notice a car parked in the street while navigating through a good storm.

Luckily there was no hail this time, though as long as it didn't break a windshield, I didn't care. I had walked over to the group home the day I met Eleanore there, and I left the funeral after her so she had never seen me with my car. These are the kinds of things an investigator keeps track of. There were small no parking signs on her street, and parking next to one was ideal. No one ever got a ticket for it, and no one would do that if they feared being noticed.

The storm lasted about forty-five minutes so that the sides of the street ran past my car with water seeking its lowest point. It was glorious. It also washed off the car. Unfortunately, that was the only upside, as there was no one coming out from the Turner home, with or without a child in tow. That's private investigations for you.

Two days later there was another storm. This time no one left the house but, as the rain stopped, I saw someone pull up on the opposite side of the street, and get out of her car, smiling at me. Dressed in jeans and a T-shirt, that desert uniform that blends in. She waved with her left hand. Her right hand was slightly behind her as she headed over. Hiding something.

When you've been in this business as long as I had, it's easy to tell when someone is going to hand you a subpoena. There's just a look about them, a friendly smile under a purposeful gaze. Someone in the Turner house had spotted me, and I'd guess this was a restraining order. I'd been noticed, after all. I pulled away without responding, without looking except out of the corner of my eye as her smile dropped to match her eyes. *That's OK, sweetheart, you'll get better at this and I'm not your typical sucker.* I made a mental note not to open my front door to anyone I didn't know until all these events were behind me.

* * *

There's more than one way to skin a cat, though to my knowledge no one has ever asked what that way is, nor why you would want to in the first place. And if you're triggered by this, if the image of cat-skinning distresses you, stop it. Just stop. Though I've become more of a dog person in my later years, I have nothing against cats and the saying is mere metaphor.

As I've probably mentioned many times before, I don't know that much but I know everyone who does. So I called Lynn Speth from the church that Carlo and I go to occasionally (Christmas and Easter, you got anything against that?). Lynn volunteers for a nonprofit called Aviva Children's Services. The organization does fundraising for excellent programs like assisting parents who have had their children taken away by the Department of Child Safety. Aviva helps make the separation temporary by providing drug and financial counseling to fix the problems. They also do seasonal collection drives, like one to make sure every foster kid going back to school has a new backpack and the necessary school supplies to help them fit in with the rest of the kids. Lynn is one of those women who acts as a mother to multitudes.

Turned out that—no matter how close we were or how much she trusted me—Lynn wasn't allowed to release the whereabouts of a child being fostered without the permission of the Department of Child Safety and the people doing the fostering. *Pretty please* wasn't going to work in this case. Lynn is a hardass rule-follower.

I reasoned with her. "Could it be different if the child is in respite care with a different family?"

"I still don't think I'd be able to tell you where the child is, even temporarily, for her own safety."

I made my tone as non-pushy as I could. Pushy doesn't work for women like Lynn. "Could you double-check? The name of the child is Ramona Gleason."

Lynn called back just a half-hour later. She was able to say only that Ramona Gleason was not presently with the assigned fosters.

"Another family?" I asked.

"It doesn't matter how you ask the question, Brigid. I can't say."

One more try. "Do you happen to know the Turners? Ian and Eleanore?"

After a pause, Lynn said, "Good heavens, who doesn't? They know everyone and everyone knows them. Besides being a much-loved veterinarian, Ian's done great work on the Pima County Board of Supervisors, coming up with new ideas on caring for the unhoused. And I adore Eleanore because she's a staunch supporter of Youth on Their Own. That's the nonprofit devoted to kids who have aged out of the foster care system."

I half-listened to her as she went on. With me jumping to the question of whether she knew the Turners after asking about Ramona, you would have expected her to ask why I wanted to know. But she hadn't. There was just that pause before she answered. That's how I knew to follow my hunch.

TWENTY-NINE

I'm not sure anyone else would have followed through so quickly with finding the felons a place to stay while they fixed the kitchen in the group home. I was motivated. Able to get them into three rooms at the small motel in Catalina. That taken care of, and finding that the Pima County Board of Supervisors was meeting, I went to their meeting room and took a seat in the audience.

As is usually the case, the meeting went on forever, with Ian Turner sneaking looks at me that he thought I wouldn't notice. When all the windbags had done all their posturing (not to say they didn't make good decisions, because they're a really good group), I went up to the long bench where the five of them sat and said hi to Ian. He couldn't brush me off because the other supervisors were curious.

The presence of others could be a benefit, so I didn't waste any time. "I'm looking for Eleanore," I said. "You might remember us meeting at the gallery."

"So call her," he said, while gathering up some papers.

I put my hand on the papers. "I tried. She's not answering her cell phone."

OK, that was a calculated lie, but it turned out to be a good one. Glancing at the others who were glancing at us, he said, "She's at Miraval for a few days."

"So I hear."

"Needed some alone time. Didn't take her phone."

"Ah, that's the reason she didn't call back. I tried calling the reception desk but they wouldn't acknowledge she was there. So just on a whim I called back and made a reservation in her name. They wouldn't do that if she was already there."

Now he looked somewhat concerned. Ian got out his own cell and called what was presumably the Miraval number and asked to leave a message for her.

Now he looked alarmed. He was either genuinely worried or did "alarmed" very well.

"Told you," I said, making an effort not to sound smug.

"Where the hell is she?" he asked no one in particular.

"Exactly," I said.

The others had drifted away so as not to look too curious, so Turner could grasp my wrist and lift it off the papers on the desk without appearing to assault me. He held it now and the grip was strong. "You're involved with that woman she's mentoring, aren't you?"

I didn't deny it, just waited for the point.

"I told Eleanore not to mentor her. A woman kills her husband, how can you be sure she isn't dangerous?"

"Slight jump to a conclusion?" I asked. "Or do you know something I don't?"

He let go of me then, and picked up his cell phone which had been lying on the desk. He pressed three buttons on his phone, either 9-1-1 or maybe Max on speed dial. "I need to report a missing person," he said, running the fingers of his left hand through his hair plugs.

Maybe he expected me to leave, but I stood my ground and listened to him give all the details to whoever was on the other end of the line, if anyone was. You don't trust a guy about one thing, you don't trust him about anything. When he finally saw I wasn't going anywhere, he disconnected and said, "What else?"

"Oh, let's see. Slipping my niece a roofie, for starters. Sexual assault. Suspicion of pedophilia. I think they could get you for something."

Ian didn't bother to deny anything. He didn't even go with the typical who-will-they-believe. "You know," he said, "Trump's not the first horndog in the White House. There have been lots of presidents who took advantage of their power to get ass on the side. But you know the difference? In this era nobody asks, 'Did he do it?' It's more like, 'Who cares?' Seriously, even if I didn't have the whole county to vouch for me, hashtag me-too is . . . so three years ago."

* * *

There was nothing more to be done for the time being. I went home and microwaved a couple of prepared frozen chicken cordon bleus with a salad. Pretended to eat in front of the evening news with Carlo, Peg on the couch between us. I had the sense she didn't miss Al the way Carlo and I did. This way she could be petted by both of us at the same time without Al being in the way.

Halfway through the BBC report on the civil war in Sudan, a loud rap sounded at the metal screen door in front. The doorbell is broken and we should have it fixed. I could tell from the repeated rappings that this person really wanted me to answer the door, and wouldn't go away. I looked out the front window next to the door as I wasn't in the mood for a Gemma-Kate attack or someone wanting us to change our internet provider. It was, I noted with some surprise, Nicki.

She cringed at the sight of me in the window, also surprisingly.

I threw open the door. "Nicki! I'm sorry I startled you. Do you want to come in?"

"Is your husband here?" she asked.

I assumed this might be private, that it wasn't Carlo she wanted to speak to. "Is that a problem? We can talk on the back porch."

She shook her head no. In the heat of the early evening, still ninety degrees with the sun setting, she was shivering. "Are you ill?" I stepped toward her, put the side of my hand on the side of her head to check for fever, that reflex whether you were ever a mother or not. She jerked away.

"OK, let me get my stick and let's take a little walk." I grabbed it from the stand in the front hall, along with a small flashlight from a drawer in the credenza in case we needed it. "Do you want water?" People are always asking that in the desert. She said no and we headed east down the hill on Golder Ranch.

"It's good to see you," I began, starting with something easy and personal rather than jumping into my many questions. "I thought maybe I'd said or done something that bothered you. Hurt you?"

"No. I'm . . . I've just been busy."

I waited. As we walked down the steep incline toward the big wash, Nicki was staring at the ground with a please-don't-make-me-tell-you expression. I remembered seeing it when she'd first come to Desert Doves and wanted my help without having to admit that her husband was a colossal asshole who put her and her child in danger. I waited the way I had the first time.

No big reveal, just a conversational opener on her part. "So. Have you seen Eleanore Turner lately?"

That was interesting. Nicki comes over in mid-panic attack and the first thing she says is have I seen her mentor. Like it couldn't wait until morning. Had Ian Turner called her? Had Max?

"Not at all," I said, without sharing what I'd gathered about Miraval, because (and this hurts to say) I wasn't sure I could trust her anymore. "Have you?"

She shook her head.

Without giving my opinion that this might be a little wonky, I ventured, "Why are you asking?"

"Eleanore always told me to try to make good decisions."

"Was she talking about anything in particular?"

Nicki clasped her hands so tightly over her middle, her knuckles paled. Still, the tremors rippled out from there, as if her hands were the epicenter. "Eleanore's not so bad, you know?"

"I never thought she was."

"I know she talks a lot and everything, but when we were writing letters when I was in prison she was really interested in me. And she encourages me to talk when we're together."

Ignoring that Nicki seemed disturbed by the lack of Eleanore in her life, I let her go on while waiting for the bigger talk that must come. "What is it that you do together?"

"All kinds of things." Nicki stopped dead, one of those points where someone is about to say something and then doesn't. Maybe one of those times when Eleanore had told her to make a good decision. After a moment, she went on. "She's taken me shopping, not just to Ross or T. J. Maxx, but to the really good stores. Like Macy's. And she bought me things that weren't on sale."

"Fabulous," I said. "What else?"

"Well, we go to the movies. She doesn't like the *X-Men* stuff—"

"I love *Wolverine*."

She nodded her agreement; apparently just talking about Marvel soothed her a little, too.

"And we go to lunch. Like the shopping, not Denny's, but places that are just . . . just . . ."

"Not chain restaurants," I supplied, wanting to scream at her to get to the point. "Where have you gone?"

"Downtown, on Fourth Street. Have you ever had vegan food?"

"Maybe once or twice," I said. "Have you tried calling her and asking her what's up?"

"Yeah. She's one of those people who doesn't like to talk on the phone so we text. But it's different."

"What are you getting at, Nicki?" I asked, beginning to lose patience with the small talk. "Is she ghosting you?"

"What's that?"

Sometimes I forgot Nicki had been "away." "It's when someone ignores you, doesn't return calls or texts."

"No, she texts, just to say she's really busy. I asked her if I did something wrong, if I'd made a bad decision, but she says no, Nicki, you're doing just fine."

Who was this Eleanore? Enough skirting the issue. I cared, but if we weren't going to get to it, I might as well go back to Carlo. "Nicki, how's Ramona? What have you heard about your daughter? Surely, with all the excursions Eleanore has you on, some include visiting her."

No answer was her answer.

I took a deep breath and jumped. "Nicki. Do you know where Ramona is? Who has Ramona right now?"

That's why Nicki was here. She was thinking the same thing and couldn't bring herself to say it.

I climbed out of my brain and took another look at Nicki. She was more and more a frail, thin, bag of woman. I said the usual empty things, was she being treated OK, she should eat to keep up her strength because when this was all over, she had a daughter to think of. I pretended that it didn't break my heart to see her no better than she was when she first came to me at Desert Doves. Circumstances beyond her control had abused her no less than her husband had.

We got to the bottom of the hill and turned right on Lago del Oro Parkway. No one here to see us, only a couple of houses way up the hill to our right, and the big wash to the left. I stopped and made her face me. Her head sagged, but not so much that I couldn't see her eyes swing back and forth, the only sign that she might be looking for some hope from me. I wished I could give it to her, but there was only one way. This was going to hurt.

"Nicki. Where's Ramona?"

Her head shot up and she dared to stare at me for just a moment before wrenching to the side. "She's fine."

"I don't believe you," I said. "I talked to someone who knows the system, and they won't tell me where she is."

"Happens all the time with DCS. They have so many kids in the system, they're bound to lose track of some for a while."

"That's not what I said. But you're sure she's fine. If she's fine, why won't you tell me where she is?"

She shut off again.

"You're lying. And while we're on the subject, where *is* Eleanore Turner?"

Nicki's eyes cut down. "She's doing time at Miraval."

"Another lie. Why can't you tell me where she is? What are you afraid of? Is it because Eleanore told you she has Ramona? Did she threaten to hurt her? And why would Eleanore do that?"

Nicki was weaving a little, someone on the ropes. I'd always been so gentle with her and she wasn't taking my pressure well. She all but shouted, "Well, maybe I killed her. Have you thought of that?"

This wasn't a woman who was guilty. This was a woman who was terrified. I went to take her hands but she pulled away, the threat that a touch might wound. "Nicki. Don't say those things." I thought about testifying under oath at her trial. "Not even to me."

"Why not? You believed me four years ago and look what happened. Has it occurred to you that I might just be a fucking liar, putting one over on you and everyone else? Like that note."

"What note?"

She squinted and gave a puzzled frown. "The note I gave you when we were all over at the house."

I vaguely remembered. What with the business with Al dying and Gemma-Kate's attack, I'd forgotten about the note she'd passed to me across the table, folded into a secret. I had put it in my pocket. "What did the note say?"

"Never mind. I was being crazy."

What was I wearing that day? Those jeans that are supposed to look like regular jeans but have an elastic waist. "Come on, I've got the note. Just tell me what it said."

"Don't trust ET," she whispered. "You didn't do anything then."

"That's it?" I asked. "ET. Don't trust Eleanore Turner? Why not?"

"I was just frustrated. I lied to get her in trouble. I'm a fucking liar. I came to tell you not to do anything. You've caused me enough trouble."

I realized that of course, it had occurred to me that Nicki was lying about something, though I hadn't articulated it even in my own mind until now, let alone what the lie might entail. But admitting it wouldn't serve a purpose. "For God's sake, don't talk to anyone else about this. You can't trust anyone, Nicki. Except me. You have to trust me, Nicki."

Nicki snarfed. I noted but ignored it. "There's evidence to implicate you in Dorita's murder—your argument, that concrete block that ties someone at the group home to her death, maybe you. If something happens to Eleanore, it will be three strikes against you because of your relationship with her as a mentor, don't you see? At the moment, there's no real suspicion about Eleanore being in trouble, even though her husband called in a missing person's report. She may have just taken off somewhere without telling anyone. What I want you to do is not say another word, in your defense or otherwise. No late-night confession to someone else in the home. You can't depend on them either. Forget it if Eleanore has gotten you an attorney. I'll get you one you can trust." One look from her made me add, "Better than the first one."

She folded in on herself again.

"Nicki, did you hear what I said?"

She turned around and started to go back the way we had come. I realized we were very near to the spot in the wash where I'd killed Gerald Snesil.

"Nicki, wait. Hear me out."

"Hear you, sure. What makes you think I can understand anything? Haven't you heard, I'm a moron and I make bad choices. What makes you think I even deserve Ramona?"

I've never been the most patient of investigators, and lately I was repeatedly hitting as many dead ends as an Energizer bunny in a box. It was only my talk with Gemma-Kate in the hospital that gave me my first good lead, and I wouldn't let go of it. That's no excuse for going after Nicki the way I did.

"We never really got to know each other that well, did we?" I said. "Here's something you might not know about me. I hate being suckered. And I hate going to prison because I'm trying to protect the very person who's suckering me."

Nicki couldn't have known what I meant, that I'd be trading my freedom for hers. But neither did she insist on her innocence. From the thousand-yard stare in her eyes, I wasn't even sure she understood what I was saying. Maybe she was thinking of someone else. Or another lie. "You lied about the front door of the house being unlocked."

"No, I . . . it was unlocked."

"That's because you unlocked it after the guys left. And you knew to go in the bathroom. You knew to stay there until a specified time and that's when you called nine-one-one. Before you were supposed to even know the other sucker was in the house."

Nicki started to cry. That's when I went full bully on her. "You set up the whole thing, didn't you? You probably found the guy. I bet you know a lot of druggies around Catalina, maybe even a contact from prison. Or one of those sometime workers who stock the shelves at the grocery store for drug money." I was talking and watching at the same time. That's why I saw her fingers curving into fists. *Come on, Nicki*, I thought. *Let's do this. Let's see if you've still got it in you. Let's see if I was a sucker all along.*

"The only remaining question is why. Why did you set the guy up? I suppose you were planning on letting him get killed by the SWAT team, I mean that's what they're there for. And you made his death more certain by telling them he had a gun when you called, before you could have known he had a gun because the bathroom door was closed. Hell, you couldn't have even known it was a man, or that it wasn't one of your roommates."

You had to be watching her very carefully to see the tremor in her head, how I was working at her, daring her. Just a little more. "Only you're too stupid to think that he might have said something before he died. Last words. What was it he said? 'I didn't put in for this shit.' It was your shit, wasn't it, Nicki? He knew you, was burglarizing the house because you had him do it. And the only account we have is what you told the police later. It's all you. Only you're too stupid—STUPID—to devise a foolproof plan. Because that's what you are, Nicki. A goddamn fool." I pretended to wring my hands in the manner of a swooning belle and whimpered, "'Oh, Brigid! I'm not a monster, am I?' But you are. And while we're on that subject, you even had the wherewithal to kill Dorita, though I haven't figured out the details of that. Or the question: Why did you do it? What's your motive?"

I didn't know how long I could have gone on that way. I was running out of words, let alone valid accusations. Luckily, it was enough. Nicki attacked.

I grabbed her forearm as she was attempting a punch to my midsection. We struggled, and she hadn't forgotten everything I'd taught her. But pushing her arm back while hooking my ankle around hers and jerking back, put her off balance on the side of the road. I knew how to do it so I'd catch her head before it cracked on the packed dirt. If she'd been seriously injured on this road where there was very little traffic, I don't know what I would have done.

She looked a little dazed flat on her back, so I left her that way until she could recover, and sat down cross-legged beside her. "You're not hurt, are you, Nicki?"

She was certainly more docile, maybe having burned through her anger. But she stayed quiet, blinking at the dark gray sky.

"Give it up, Nicki. Now. We don't have the time."

"I can't."

"OK, I realize you're protecting someone. You were ready to hurt me rather than let that person come to harm. You wouldn't do this to protect anyone but your daughter. Where is Ramona?"

"I don't know."

"I can help you."

"I don't think you can. I don't think anyone can help me anymore."

"OK, how about I tell you something you might not know. Dorita was a realtor responsible for pre-sales of the houses in that development next to the group home."

"I never knew that."

"It was Eleanore Turner's money, her deal, and Dorita was selling the houses for her. Dorita was afraid the group home would inhibit people from buying, so she wanted it rezoned for residential only. They tried to stir up some problems with Dorita complaining, getting signatures on her petition, but the rezoning was going too slowly. That's when she, or they—I'm not sure whether Dorita was in on it or whether that was just Eleanore—decided to make things more serious by having the junkie killed. But not even that moved the needle on rezoning, and apparently closings of home sales *really* tanked after it. Another question is, why did Dorita have to die? Why?" I picked up a few stones and threw them across the road. I think better when I'm doing something.

Nicki said, "I don't know! I really don't know anything more. After Dorita's murder, Eleanore started to get sort of jumpy and standoffish. She wasn't around as much, didn't offer to do things for me the way she had at first."

"She still held the gallery showing," I said, throwing another rock at that thought.

"She couldn't get out of the gallery thing because it was already promoted and would look suspicious if she cancelled it. I started getting scared. It felt like if Eleanore lost interest in me, I'd lose chances of getting Ramona back. I don't know why I made that connection. I started to blame myself, wonder what I'd done that she didn't like. Her attitude was more, I don't know . . ."

"Like you said. Standoffish. Maybe even a little angry?"

"Ghosting, you said. Yeah, maybe that's what you'd call it. When she was still in contact, she said things about Ramona, how if I got into trouble again I'd never see her for the rest of her life. But she said it all like she cared, like she wouldn't want that to happen. And she really did promise to get me a lawyer. I told you the truth about that."

I tried to hit the rock I'd thrown before. Missed. "Killing you would have been one too many deaths. And you might come in handy as a scapegoat. So one possibility was that you were beginning to feel threatening to her. You got too nervous, and she wasn't sure she could trust you to keep quiet."

"But like you said, the gallery show. And the lawyer," Nicki said.

"That would just attest to her own innocence, and make it easier to frame you. Or maybe Dorita posed a threat we'll never know about. Maybe she was the one threatening to tell. Blackmail, maybe."

"It's all so complicated."

"That's why you were both, to put it mildly, on edge at the funeral. Eleanore forced you to go to make herself look good, and then got concerned trying to make you not freak out."

"Something like that."

"The thing is, if you didn't do what she told you, she'd pin Dorita's death on you. This time it wouldn't just be prison time. They'd go for the death penalty."

Nicki lifted her back off the ground and sat up with her knees drawn to her. "Hell, I've been thinking so many crazy thoughts, I even wondered if she had Dorita killed as a threat, just to keep me from telling anyone that the group home burglary was a set-up. Crazy, right?"

"I've seen crazier. And you're not crazy."

Nicki started to cry at that. I gave her a tissue that was hardly used from my shorts pocket.

"Hey," I said. "You realize I just said all that shit to you in order to push you to tell me what's going on. I know how smart you are. I'm sorry, but I was at a loss."

"You were being honest. I'm an idiot. Just a fucking idiot who can't tell whether someone is good or bad, just whether they're nice to me."

What to say, if anything. Sometimes you don't know whether to offer advice or just listen. "You know, Nicki, if Carlo was here with us, he'd probably say that that's a pretty nice person to be, someone who can't tell whether people are good or bad. He would say that a lot of saints are that way. And you know the way I see it? I see you as just like anybody else who loves somebody. You'll do anything for Ramona, even kill. Maybe only the best people can be idiots that way."

Nicki was thinking hard, I could tell by the way she stared through me. Admittedly she wasn't a higher-concept kind of gal, but that didn't make her any less. Maybe someday if we got through all this without one of us dying, I'd tell her more about myself, my own flaws. For now it was just, "Would it make you feel any better to know I'm an idiot too?"

Nicki started to cry again. The sodden ball that was my tissue wasn't enough anymore, and she wiped the tears off her upper lip with the edge of her T-shirt. More than the tears, I found her face no longer seemed static, frozen. It became more and more expressive the longer I knew her.

When she could speak, she said, "Terrific. The only person I'm supposed to trust is an idiot."

The light was dying in earnest now and, using the flashlight to make sure we didn't surprise a hunting rattlesnake, we headed back up the hill to the house where she said no, she didn't want a ride to work. I watched her walk toward the grocery store until she disappeared in one of the dips in the road.

Remembering what she'd said about giving me that note, I went into the bedroom closet where we kept the laundry bag. I rifled through it, found the jeans in question. Thank God I'd been too preoccupied to think of doing laundry.

I felt the crinkle in the pocket and reached in, remembering the moment, when the felons were all at the house, that Nicki had passed me a note like in school. I opened the note and read, as she had told me, "Don't trust ET." It didn't take a genius to see that the initials stood for Eleanore Turner. Did Nicki mean to disguise the name because she feared Eleanore? Or was she sending another message, this one about a connection between *E.T.*, the movie with the cute little alien, and Phone Home, the realty company set up to sell the homes in that new development beyond the group home? Was it a coincidence? Nicki might have some mental challenges, she might behave foolishly, act impulsively, but that didn't mean she was stupid.

I still felt the weight of her around me, as if I was swimming with her body to a shore I couldn't yet see. That hopeless immobilization that settles into our bones when we despair. If Nicki gave up, the way it looked like she might, I might not be able to prove she hadn't killed Dorita after all. And how ironic it would be if, by offering to make my own confession to Max, we both lost ourselves, our lives, in the process.

But before any of that happened, it was easy to look up Phone Home and find that it was incorporated under Ian Turner's name. He may have used Eleanore's money, but he would be the one to lose it. And that made me remember what Nicki had said about Eleanore texting her. *No, Nicki, you're doing fine.* Eleanore always called her Nicole. A small item in the midst of this mess, but it made me think.

Eleanore was missing.

Ramona was missing.

Ergo, as Carlo would say . . .

TWENTY-EIGHT

You tell Brigid a bunch. That Eleanore was so nice to you, managing to pull some strings, she said, that got you into the group home. That she promised to ease you back into society and all that. That she would make sure everything went smoothly with getting Ramona back from the foster family where she was staying.

You're grateful. Eleanore was nicer to you than any person you'd ever known.

After talking to Brigid, being more honest, events start coming back to you. At the beginning it didn't occur to you to wonder why Eleanore was so nice. You told yourself she was a good person and that was all there was to it. Eleanore started to tell you what to do: little things at first, like buying paint supplies, taking you to the theater, telling Henry he should build a wall on the side of the group home to hide the garbage bins. What could be bad about that, right? She coached you with your parole officer, how you should tell him what was going on, that you were doing fine but were worried about the other people in the group home. It was true, you weren't worried actually, but a couple of those guys could be pretty rough and you hadn't been around men much since you went to prison.

One of the nicest things that Eleanore did was the pool party at the Turner house. She said she got permission to have Ramona there with you. Only now, telling Brigid, watching her face, you can see it was just another thing you could be in trouble for. You probably shouldn't have trusted Eleanore.

During the party, you were alone with Ramona in the pool and she asked for juice. You were very responsible, telling Ramona to sit out of the pool until you got back. Toweling quickly, you went into the kitchen. There you overheard the Turners talking. They were angry at each other. It was something to do with Dorita Gordino. Eleanore's face was red and her mouth twisted in a way you had never seen before. Even Ian looked pale at the sight of her. Then she looked at you and stopped talking, asked what you wanted. You said, juice.

You were a willing participant with that junkie. Well, not entirely willing. OK, not willing at all, but what choice did you have? Doing what Eleanore suggested, that went on until she said you should unlock the front door and call 9-1-1 about someone in the house. You asked a few questions, but whenever you did, Eleanore just smiled, and even if she didn't you felt like she was patting you on the head and you were ashamed that you didn't mind it. She didn't tell you that poor man would be killed. You swear you didn't know that would happen. Once it happened, you were sort of in deeper than you wanted to be.

So there you were in the bathroom with your cell phone, ready to call the emergency number to come get that guy, without him having any idea that you were in on it. Eleanore told you there wouldn't be a gun involved, that he would only have a box cutter, and if you did whatever he said to do he wouldn't hurt you. Apparently, the guy was such a loser, doped up on who-knew-what, that it would be easy to stay out of his way.

Well, Eleanore was wrong about more than one thing—you weren't able to totally stay out of the idiot's way, and he nicked you with a bad shot from the gun he had, the one he wasn't supposed to have. However, Eleanore was right when she said how things would shake out. The SWAT team came in and killed the guy because you said he had a gun. Now he wouldn't be able to tell his side of the story.

And that argument with Dorita that made them suspect you might have killed her—it never really turned into a fight the way someone in the group home had said—that was something that no one could have foreseen. You were taking a walk and Dorita said something about "trailer trash." Trailer trash. When you moved in with Vincent, you thought his trailer was a fine thing. A mobile home is what he called it. You are now ashamed that you thought that trailer was a fine thing. Your shame made you angry. You challenged Dorita to come out, and you'd show her trailer trash if that was what she wanted. It was stupid.

And it was all so confusing! But Eleanore was good to you, too, helping get that gallery showing that put ten grand in your bank account and promised even more. Because of her, you were a professional. An artist. You hadn't imagined that it would come at the cost of Dorita's life.

You hope you hadn't told Brigid things that could get her killed, or put Ramona in danger. Of all the things that weren't certain, like whether Eleanore was mostly good or mostly bad, you were certain you'd do anything for Ramona's sake. Like Brigid said, even kill.

TWENTY-NINE

Eleanore Turner was a willing participant. She had built a reputation as a philanthropist, donating to various nonprofits throughout southern Arizona. It was all done out of real goodness inside, not because she craved praise or needed to be on an upper rung of society. Though that wasn't a bad thing. Working as a mentor for women released from prison was her favorite. She'd gotten involved with that after hearing a speaker at her church, an Episcopal deacon who was assigned to Perryville Prison. She had brought art works done by the women there. Eleanore even bought one, a work in relief of an owl, done by curling slips of beige wood to form the image on a piece of cardboard painted black. She talked to the deacon after her speech, ended up filling out an application to be a mentor.

The first three women, who she helped over the course of two years, went so well. Since then, they had all found jobs and a place to live and had merged back into society, even the one who had drug-abuse issues. She was clean now. Eleanore could claim some credit for that, right?

Then there was Ian. She convinced herself over the years that it wasn't just her inheritance. That he loved her. She was loved.

Ian wanted Eleanore to do something for him, and it seemed so easy. To cultivate a specific mentor–mentee relationship to help with a business scheme apart from his veterinary practice and his political goals. Had something to do with the housing development in which he was the sole signatory. It appeared that a house one block from the development being built had been turned into a group home for formerly incarcerated individuals. Word of it got around and pre-sales of the homes were affected. It was all sort of complicated, and it was her money he was using, but what harm could it do? Ian had begun to lose interest in her lately, and now he was being so sweet. She would take it any way she could get it.

After Eleanore agreed to do this, the first woman she mentored didn't work out right. She had been doing time because of some animal cloning fraud scheme. That wasn't what made her all wrong, except that maybe she was smarter than the woman Ian was looking for. What made her wrong was that she had a lot of family in Green Valley, and probably wouldn't agree to do anything Eleanore wanted her to do. It had to be handled delicately, but she was able to relinquish the mentoring and the woman (Georgette Something?) took it with good humor.

The next woman she was given to mentor, Nicole Gleason, turned out to be the perfect candidate for what Ian had in mind. Eleanore was proud to be able to give her husband what he wanted, like being part of the team. The two of them had been drifting apart for years, Ian with his business and her with her charities. She even suspected he'd had an affair. Or two. Recently he had been much different, knowing how helpful she could be. He even bought her a vintage Jaguar and got reservations for a Galapagos cruise next fall. People who knew her seemed to think that she was such a strong woman but, when it came to Ian, she was not. It's a secret she can keep from everyone but herself.

Eleanore didn't want Nicole to get in trouble. It's just that everything went south and she couldn't control it anymore.

Nicole had something called fetal alcohol syndrome on top of being convicted, a disability she got from her mother drinking too much during pregnancy. Eleanore's understanding was that it meant her IQ was lower than normal. When she looked up the syndrome online, she found that the victims with FAS lacked something in the part of the brain where executive function resided. That's the ability to make logical decisions, to do the right things. To make the choice perfect, Nicole (or Nicki, as she liked to be called) didn't have any known family at all, and had even killed her husband in an argument. She also had a small child who could be used as a mode of encouragement—or deterrence—if that became necessary to keep Nicole from repeating anything she might know or suspect.

Eleanore knew the foster family where Ramona had been placed. Of course, given all her philanthropy, she knew lots of people in DCS. They trusted her. Now she was here. Despite all that do-gooding, Eleanore was here. How did she end up here? In the first hours of her captivity, she screamed and pounded on the walls. But the only result was that the activity made her thirsty. That made her cry with frustration, tears that she would later wish she had saved. There was no air conditioning, and without insulation the temperature inside must have been a good twenty degrees higher than outside. Outside it's 107 degrees Fahrenheit. And the humidity is under 10 percent, which makes your perspiration dry the moment it emerges from your pores. At the beginning she didn't think about all that fluid leaving her body, what she had always taken for granted.

Of course, there was water! Eleanore went into the tiny bathroom in which there was a toilet, a sink, and a shower stall. She turned on the tap, only to find that the water wasn't running. Nice detail, she mused, annoyed. If she didn't know better, she'd think she was in real danger. But for the time being she reasoned this was just a threat. If she behaved, did what was required of her, the door would be unlocked and she would be released.

Nonetheless, at first her yells were belligerent: "Let me out of here, dammit!" And, "This isn't funny, I'll fucking kill you!" Then, as time went on, she heard herself becoming more plaintive, until she said, "Please," in a voice that no one could hear. Even now, Eleanore wasn't the only one on her mind. Ramona invaded her thoughts and wouldn't let go. The "please" was a prayer that this wouldn't happen to the child, that she wasn't locked up somewhere else without food or water.

That's when Eleanore regretted everything. The decisions she made, the actions she took, the hurt she inflicted for the love of Ian. For the first time in her life, she fell to her knees. If that wasn't enough, she bent at the waist to make sure that whatever was watching saw how remorseful she was, and how much she'd do everything, *everything* differently if only she had one more chance.

The sun must have been well over the house by this time. Eleanore couldn't see it from the one small window in the side of the building, but she saw by her watch that she had been in the casita for ten hours. It was early evening, and so far no one had shown up. Should she break the window? What if no one could hear her screams even then and she'd be punished even more? With a small chair she finally did break the glass. The square was too small to get her body through, but she called, "Help! Help!" Not as loudly as before because her throat was dry and she couldn't imagine the croak reaching more than halfway across the yard.

Eleanore decided to lie down on the couch and wait for morning. The charade would certainly come to a conclusion then, and she would promise to do as she was told.

She should never have threatened to go to the police.

She drifted off to sleep, and when she woke the sun was blasting hot. Her watch said five fifteen. That's how it is in Arizona, no daylight savings time, so even though you're in the southern part of the country, the sun still comes up earlier than in other states south of the forty-fifth parallel.

Eleanore stared at the watch. She had a smart watch and could have called for help with it. But Ian had been so pleased with finding this beautiful antique time-piece that she had taken off the smart watch. Her mind was foggy, and she couldn't remember when that had happened, how long ago he might have begun planning this.

After the consciousness of the light, the thirst is what next hit her. Her mouth so dry she couldn't peel her tongue from the roof of her mouth. She had a headache, without knowing it was a consequence of her brain having contracted slightly, causing it to pull away from her skull. She remembered reading a thriller about someone lost in the desert. They held on to their urine rather than peeing, so that it would be reabsorbed, and survived until they were rescued. Who was that writer? She used to remember.

What if no one came to rescue her? How long could she

last? Eleanore had heard about people dying in the desert within a day and a half, but surely you could last longer in this building with . . . she went into the bathroom, tried the tap at the sink again, to no avail. Then she eyed the toilet. She took the top off the water tank and found it full. Good thing she hadn't flushed it or she'd be out of luck.

From the alcove that served as a kitchenette, she took a glass out of the cupboard and dipped it into the tank in the bathroom. She might have roughed it before, camping as a kid, but nothing ever topped this one. *Now that's something to write in your gratitude journal*, she thought as she drank three glasses. The water made her feel less desperate.

For a while.

She got a bowl out of the cupboard, put it in the corner and peed in it. The urine wasn't too dark yellow, what happens in the later stages of dehydration. That was a good sign. With her newfound comfort, though, she was hungry, and there was no food in the place. Ian had thought of everything. She noticed that someone had left a book on the floor next to the couch. A Lisa Unger novel. She wasn't in the mood for domestic thrillers, really, it was always the husband.

It's always the husband. Why can't someone figure that out and come rescue me?

She fell asleep thinking of potato chips. Was there something about losing sodium that intensified the effects of dehydration? She had read that. Everyone living in the southwest U.S. knows a little something about dehydration.

Eleanore should have rationed the water. But how could she know that her objections to the plan would be taken this seriously? The toilet tank was so low around mid-morning of the second day that she was scraping the glass along the bottom and was only able to get an ounce or so. She wouldn't drink out of the bowl, she hadn't become an animal yet, but she lifted the lid and looked. It was empty, the water having flowed back into the tank. She'd been drinking water from the bowl whether she wanted to or not.

She had thought drinking out of the toilet like a dog was the worst. But the worst was the morning of the next day when she thought of her own urine staving off death. No, now she was maximizing. She had a tendency to do that, which was probably why she was in these straits to begin with.

She couldn't remember the last time she thought of Ramona's safety, let alone cared about her. That was how it was, dying from dehydration. All that's left is your own animal urge and you can't think about anyone else. Like an addict, Eleanore thought, only interested in your next fix, and the drug of choice is water. Like that poor boy who was paid off with a thousand dollars in cash and the promise of drugs to break into the group home to find more. Did she know he'd be killed by the SWAT team? She should have known it could happen. She was incredibly stupid. But even if she had known he'd be killed, what decision would she have made? There was the child . . .

At the end of the second day, she sipped her own pee, just a tiny sip. It wasn't bad. Because she stupidly drunk so much in the early hours of her captivity, this was mostly water. It tasted a little salty and made her think again of sodium levels dropping. *How much did you lose through perspiration?* When she licked her forearms, she could taste a little on the skin. *How much sodium can you lose before it becomes dangerous? What will happen then?* She had checked the salt-and-pepper shakers in the kitchen. Empty, but just the same she licked the top of the salt-shaker, knowing that it would make her thirsty, but willing to risk it. Rather than pee any more in that bowl, to conserve the diluted urine, she did it in the empty toilet bowl. The urine had become a brownish-orange color. Too weak to walk back to the main room, too proud to crawl, she dropped to the bathroom floor, where she sat and gazed at what was in the toilet with detached interest. Her shoulder and head sank to the linoleum, which was cooler than the thin carpet in the rest of the place. *Yes, better this way.*

Without knowing how long she had been lying down, she came to, and with some effort pushed herself off the bathroom floor into a semi-sitting position, resting on one hip. Her head was another matter; it felt too heavy and drooped forward. She felt unexpectedly cool, though there was no reason to think the temperatures inside or outside had dropped. Even the nights these days barely slipped under 100 degrees.

No one to see, no one to say you look funny, so she crawled out of the bathroom. Daylight came through the broken window. *What time? What day?* Eleanore's vision was blurred so that it was hard to read the watch dial. At that point her body had absorbed water from its cells in order to keep her blood pressure sufficiently high. As a result, her eyes had contracted in the same way that her brain did. That's what was affecting her sight.

How long had it been, if she measured day and night? Certainly, more than forty-eight hours, now well into her third day.

So tired, but she grasped the edge of a coffee table and forced herself to stand. From there she grabbed the edge of the window, cutting herself on the glass that remained. With detached curiosity, she noticed that her blood didn't gush from her palm, but slowly seeped. She smeared it on her khaki shorts and looked again. It had stopped now.

She looked outside the window. There was no one hiking in the area behind the casita. There never was. She noticed a couple of javelina, those wild pigs that live in the desert. She almost wished she could call to them, but her throat was too dry to emit sound, so all that came out was a croaky "oaaah." Nevertheless, the javelina looked up. She had never wondered how animals like that find water in the desert. Maybe they lasted longer without it. Eleanore had never felt such a kinship before.

In her confusion she lost all track of time after that, and lost control of her body as well. When she dropped to the floor this time, it was impossible to get back up again. She was able to crawl over to the bed but only to roll over next to it. Just not worth the effort.

Important electrolytes like potassium and sodium were entirely depleted. Atrial fibrillation is the first sign of that lack which gives a victim the heartbeat of an alarmed cactus wren. Then involuntary muscle contractions begin, first in your calves, then in your upper thighs. She wants to massage her muscles but her hands are cramping too. She's too weak to do anything but endure the pain. In a moment of consciousness, she tries to close her lips over her teeth to hold in any moisture remaining there, but is unable to do so. Her lips have shrunk along with the rest of her. She is becoming a desiccated piece of meat.

Sometime in the next hours, paralysis begins to overtake her respiratory muscles, which makes breathing nearly impossible. Her breath, when it comes, is in rapid little puffs that reach only the top of her lungs.

She may have had a seizure but, if so, she didn't notice.

It's probably too late now. If she were to drink all the water she craves (she mustn't think of that), it would result in hyponatremia. Her liver and brain would take on too much water and swell rapidly. This would likely kill her.

Time elapses. Even though she is now near death, there is vague awareness of something happening, something different. The door of the casita has opened and someone enters. She knows this because she's in direct view of the sun in its western slide. Her eyes are slightly open and the sun glares at her. Because of the sun in her eyes which no longer blink, she can't see who the person is, only a small figure blocking a bit of the light. And another figure. Is it Ian? Is it the person who will save her? She doesn't even know if they are really there. It could be a hallucination.

The door closes again. Is that a sob she hears? Yes. Her last act is to reach out her hand toward the small figure, but it falls to the bed. She doesn't remember closing her eyes, but all the same her vision recedes, fades to white, then black.

THIRTY

I called Max. "It's not Nicki," I said when he picked up. "It's Ian Turner."

"Who says?"

"Nicki. Well, Nicki plus a connection between Ian Turner and everything else."

"What makes you think she's telling the truth?"

"Because of what she confessed to me. I've got the whole story and it hangs together, Max. But we can't waste time explaining right now because I have a hunch Turner is going to be making a break for it. I went by his house and looked around, but I don't think anyone is at home. I didn't hang around after that. So it's up to you."

"Do you have any idea where he's going?" Max asked.

I remembered that Gemma-Kate had lost her cell phone at the movie theater. She said she had it in her hand when she was attacked. But the cops didn't see it.

"I bet you anything Ian Turner took her phone so she couldn't use it to call for help. Maybe he held onto it for some reason. Trace it." I gave Max her number and told him I'd be picking him up.

Max was standing outside his office when I pulled up. He got in the car and said, "It's at the Turner house."

"He can't be there. I was just there. Had an empty feel. The place was empty, goddammit."

"That's the only lead. You gonna follow it or what?"

It was just five miles away and nothing to lose so I drove there. We jumped out of the car, Max with his gun drawn. Up to the front door, "Sheriff," he called as he knocked. "Open up."

Nothing.

Just for what Dad used to call shits and giggles, I tried the door. It was unlocked. I looked at Max.

"We don't have a warrant," he said.

I threw open the door. "Put it on my tab," I said.

Gemma-Kate's cell phone, with its lavender protector, was on the kitchen counter. Turned on, it was a decoy to bring us here and stall for time. We split up and bolted through the house to find it barren. Some clothes and a large empty suitcase in the master bedroom. "I bet he decided to travel light," Max said.

"He's not as stupid as I thought he was," I said. I ran to a door off the kitchen that led to the garage. Both cars were there, the Jaguar and a Mercedes. "He's definitely in the wind," I said.

"Airport shuttle?"

"Right. Phoenix or Tucson?"

"Phoenix has direct flights everywhere."

"Tucson is closer and has a flight to Hermosilla."

Mexico was a possibility. We have an extradition deal with Mexico, but that was only if we could have found him first. It gets a little harder to find someone in a different country. Plus we figured every minute he had Ramona with him, the more desperate he became at being found, the more he stuck out with a child in tow, the less value she would have for him.

We headed toward the Tucson airport, Max on his phone calling TSA at Tucson International. Turner had checked in. TSA was alerted and he was delayed going through the security checkpoint. Americans are kind of skittish when it comes to airport security, so it's easier to detain someone at the airport than outside of it. The agent reported his ticket said Toronto, not Mexico.

"What do we have on him?" Max was asked on his phone while we were on our way.

I thought, then said, "Abduction."

Max spoke, then listened. "TSA says that's not national security. It's local law enforcement. And abduction of who?"

"Tell them to hold him till you get there and take over. Tell them child sex trafficking. Possibly transporting a minor across the border and they'll be in big trouble if he gets away."

Max looked at me. I shrugged. He repeated on the phone what I said, and added, "Just hold him till we get there."

First thing I did, before anything, while Max was still communicating with airport security, was call Nicki on my own phone to let her know.

"Thank God," she said when I told her they had Turner in custody. "It's over."

"It's over," I said, and then squirmed a little inside my head because I knew her next question.

She asked, "You got Ramona. Is Ramona OK?"

Shit, I should have waited to call her. I didn't know enough to confirm that without reservation, really, and I shouldn't have spoken with certainty until I had the full picture. Nicki needed to be able to trust someone. "I'm not at the airport yet to see her with my own eyes. I'll call you back." To Max, I said, "Ask if Ramona is safe."

He put the TSA guy on speaker. "Is the girl unharmed?"

"Girl? We don't have a child in custody."

"Search the airport," I shouted rather than going through Max. "Maybe she bolted while Turner was taking his shoes off or something." I gave them a description. I imagined security rushing off in all directions. Tucson International isn't that large an airport, just one concourse with ten gates, one level for departure and one for arrivals, and even if Ramona had run outside, she couldn't have gotten far without being spotted. A girl about three feet tall, alone. Terrified enough to run.

I'd been trying to work all the angles but had missed one, only to impale myself on its point as we pulled up in front of departures.

"Wait a sec," I said to Max. "Turner was going to Toronto. What are the odds that Ramona has a passport?"

"He's traveling alone," Max agreed.

"Fuck." That was my brain going through all the scenarios possible, and none of them were hopeful. "Where are they holding him?"

"The TSA office."

We ran down the escalator from the departures level to baggage claim, where the TSA office lurked discreetly in a far corner of the area. When Max and I burst through the door, a belly with a TSA uniform covering it looked up in alarm and nearly drew his weapon. "You can stop searching the airport, the girl isn't here," I told him, and let Max take care of showing identification while I went straight for Ian Turner, handcuffed to a chair. The first thing I noticed besides the handcuffs was an over-sized Band-Aid on his right cheek. I ripped that off to reveal two crescent moons in a mirror reflection. One of the crescents was a little more pronounced than the other. Unmistakably a bite mark. I'd deal with him later about that as I knew Gemma-Kate was safe. But first, "Where's Ramona Gleason?" I asked.

"Who?" he said.

I could tell it was bravado, that Turner knew he had been outrun. But that didn't stop my reflexes from engaging. He fell out of the chair trying to get away from me, his cuffs preventing him from getting back off the floor.

"Brigid, hold on," Max said. "There are witnesses."

That comment made the TSA officer start to go for his phone for back-up. Max put up a hand to stay him. More people would only make the situation more complicated, and that would delay us from finding Ramona for too many precious minutes.

From his awkward position, back against the edge of the chair and legs splayed out in front of him, Turner said, "Look, I was just getting out of town for a bit because I've been so worried about where Eleanore is. That's it. You can't hold me without a charge or suspicion. My lawyer is on the way, so you better get me off this goddam floor before I sue for police brutality. This way it looks really bad."

"Except who bit your face?"

"I cut myself shaving."

Turner was right. Once the lawyer got there, he was off to Toronto and who knew where else from there. At this point I couldn't care less, let the fucker go. I was more interested in saving Ramona, and possibly Eleanore, than I was in seeing Turner charged with any crime. He might continue on his trip, or he might double back to his house to hide some evidence. I stopped short of imagining what that evidence would be.

"I'll get his keys," I said. "Maybe he hid a body in the trunk of his car."

"Hey! You can't do that," he cried, squirming on the tile.

I bent down, went through his pockets and found them. "Like you said, sue me."

The TSA agent was trying to hoist Turner back into the chair, but agreed to delay letting him go as long as possible until we could get back to him with some evidence.

The training of TSA agents may be lacking somewhat. Turner had been cuffed but in front rather than behind so he could sit more comfortably in the chair. This is what allowed him to grasp the revolver out of the agent's holster and point it at me. It was as if he had read my mind about my top priority being to find Ramona.

"Just tell me where Ramona is," I said. "You can't shoot all of us with that thing. One of us will take you down and, if you live, you'll be charged with assaulting an officer of the law."

"Alternatively, if I've hidden them somewhere and you kill me, you'll never find them," he said. "Let me go."

Them. It was an easy guess. Ramona and Eleanore, too? "What did you do to your wife? Wasn't she cooperating?"

"Let me go," Turner said. "I swear Ramona was alive when I last saw her, but possibly not for much longer."

I couldn't help but ask. "What about Eleanore?"

Turner said, "Let's make a deal. Forget Canada. Give me a car and one hour to make it over the border and I'll tell you where they both are."

This was new to me. I've seen some pretty revolting stuff from people, but had never seen anyone use the life of a child as a bargaining chip. And ultimately it was all about money, the getting of it. You know, I don't know what Max would have done in that moment but I would have let Turner go. Ramona was more important than what would amount to a few more hours of freedom for this scumbag. But the TSA agent had jurisdiction and he was playing by the rules. "We can't do that," he said.

Max's hand was slowly slipping down his side to unclip his own weapon. As he did so, he said. "What about we go to your house first and take you along with us?"

The idiot rookie agent said, "That can't happen."

In the skinny minute that was all we had to change the outcome of this situation, Turner's glance shot to Max's gun. I saw something in that glance that spoke of decision. Decision, resolve, and despair; all those things I'd seen time and time again. Turner knew it was all over and he was going down for some real bad things. He confirmed this as he lifted the gun to his head.

I lifted a cautionary hand, trying to stop him and get more information at the same time. "Wait," I said, partly wanting to know and partly wanting to distract him. "Let's just talk this through. Admitting your guilt for Dorita's murder will go a long way toward saving your life. You have some room to negotiate here. A lot of room."

It was too late and he could tell from my eyes that I was lying as much as he was. Like they say, the knowledge that one is about to die concentrates a man's mind wonderfully. With a last wide-eyed look, Turner lifted the gun as far as he could, given his cuffed wrists, and pulled the trigger.

THIRTY-ONE

Ian Turner had been hemorrhaging money. It wasn't a good look for someone wanting to run for mayor and more, maybe the U.S. Senate. He had lost a ton of Eleanore's inheritance on some mining deals because of environmental regulations, and the housing development in Catalina was his last chance to form a political war chest. Ninety upscale homes at a hefty profit after taxes and realtor fees. That was going well until the surrounding neighbors began screaming about the presence of a group home. The burglar set-up was supposed to get the home rezoned, but even that blew up in his face.

Then there was Dorita. She had been fine in the sack, whether she did it for love or the money she was hoping to make by selling the houses in Ian's new development. With that mouth of hers, and her self-interest, she was a natural for stirring up trouble in the immediate neighborhood and beyond. Because she lived so close to the group home, no one questioned why she was upset about the people living there. No one had to discover she was selling properties one block west.

The state promised to investigate but did nothing, hoping things would just quieten down. Government, only there when you don't want them, with their hand out. For her part, Dorita then created a fake name and posted the goings-on around the group home on the Neighbors social media site. Some of what she posted was true, or at least a real event, like an argument in the front yard of the home, embellished to sound more like a shouting fistfight. She was also the one who called out the police continuously, until they stopped responding.

So that was when Ian got more creative. It was easy to find an addict in Catalina. They were literally on every corner. One day, when he was leaving Ace Hardware with some pool supplies, he found one sitting right there on the curb in the shade with the sign that said "Homeless. Hungry. God Bless."

Toothless. Black. One indicated a meth addiction and the other, well, that was just a bonus considering what he'd be used for.

The man was taking a break from the heat, looking at his cell phone. Ian had never mixed with this class of man before, but it's instinctive, how you could tell he was more than just your everyday lunatic, that cell phone. This was something Ian could work with. He looked around to see if anyone spotted him talking to the man, but it was hot and there was no one else around. Any other time he would have told the bum there was a food bank two streets over, but this time he said, "How would you like to make some money?"

The man looked up with interest, keen. Ian told him of a house where there was plenty of drugs. Plus, there was a thousand in cash up front if he did this job. All he had to do was go when and where he was told. The man agreed and asked for a number, but Ian said, "No numbers, no names. Do you have a gun?" He said no but he could get one. Ian told him he'd meet him the next night after dark, in front of the same hardware store when everything was closed. That was when Ian paid him the thousand in cash, small bills. It was a small risk, but if the man didn't follow through, Ian was only out one grand.

That was a few months after Eleanore had gotten Nicole Gleason moved into the house, and told her what was expected of her. These things took time unless they wanted to get into trouble.

Things went so much better than Ian could ever have anticipated. It would have been fine if the junkie had lived. He didn't know who had paid him to break and enter the house, and even if he told what he knew; no one would really believe he wasn't just after the drugs. But the SWAT team killed him. Perfect. If anything would get those people out of the neighborhood, it would be this, especially when Dorita created another persona on the neighborhood social media site and helped stir the shit. Outrage was so easy these days. Maybe it always had been.

But before things could play out, with enough uproar to uproot the group home, there was the issue of Dorita. Who could have anticipated that she'd fall in love with Ian? These women and their "falling in love." First there was the pressure to leave Eleanore for her. Then there were the threats to tell Eleanore. And if Dorita did that, who could say that Eleanore wouldn't spill the beans on the junkie? As someone has said, "Hell hath no fury like a woman scorned." The vintage Jaguar he bought for her birthday present helped.

That's why he killed Dorita. Made it look like it would have taken more than one person to do it. Getting Eleanore involved, even as a witness, was a stroke of genius because it meant that—no matter what happened—she couldn't incriminate him without incriminating herself.

Ian told Dorita that he was coming to visit her and would bring Eleanore. He told her, "We'll tell Eleanore together that we're in love."

That night, after sunset, parking behind the wall in her backyard so none of the neighbors would see them, they all got good and drunk together. Or at least Ian made sure they were drunk. He had taken one of the concrete blocks from the yard at the group home that they were going to use to build a wall to hide the garbage bins. He also had a gasoline-soaked rag in a plastic bag. And he brought the battery-powered lighter from the gas grill in the backyard.

While the women were being cordial on the back porch, Ian wandered into the yard, poured gasoline onto the wood in the fire pit, and lit it. It gave a nicely dramatic backdrop to the scene. As the women approached, he told Eleanore, in front of Dorita, that he'd discovered Dorita was a traitor. "She plans to turn us both in to the police for staging the fake burglary," Ian said.

Dorita, after a moment of stunned silence, yelled at Eleanore, "Bullshit! Ian and I have been fucking for months!"

As Eleanore looked doubtfully from Dorita to Ian and back again, he made a half-astonished half-regretful face that she could read as *poor lying deluded woman.* Ian simply shook his head, not bothering to defend himself, which was the best defense.

Dorita was so shocked by this reversal, by Ian's betrayal and lies, she lunged at him. He anticipated it. She was always so reactive. It was easy to put her off balance, so that she fell face down in the gravel.

Ian rolled her over, straddled her, and told Eleanore to get the concrete block. Eleanore was drunk. Without knowing quite what he would do next, and having lost the ability to think for herself, she did as she was told, straining to lift the block. When that proved difficult, she dragged it to him.

Ian was stronger and also more sober than the two women. He lifted the concrete block and dropped it on Dorita's face once, twice, then stood up and repeated the action from a higher point to make sure she was dead. Then, as if to hide evidence of the murder weapon, he put the gasoline-soaked rag in the hole where her teeth had been, and lit it with his lighter.

Eleanore stumbled about in the background, stunned with disbelief at what was happening. It didn't matter whether she'd helped kill Dorita. She was implicated as an accessory to murder. Until recently, Ian had been sure she wouldn't talk.

Using his shirt to avoid leaving fingerprints, he grabbed the hose from where it was hooked up on the side of the house and turned it on Dorita's face to put out the fire. The sight of the water cascading over the blackened face, turning it to sludge, set off Eleanore more than anything that had come before. She started moaning, "Ohhhhh, ohhhh, ohhhh," at a volume that was almost as loud as a scream.

Ian briefly turned the hose on the concrete block to wash most of the blood off, then dropped the hose and clapped his hand over Eleanore's mouth. He pulled her from the backyard around the side of the house to where the car was parked. There she had a delayed reaction, screaming about what had happened. Good thing the yards were big, and the windows of the Jaguar solid enough, so that her cries were muffled even if someone was standing just outside. Moving quickly in the dark, Ian circled back and got the concrete block from the backyard. This was critical. It had a little of Dorita's blood on it. Good. He had made a calculated guess that the roughness of the concrete would hide his fingerprints. Interesting how a person can distance himself from such a heinous crime, can think so logically in the course of committing it. He congratulated himself.

The group home was just across the street from where the car was parked. It was risky, but he placed the block near the pile of other blocks. If the forensic investigators were just smart enough, they would be led to this pile and find the bit of blood.

From watching all those cop shows on TV, Ian knew he'd planned it well.

Motive: Dorita trying to get rid of the group home.

Means: The concrete block and enough felons to drag her outside with the rag stuffed in her mouth so she can't call for help.

Opportunity: Middle of the night and no one else around.

And Nicole Gleason wouldn't talk because she was part of the plot with the burglar. If she was connected to the burglar, she could be connected to Dorita.

The Molotov cocktails thrown into the group home, the death of one of the residents—Ian didn't do that. It was the social media mob, previously ginned up by Dorita's virulent postings, that did it. Ironically, Dorita was helping to keep suspicion off Ian even after her death. After the HOA meeting, where he stood just outside the door at the back of the hall, he set the fire in the garage of one of the unfinished houses in the development—that was just a little something extra. He didn't care whether it was blamed on the group home or on someone who hated the development. As long as no one got suspicious of him.

Attacking Brigid Quinn's niece was foolhardy, and she bit him before he could finish the job, but so far the kid had not identified him as the assailant.

And of course, there's Ramona. Ramona is his ace in the hole; she'll make certain that Nicki continues to stay silent about the burglar, and about anything else Eleanore might have shared.

For Eleanore, it would just take a little more valium and Scotch than usual.

Except. The sedatives and Scotch weren't enough. Eleanore

apparently wasn't cut out for murder. Every day she would spend more time staring out the back of the house, less time going about doing good; so much so, people thought she had disappeared even before he locked her in the casita. If she had had a champagne personality before, it was obvious the bottle had been left open, the bubbles flat. When had she stopped brushing her hair in the morning?

In a reversal of Macbeth, it had become clear Ian couldn't trust Eleanore; she was too weak. It might appear that she was only trying to protect Ramona who, should anything happen to her, would be collateral damage. But none of that, not even Eleanore's money or his connections, could keep Ian's ass out of prison. He was willing to do whatever it took to stay out of there.

The day before yesterday, he had poured a cup of coffee spiked with 40 milligrams of valium and took it out to where Eleanore was sitting on the edge of the pool, dangling her bare feet and rubbing her palms raw on the coping, a recent habit. That's what had made him think of Lady Macbeth.

Ian sat down next to her with his own mug and said, "Dear, you're going to have to get a grip."

She looked at him and laughed. It wasn't with amusement. He could tell that "getting a grip" wasn't going to be in the picture. He had thought of drowning her, but then what to do with the body? Better to keep her alive until things settled down, until he could figure out how to pin her disappearance on, say, Nicole Gleason. That was when he happened to look at the casita behind the pool, with its padlock on the door to keep transients from sleeping in it.

At first, the lie about Eleanore telling him she'd gone into rehab worked. But at the Pima County Board of Supervisors' meeting, with Brigid Quinn listening to him make the call, reception said she never checked in. He couldn't use that excuse for her disappearance any more. He called 9-1-1 to report a missing person. Not sure it's an emergency, he said. He got the feeling Quinn didn't believe him even then.

He'd made something of a mess of things. He regretted putting Ramona in the casita with Eleanore, but that was insurance in case he needed to bargain. Now it was time to get out of the country. Maybe when he was safe, he'd call the authorities anonymously, let them know where the kid was.

THIRTY-TWO

Fortunately or not, the cuffs on Ian Turner's wrists made it awkward and he only succeeded in shooting off the side of his skull. He could have lived with part of his head missing, even though he would have lost much of his attraction. The noise in the small space of the room coupled with the spurt of blood from his wound stalled us from reacting, and gave him the time he needed for another try. As he struggled to bring the weapon around to the front of his face and maneuver it so that his thumb could press the trigger a second time, I was the first to leap forward. The TSA agent and Max followed like the defense line of the Arizona Cardinals (team, not birds). We were all close enough and in such a muddle, it was impossible to tell the result of the second shot.

But the end of any struggling made that apparent. As quickly as we had gotten into the tussle, all four bodies broke apart and were still except for a little heaving breath. I suppose we all took a second to determine if we'd been wounded by the bullet. It could have hit Turner and one of us as well at this close range. Then three of us rolled away from the body, leaving Turner lying on his back, his open mouth a bloody maw. Max said, "Nobody hurt?"

The TSA agent appeared to be in mild shock, but otherwise was able to nod his head as he stared at the ceiling tiles rather than the corpse lying next to him. Then he rolled over again and threw up.

"Look at that," I said, temporarily distracted from my main purpose by death: that is, the shock of Turner's and the near escape from my own. "I always thought stress-induced vomiting was something that only happened in the movies." And to Max, "Re. Dorita. I'd take what we just witnessed as a confession, right?"

"Open and shut," said Max. "Three witnesses."

"Damn," I said. "Damn and fuck. I really didn't want this bastard to die." That was unlike me, usually. I had relished the death of a bad guy on a number of occasions, either by my hand or lethal injection, but not this time. This time I needed him alive.

I shook my head to clear my ears and brain. Max and I both got up from the floor and weaved a bit until the mild vertigo from the noise of the gunshots eased and we got our balance back. Then Max gripped the hand of the TSA agent and pulled him up after us. There was no time to check Turner's pulse or what might have remained of the back of his head. Depended on how far the barrel had been into his mouth. From the absence of teeth, I thought not very far.

I was already heading out of the door. "You'll take care of this," I said to the TSA agent who had a "what the fuck?" look on his face. But Max understood. He was a little more compassionate. "Are you sure you'll be OK alone here? I'm sure the entire airport security force will be responding to the gunshots in less than thirty seconds, and we can't wait around to be questioned. We have to find a missing child and a missing person."

"Go," the agent said, "I got this." He wiped something from his mouth with the back of his hand and seemed to get taller in that moment.

We must have missed something. We were about forty-five minutes away from the Turner house and operating on sheer intuition at this point because we had no other place to go. Max went with lights and siren and that shaved off about fifteen minutes. People in Tucson are great about giving way to cops and fire trucks. Except for the drivers who had the air conditioning and music blasting, they all pulled to the side of the road.

When we got to the house in Oro Valley, it looked just as quiet as it had before. You couldn't tell there might be two people held captive there. Because where else? Maybe with the two of us searching and some extra time, we'd find a secret room that we'd overlooked the first time we were there, an address traced in blood on the floor or, third choice, Eleanore's body.

First, we went back into the garage, using Turner's keys to check both of the cars. Trunks empty. We came back inside and stopped in the living room to get our bearings. I hadn't noticed them the first time, but now I recognized the gigantic Foo dogs that Gemma-Kate had mentioned.

They were laughing at me.

I yelled Ramona's name. No response, no small yelp or wail that could come from a child. We tried searching the whole place more thoroughly this time, splitting up, each going to a far end of the house, looking for a little girl. Looking for a hiding place. Under the beds where only a small person could crawl. In closets. In desperation, even in kitchen and bathroom cupboards. Maybe she was hiding and afraid to answer when we called. But nothing.

We met back in the living room that overlooked the pool and expansive backyard through sliding glass doors. "It's a big fuckin' city," I said, trying to think of where next to go. And here I'd let Turner kill himself without telling me where Ramona was. I called that one wrong. Psychopaths don't commit suicide. One more thing to never forgive myself for. Again, I would have plenty of time to dwell on that regret later.

"And a bigger desert," Max said, thinking. "The only good thing is that without the rains, the soil is still as hard as cement, so it would be difficult to bury a body."

There's a lot of open land around here, and bodies have been found years after their owners disappeared. My chest tightened, my heart dropped. I kicked the ceramic Foo dog because I didn't like the way it kept grinning at me. It toppled over and was more brittle than you'd expect.

Max didn't react at all. "Look at that," he said, as if my temper was anticipated and something to be ignored. I looked at him pointing to a casita off to the side of the pool. He threw the latch on the sliding door and we both ran out to the building, much like the one we'd built in our yard. Also like ours, it was just sturdy enough. I pounded on the flimsy wooden door. “Ramona!” I called, and if not her, “Eleanore! You in there?” They could be tied up. “Kick the wall,” I yelled. “Stomp your feet or something!” All quiet.

“I don’t believe there’s anyone in there,” Max said.

I knew he meant anyone *alive*. I handed him the keys I’d taken from Turner and walked around the side of the casita and found a window. Typical for desert buildings, the glass was double-paned to keep some of the heat out. On this one the outer pane was intact, but I could detect a crack in the inner one. I peered into the room, but the bright sun had blinded me just enough that I could hardly see anything in the darkened interior. Wait, was someone on the bed? I called Eleanore’s name but the figure didn’t move.

I moved around to the front door where Max was trying all the keys on both the spring and the bolt lock. “Not here,” he said, jangling the keys.

“There’s a broken window, just the inner pane. It’s dark in there but I’m pretty sure I saw someone on the bed,” I said. “Unresponsive.”

Max pulled his weapon and shot off the lock. At the sound I yelled, “Don’t be scared, Ramona!” Though I still hoped she wasn’t the one on the bed, unable to respond to my call.

Max tried the handle of the door and pushed, but it still didn’t open. “I think there’s a bolt on the other side,” he said. Clearly with every muscle in his body, he kicked at the door with the heel of his boot, part strength and part frustration. Contrary to the way it happens in movies, the door stayed shut. “You know it could be booby-trapped,” he said.

“Do we give a fuck at this point?” He stared at me, and just like old times we were suddenly communicating. When I said, “OK, one, two . . .” he got me. Three, we both butted the door at the same time with our shoulders; the door held but the flimsy frame splintered and gave. The door fell inward and we stepped over it.

Like the casita behind my own home, this one was small, one room plus a bathroom. So it was easy to see what was left of someone who must have been Eleanore lying on the bed. The stench billowed out at us as if it had been waiting. Both

Max's and my gag reflex kicked in, not only from the smell of the decomposing body, but also at that from a Pyrex bowl on the floor with a half-inch of orange-brown fluid that was unmistakably urine. But the smell wasn't the worst of it. The woman looked like she'd been there for some time before death, maybe longer than after. Early decomposition had begun but the corpse was darkened, emaciated, as if it had spent some time in one of those kitchen appliances that desiccates meat. She looked like a large slab of beef jerky. There hadn't been a whole lot of fluid to make the body swell. No trauma was immediately apparent but that would be for Fressler to determine. I kind of hoped for something like that, a bullet in her heart so that she wouldn't have suffered one of the worst ways to die.

But having seen the man, I had no doubt that Ian Turner might have simply locked her in the casita and let her die from dehydration. In the desert's low humidity and summer heat, it only takes three days without water. The building was set off in the back of the yard overlooking a deep arroyo, apart from any neighbors who would hear her calling for help. We could have conjectured what she died from, but I got the sense that neither of us wanted to open our mouths unnecessarily.

Saying he would call for back-up and an ambulance, Max stepped outside. Trying to take breaths small enough to keep a hummingbird alive, I took one quick look around and spotted another door. Bathroom, probably. "*No,*" I thought. "*No, no, no.*" It wasn't locked from the inside. When I opened it, I saw the little person curled up in a ball in the shower stall. Trapped in here with that thing on the bed for God knew how long. "It's OK, sweetheart, everything is OK."

"Max!" I yelled. "In here!" I heard footsteps and had the sense of someone behind me, then it was gone.

Ramona hadn't turned around or looked up, just kept her forehead on her knees. I saw her back go up and down, breathing small rapid breaths. I could have told her that did only so much good. The smell of Eleanore had already crept into my own mouth and up into my brain. When I got into the shower with her and sat down, I noticed a little bar of bath soap balanced under her nose. It was all she had to counter the smell of Eleanore. The presence of that bowl in the other room and the empty toilet bowl to my side told me that Turner had turned off the water. Eleanore didn't stand a chance, and if we hadn't got here in time, neither would Ramona. For now, she was alive, and I hoped the paramedics could keep it that way.

"Ramona," I said, everything focused on her rather than wishing Ian Turner was still alive so I could lock him in this house without water. "It's over. I'm going to take you to your mom now."

She dared to lift her head and I saw her eyes were sunken, her lips dry and cracked. Like Turner had said, it was almost too late. It might already be too late. You don't just give someone water after severe hydration and expect them to live. It depended to what extent the organs are damaged.

Ramona whispered something that she had to repeat before I could detect, "Which one?"

It would have been simple to answer her if she hadn't been vibrating with terror, if her teeth hadn't been chattering. She could have been referring to her foster mother for the past three years, but for all I knew she thought I might be forcing her to go to the dead Eleanore.

"Your real and true mommy, my love. The one who named you when you were born and has loved you even when she couldn't be with you. The one who protected you no matter what. She won't let anything bad happen to you ever again. Your job right now is just to stay with me, hear?" There would be a few issues to think through regarding Nicki's involvement but that's not what you tell a child, right?

Then, arms hanging limp by her sides, Ramona fell against me, as if she would have hugged my neck but was too weak to do so. I could feel her rapid heartbeat, syncopated with my own. I picked her up—less than forty pounds, I reckoned, not much more than Achilles. I buried her face, cool and dry, in the curve of my neck so she couldn't see the body, walked quickly through the almost visible molecules of stench, and brought her out into the yard where the paramedics were already wheeling a stretcher up to the casita door at Max's direction. He was on the phone at the same time, looked up when I passed by to say, "I've notified the sheriff and TSA."

I told the paramedics it was likely Ramona was severely dehydrated, even though they could tell that at a glance. They would have seen it before in this part of the world. They confirmed they'd take Ramona to Oro Valley Hospital to "check her out" and rehydrate her slowly. We all knew too fast could kill her. It was awful, having her go off with yet more strangers, but necessary.

Ramona reached for me, might have cried if there was anything in her tear ducts. I grabbed her foot and wiggled it playfully now that I knew she would live. "Don't worry, sweetest. I'm going to be right behind you."

This was my purpose, is what I live for. No matter what the consequences. While Max took me to the house to get my own car, I made a bunch of calls; first one to Nicki, of course, telling her that Ramona was physically stable but would need a lot of trauma counseling. Then to Carlo, not to wait for me to get home but asking him to pick up Nicki and take her to the hospital. I thought to call Gemma-Kate, too, because she'd been so interested in the case, but before I could elaborate on Ramona's condition, she said she was busy studying for an exam and would call back some time. That was fine, I had more important things to think of. Like calling Lynn Speth from Aviva Children's Services, so she could contact the foster parents who were still on vacation at the Grand Canyon. Lynn would know what to say so they wouldn't be alarmed.

I got to the hospital a few minutes ahead of Carlo and Nicki, and so was able to watch the mother and daughter reunite when they arrived. When they'd had some time together, I took Nicki aside and told her everything because I knew she was strong enough to take it. How Ramona had been locked in with the body of a rapidly decomposing Eleanore. How she had been in danger of dying from the heat herself.

I knew Nicki's story, how she had nearly lost Ramona in a hot car when she was a toddler. Neither of us had to speak of this, we could see it in the other. Because she had also shared everything from her life with Eleanore, trusting her, Turner would have known this as well. The rage in her face told me it was a good thing that Ian Turner was already dead, or Nicki would risk another go-round in Perryville Prison.

Carlo got to see them both together for the first time. He and I stood at the curtain that provided some privacy in the emergency area as Nicki, given permission to approach her child, knelt down beside the hospital bed so that her face, that unusual face, was a little lower than Ramona's. Nicki took the child's hand, the one with intravenous fluids slowly coursing into it, and kissed the wrist with something like veneration.

I said to Carlo, "I want you to know. I'm not only a monster. I do good things. I did this, too."

Without asking what could have been a thousand questions, Carlo just put the flat of his hand on my back. My own question might have been what I'd done to deserve this man, but I knew I didn't. Deserve him, I mean.

THIRTY-THREE

There would be plenty of time for Nicki, with my help, to take care of the Business of Living—finding a more suitable place to live, maybe one of those tiny houses the city was constructing out of cargo containers, loaning her one of our cars so she could find a better job. Making sure she got the best child advocate to ensure she could eventually have Ramona live with her even if they had to be monitored. Through my contacts, she had a lot of people to vouch for her protection of her child. And the only people who could say how much she knew about the Turners' crimes were dead. After all, Nicki hadn't done anything wrong except know the burglar was coming and calling 9-1-1. That would never have to be shared. I made a note to call a friend at Emerge, a local nonprofit for victims of domestic abuse, not only to get a place furnished for Nicki, but maybe to get her a job. She'd be a great spokesperson. Lots of things to take care of. I almost teared up imagining one of those tender movie scenes where the courtroom would be filled with people on Nicki's side and the judge would decide for her with a sharp rap of the gavel. Time would tell.

For today, the felons gave Nicki and Ramona a beloved celebration at the group home and Henry went out for pizza and wings on my dime. They decided on pepperoni, which I think is boring, so instead of staying I went home with Carlo and told him I had something to share with him. Maybe it was the way I said it, like ripping off a Band-Aid, because without hesitation he sat on the couch, with the two dogs, Achilles and Peg, prepared to listen. I stood before the three of them as someone auditioning for the role of wife, and really sucking at it.

I told Carlo everything. I went back decades, back to the rookie agent I trained and then lost to a serial killer, back to killing my corrupt boss, back to the rapist I killed in the wash, then finally ending up describing what I had found in the casita. I talked about Nicki and Ramona. How, because I thought fighting your abuser was the only way to go, I had failed them once but didn't fail them when I had a second chance. I talked about how I should have known sooner that Eleanore was largely a victim rather than a villain. How when I saw her in the restaurant, and considered that she was being abused by Ian, that it was true in a way I couldn't guess at the time. I shouldn't have lost Eleanore. I should have known sooner. I failed.

Carlo let me go on and on without interrupting. How many people do you know who would do that: let you talk and talk and just listen without shooting out some less than useless affirmation? When I had spilled it all, I said, "This is who I am, Carlo. It isn't that I enjoy being me. I wish I could have been any number of the other women I've known. But it's not a choice. It's a calling, you get that, don't you, the whole priest thing." Carlo didn't so much as nod his head but I could tell he was still paying attention. "Only my calling is uglier than I can ever express to you, no matter how much I detail events. Nicki, Ramona, these people find me. I don't know how, and I don't think it's going to stop. But I also understand if you can't live with that. I'll always love you however we end up."

Carlo didn't draw away this time, didn't flinch the way he had once. I still remembered that flinch that had driven me out to stay in the casita because he couldn't sleep with me in the house. But he didn't respond, either.

I said, "I guess that's it, then."

"Quiet," he said. "I'm still listening."

I obeyed, and after another minute, he asked, "What happened to Ian Turner? Did you—"

"No. He shot himself. I'll play that scene out for the rest of my life. Just like all the other times I fucked up. Maybe seeing himself through our eyes, Max's and mine. That discovery, that knowing, made him unbearable to himself. Or maybe the humiliation of being seen for who he really was . . . I just didn't see it coming."

"That would be nice if it were so," Carlo said. "That the last thing Turner thought about was repentance. But I'm more concerned about you. How are *you* feeling?"

Unlike acquaintances and even friends who spit out "How are you *feeling*?" in a kind of verbal knee-jerk that makes you doubt how much they really want to know, Carlo never asked a question unless he wanted the whole answer.

So what was I to answer? That I haven't felt much since around 1995? It would be only partly flip. Turning off my emotions had become a habit for some years; it was one of the ways I survived, especially during the time when Carlo himself couldn't tolerate what he had discovered about me. But then that wasn't exactly the truth either. I had feelings for him. And he deserved knowing. So I gave him the respect of poking about in my mind and finding something I could give.

I told Carlo about the Elephant Man, how Nicki had seen pictures of him and had told me she felt like that, a monster on the outside that all the world shunned, even though her aspect was hardly as dramatic. "Nicki has always felt that she was abnormal. That stigma of disability that makes a person feel themselves living on the margin of humanity. I guess I share that with her in a way. Only a little different. I may look fine on the outside but inside I'm all wrong. And that means that if anyone really knew me, they would not love me."

I clenched my jaw. I would not cry. That would just look manipulative.

Neither did Carlo jump to assert that he would love me no matter what. What I was saying was too big for bromides. I thought some more. "Worse because now you know everything about me and I really don't see how you can stand it. Better for the same reason—I've gotten so tired of pretending to be someone else."

I thought then that I hadn't told Carlo everything. One thing I still hadn't told him about was the deal I made with Max that led to him sharing information about the case—that I would formally confess to killing Gerald Snesil if I wasn't able to prove Nicki's innocence and it turned out she was Dorita's murderer. As Carlo waited for more, I said, "I feel sad. But there's also a kind of contentment in my resignation. I feel clarity. I feel that all feelings will come and go."

"The sadder but wiser girl," Carlo said. He stopped and thought.

"You're about to quote someone else, aren't you?" I said.

Carlo didn't take offense. "Mm, Will Durant writing about Botticelli. It would have been so apropos. But I'll pass, and only say here you are, showing your true self to me, no matter how much you fear rejection."

"Well maybe it's not my *whole* true self. Don't want to get all crazy with this honesty business."

"Still, I'd say that takes some balls."

"Don't be sexist," I said, and tried to change the subject. "You know, we haven't had a chance to talk about what you learned at the retreat. Why don't you say something you learned?"

He appeared to take me seriously, then thought better of it and shrugged. "There's no place like home?" He hadn't gotten up from the couch all this time. Now he held out his arms and said, "C'mere."

"No," I said, still resisting. "If you stay with me it may involve killing. I may kill someone."

His arms stayed out.

"I don't want your sympathy. I can take anything but sympathy. If I did, I'd break."

"My arms are getting tired," he said. "What about if you try to limit yourself to self-defense?"

I thought. "Deal," I said.

When I was doing some prescribed time in Alcoholics Anonymous, one of the many handy slogans I encountered was, "Our biggest problems are the secrets we keep." Boy, ain't that the truth. I didn't know if hiding myself was my biggest problem, but I was certain I was fresh out of secrets here. So I went to Carlo. Achilles moved aside to make way and then put his chin on my leg. I'm not sure what it was that I felt in those arms—comfort, acceptance, absolution, understanding; a multitude of things but certainly not pity. The arms held too much respect for that; but whatever it was, it felt better even than love. It felt like being found. The puppy chin wasn't bad either. Then, because you can only take so much feeling at once—you kind of have to ease into it so you don't get the emotional bends—I got up, went to the liquor cabinet in the kitchen and pulled out the Crown Royal bottle. "I'm going to get numb now," I said. AA doesn't solve everything.

Carlo took a deep breath, and letting it out was in sync with him rising from the couch, like he was a hot-air balloon. "I'll join you."

I got two highball glasses out of the cupboard. "Ice?"

"By no means."

When the liquor had begun to take effect, Carlo said, "You knew I wouldn't let you go."

"I did not. I was being totally honorable in letting you know my position."

He lifted his glass but I could tell he wasn't buying it. Reassuring myself with the soft memory of Nicki at Ramona's side, I picked up my cell phone from the kitchen counter, walked into the TV room, and called Max Coyote to shove in his face that he couldn't get my confession. I was realizing for the first time that I hadn't really needed his help to clear Nicki, find the villain, or get Ramona back safely. The confession I'd offered about my killing of the serial rapist was all for nothing.

When Crystal—who still hadn't forgiven me for whatever I'd done to her husband, though I couldn't quite remember—answered the phone, she handed it to Max without saying hi. She was a tough customer but stand-by-your-man and all that. "So, Max. Just calling to confess that I won the bet."

"That's right," he said, without any indication of sour grapes. "I don't have you on murder one yet."

I should have left well enough alone, not let him bait me, but the Scotch . . . "What do you mean, yet?"

"Well, I do have you on body cam breaking and entering the Turner house, and when I pointed out it was illegal because we didn't have a warrant, you said, quote, 'Put it on my tab.'"

At any other time I might have come up with a good rejoinder but this time I was caught with my quips down. "Seriously? Come on, Max!"

"It's a lesser charge, of course. But while I've got you in custody, I can get a little oral swab to match against anything that forensics might have in evidence from the murder scene of Gerald Snesil. Did I tell you we've gotten a grant to test this backlog of DNA?"

As I was lost for an answer, Max said, "But no rush. I'm thinking we could get you in around mid-December. Make it an early Christmas present."

Need I remind anyone that was six months from now? Six months to worry about how this would go down. If not six months to move out of the country. "You fuckin' bastard," I said.

"That will give me plenty of time to get this backlog of DNA tested. Plus get your help on some other cases. Like we still haven't found out who threw the bomb that killed Jackson Donofrio." There was all the silence in the world before he added, "I've got you now, Brigid Quinn." The last thing I heard was Max's cheerless laugh as we raced to disconnect at the same time.

I turned to see Carlo watching me at the door of the room. I don't know how long he had been standing there or what he might have heard. His own glass tilted slightly, which for some reason spoke of bafflement. "What was that about?"

There would be plenty of time to explain. For now, I asked, "Where does the phrase 'time to pay the piper' come from?"

Carlo turned to go back to the kitchen where he poured himself a little more Scotch. I followed suit. I'm such a follower.

He said, "Well, my dear, you may have stumped me on the source. Maybe one of those German fairy tales? I know it's a story about how a guy is hired to rid a town of rats but when he does so the town doesn't pay up. In revenge he takes all their children. Why do you ask? Does that have something to do with the call?"

"Something like that," I said. My racing mind had already left Max behind and strayed to wondering which of the felons had snitched on Nicki, about her argument with Dorita the night before her murder. And who told Max about me calling Dorita a pain in the ass?

Everything isn't neatly sewn up in real life the way it is in stories.

A lot could happen in six months, while I tried to make myself enough of an asset to Max that he would leave me alone. I remembered another story about a man, who was about to be executed, promising the king he could make his horse talk if his execution was delayed for six months. The king agrees. When a friend tells the man that he was stupid for making a promise he couldn't keep, the man says, "I don't know. In six months, I might be dead anyway. Or the king might die . . . or the horse might talk."